SAMUEL JACOBSON BOOKS

THE INVALIDITY OF OCCAM'S RAZOR

Nora, thank you so much for organizing the book launch. All the best on your adventure. —Sam

Experienced in ▓▓▓▓ Island, Canada
Begun in Pisac, Peru
Written in Bocholt, Germany
Published in Halifax, Canada

Cover Photo Credit: Josh Bruder

Copyright © 2025 Samuel Jacobson
All rights reserved.
ISBN: 978-1-0693514-0-1

For Sam Greenberg and baby Gabey

"*welcome to the dark side of my bizarre mind*"
- Malcom James McCormick

The Invalidity of Occam's Razor

Occam's Razor:

The rational man's prized philosophical concept. It dictates that when attempting to determine something's cause and effect, one should look no further than the most likely explanation. That simple explanation is most likely to be the correct one. The happenings in this story can be explained by Occam's Razor, until they cannot. Between these pages, you shall witness the theory unravel to its very bone. May William of Ockham roll in his grave.

Disclaimer:

The name of the Retreat, island, and people have been altered out of respect. Although many details and feelings are true to life, the story and its characters are fabricated. Particularly, the issues at the Retreat are dramatized or fictitious. I hope that the Retreat is not recognized. If it is, please do not let this representation skew your opinion of it.

[PROLOGUE]

This story is not one I ever intended to share. May it be for the best that my hand has gone rogue and revealed my mind. So far, I feel great relief coming in the form of these words staining the page. I hope this exorcism purges me of one haunting illness.

On the surface, this story is no more than a colourful recollection of the time I moved to British Columbia. Much lurks below this innocent facade. Some concepts found within are suffering, friendship, death, and the impossible. Much of what I have written, I have yet to understand. I expect, and have accepted, that these are happenings I will never comprehend in their entirety.

To begin, I return to a place that is far away in terms of both distance and headspace. The geographical distance is great. It is more than a tenth of the earth's circumference, or, the opposite coast of my country. The headspace is that of searching. Okay, maybe the headspace is not so far away, but is it ever? Anyway, this is where our story begins, in a brighter and happier world. For clarity's sake, it is not the world at large that has lost light, only mine. While my world is rocked and forever shaken, the world at large has paid no mind. I do miss the way things were before, when Occam's Razor could be relied upon. The universe's unpredictability has rendered the tool less than useless.

[CHAPTER ONE]

The East Coast of the land that we refer to as Canada is a truly lovely place. Admittedly, I am as biased as can be, but please, I encourage you to come and take a gander for yourself. If you do happen to make the trek from wherever in the world you may be, I can assure you the odds are high that you will be greeted upon arrival with a genuine smile. You may find yourself shocked by our affinity for small talk. The first time that my uncle's German wife visited Canada, she sure was. As the pair strolled to the corner store, she was flabbergasted that he was greeting everyone with a 'Hello, how are you?' She incorrectly assumed he knew every single one of the people to whom he spoke. The reality was that he knew none of these people. My Uncle simply wanted to relish being in his home country, where such a greeting is met with a "Good, thanks, lovely day." Back in Germany, where they lived at the time, his friendly greeting would likely be met with a confused look and a narrowing of the eyes. Okay, back to Canada's East Coast, for now.

Atlantic Canada comprises four unique provinces: Prince Edward Island, New Brunswick, Nova Scotia, and Newfoundland and Labrador. As a proud Nova Scotian, I must take this opportunity to mention that New Brunswick is known as the drive-through province. You must literally drive through it to get to the other three. Countless lakes litter the strangely shaped peninsula that I call home. I take immense pride in the odd way Nova Scotia sticks out of North America. It looks as though we are the northern bookend to Florida's southern. I relish the opportunity to show people where it is on the map, a rather frequent occurrence when I travel internationally. Once you see the lobster-like tumour, you will forever be able to identify it.

Our small water provides a play place in both summer and winter. Warm memories of swimming and fishing at the lake fade while the temperature slowly drops. That soft, warm water in which we splashed hardens to ice almost overnight. Any snow upon the surface is hastily cleared to make way for pond hockey. It is upon these surfaces that African Nova Scotians invented our much-beloved game of hockey.

The coastal people who form tight-knit communities are both sincere and kind. The name Nova Scotia translates to New Scotland in Latin, and yes, we have a plethora of MacDonalds and Campbells. The ancestral people of this land are the Mi'kmaq, their land is Mi'kma'ki. Mi'kma'ki is divided into seven districts, of which Nova Scotia is the central. I consider it an honour to have been born and raised on this special land. Despite my gratitude, the colonial context in which I exist certainly has a dulling effect.

One thing that Nova Scotians do not take for granted is our proximity to the ocean. We have a great appreciation for the big water that provides soothingly mild temperatures year-round. We are grateful to avoid Central Canada's freeze-you-dead winters and their burn-you-alive summers. Although grateful for this blessing, the truth is that the majority of us at best have only a vague comprehension of the extent to which we should be grateful. It is much easier to appreciate something when you have experienced it firsthand, and as it is, most Nova Scotians do not possess experience with the innards' wicked weather. My point is that very few East Coasters leave, and when we do, it is not typically for central Canada.

If it is not yet abundantly clear, I have a deep love for the province in which I was born and raised, and as you know, if you love something, then you must let it go, or some shit like that. I may love it now, but I used to loathe it. By the time I was halfway through high school, I knew I had to get out. I loved the trees and the water, but not my life, and at the time, my life was too closely associated with the land. To put it simply, my early years were exciting. There were bright highs and dark lows. The kind of excitement in which a child's brain is not meant to develop. But hey, I turned out fine?

Seeking a change, while wanting to stay close to my mother and sister, I moved to Newfoundland for university. At the time that I finished high school in Canada, an adolescent's life path was simple, and the next step obvious. Upon graduation, if you could afford it, or if you had the confidence to take out a loan, then you went to university. So that is exactly what I did. For the majority of students, or at least the ones I befriended, the first two years are a pre-adult-hood transitional babysitting service. A place where the babies do some questionable things as they prepare for 'real life'. I reach by saying the majority, many do go for an education, and depending on who you ask, I did too. Life brought me there because it looked like fun. The truth is that I had no other ideas, and at the age of seventeen, fun was as good a motivator as any. Looking back, I expect that a trade would have proved more beneficial, yet I have no regrets. I met the best people imaginable and had a hell of a time. Plus, and most importantly, I came out pretty well no worse for wear. Considering how close to the edge I pushed both my mind and my body, I consider myself to be one lucky man.

[CHAPTER TWO]

The city of St. John's is geographically the most eastern in North America, and it is the capital of Newfoundland and Labrador. It is also the location of my post-secondary institution. It is just a quick two-hour flight north-east of my hometown. Fast-forwarding to the second year of my program, I was on a work term with the largest commercial real estate company in the world. Sounds cool, right? It was not. I would rise before the sun only to be rewarded by spending long hours twiddling my thumbs in a cubicle. When I initially learned that I had my own cubicle in my own room, I was filled with gratitude. Gratitude trickled out and then made itself scarce as I realized the room was windowless, talk about gloom. My lunch breaks were rushed; I ate as quickly as possible, before racing outside in hopes that the sun would bless me with a rare appearance. You see, St. John's is a foggy-gray land to begin with, so the last thing you want is to spend your day out of sight from the light. The company had little to no work for me to complete, so I kept myself busy by learning about personal investment and reading thousand-plus-page Stephen King books. By the time I made my way home, the centre of our galaxy would have already snuck below the horizon.

The semester began in January, and as time passed, the almighty beacon of hope stuck around longer. When something important is taken from you, you appreciate its return so much more, and for this after-work light, I would trade nothing. My roommates were three of my best buddies. Although I only knew one of them prior to university, all four of us were from Nova Scotia. The three of them faced off in high school hockey back home, and each would go on to play in the local Newfoundland junior league. We hosted one of their rookie parties, and I wish I could say I remembered more from that night.

By no means was it all partying for us; we would just as soon spend the day hanging around chatting and cooking. Thinking back on that first year in the house, it is likely the best living situation I will ever have; no offence to my future family. The antics were endless and arguments frequent. A favourite memory is that one of the guys took to keeping a pot and a pan in his kitchen cupboard; he was tired of feeling like he was the only one cleaning up. In his defence, he absolutely was the only consistent cleaner, sorry Leddy. However, that did not stop another one of the guys from filling those coveted pots up with water and carefully replacing them in his cupboard. Yes, it was cruel, and yes, the results were wet and comical.

One day, while I was chained to my desk, the boys discovered a gold mine. It came in the form of a small pond that was frozen over. Just a minute's walk from our house, the pond was hiding in plain sight. It was along the road that each of us drove or walked every day, but it was blocked from view by a small ditch above the road. It would have stayed hidden had the boys not spotted some locals setting up a net and skating around. They climbed the ditch in amazement, and we never looked back.

My after-work ritual became a sweet one. Balancing upon the thin line of safely speeding, I raced home. I knew the boys were back from class and in the process of clearing any freshly fallen snow from the makeshift rink. My heart rate leapt as I pulled into our neighbourhood. I snaked up the road, slowing just enough to meet the boys with an excited honk. A barrage of shouts, smiles, and waving sticks happily responded. To an innocent bystander, you would think I was coming home from war.

I floored the accelerator, ripping around the corner and into the driveway. A mad sprint into the house yielded my dress shirt swapped for a bright red Washington Capitals jersey, 'Ovechkin' plastered to the back. Skates in one hand, stick in the other, I breathlessly ran back to my brethren. I slid dangerously down the far side of the ditch before lacing my skates as quickly as possible. With the boys urging me on, I hit the ice. Eager as ever to stretch my spine after a long day of sitting. My presence often evened up the numbers, and so our game would begin.

The net consisted of repurposed wooden boards and an old fishing net that was hastily nailed together. It was perfect, an East Coast classic. The already small pond felt even smaller due to our size. Consider that I was the smallest of the group, and still over six feet tall. A couple of our buddies from around the other corner would often join; a friend named Chris is worth noting. A stand of pines formed a ring around the pond. Standing tall, they would work with the ditch to protect us from the wind. If the trees had eyes, they would see a blur of colours and shouts of joy. Once the final light faded, we were cold and worn. As one, we returned to the warmth of our house, smiles wide, and chirps loud.

Like all good things, it could not last. Warmth spread from within, and ice made its annual transition to water. My summer semester began, and I moved into a new house closer to campus. Another change was that one of my fellow pond hockey players decided his future lay elsewhere; it was the aforementioned Chris. When he told me his plan, I was both impressed and a bit jealous. He was heading out to 'Beautiful British Columbia', Canada's fabled West Coast. He was a fellow Nova Scotian, and so this was some distance away. The capital of Nova Scotia, Halifax, is closer to Barcelona than it is to Vancouver, the largest Canadian West Coast city. His adventures would take him to the hippie haven of Tofino for a summer of surfing. Winter would be spent snowboarding in the Rocky Mountains. Both places were riddled with thrill-seeking tourists, so he had no problem finding jobs in the industry. As I watched my friend march to the beat of his own drum and explore the unknown, I was stuck with another two years of school. Witnessing the flawless execution of his ballsy plan, my jealousy turned into a yearning.

    Chris's change of heart and plans may have been rather impressive, but they were not new. Despite Atlantic Canada possessing beauty and serenity, it lacked the drastic landscapes and rainforests out west. For my more adventurous peers, it was relatively common to follow the long road in search of snowboarding, mountain biking, and or climbing. The mountains were bigger, and the adventure communities better developed. Another strong yet simple pull was the stark differences in culture and climate. Some people run towards change, especially from what they have always known. While university in Newfoundland had certainly been a change from home, at the end of the day, it was still the familiar East Coast and well within my zone of comfort. I followed Chris's adventures as closely as I could, and years would pass before we would meet again. It would be in uncharted territory that we would reunite, and under extreme duress.

[CHAPTER THREE]

    The subsequent completion of my Bachelor of Commerce provided little in the way of excitement. Upon graduation, I had no interest in joining the world of business; if anything, it made me sick. I gained a fair understanding of corporate greed and possessed no intention of climbing a ladder or spinning a wheel. Overall, my mental health was suffering as I drowned in the indecision of what to do next. I chose that particular degree expecting it to open doors.

To my dismay, it opened far too many. The options seemed endless, yet none of them stuck out enough to be chosen. I could have done my CPA, the direction in which so many of my classmates had opted. That or a CFA certainly would have lined up with society's norms. I am certain that many of my classmates and friends felt they had no option other than pursuing a clear cookie-cutter career, and I do not blame them at all. There was a brief moment where I wanted to move to Toronto to knock on the finance industry's door, but that idea was deader than a dead kid playing dead. Maybe things would have worked out better had I decided to stay colouring between the lines, we will never know. For better or worse, being anyone other than myself has never been an option.

One of the most important things Newfoundland gifted me was a deep appreciation for nature. On the big glacially shaped rock, there was little else to do other than explore it. I connected with important parts of myself along rugged mountain top trails that wound above the Atlantic. I spent many nights camped out under the stars with both friends and lovers. I watched icebergs float down from the north and whales play amongst them.

My final semester was completed while I was living at home in Halifax. It was just my mother and me, and so I often looked to her for advice. She recommended that I find what I was passionate about and follow it. Solid advice, but as with the best, it was easier said than done. Although grasping desperately at straws, my passion seemed to be connected to nature and the environment. The idea of protecting it has always been a sexy one, so why not wield the sword for what I had grown so fond of? The idea was broad, but I simply needed to point an arrow to quell my growing despair.

    Borderline depressed and continuing to struggle with post-university blues, I stumbled upon a federally funded volunteer program. It offered a variety of environmental placements. I immediately identified it as something that could help narrow my scope. Even better was that it offered the opportunity to relocate to Western Canada. I felt a lifeline and wasted no time in applying. Considering that I read few people were typically accepted, I was ecstatic to be quickly approved for the program. I was immediately flooded with relief. The importance of having something to look forward to cannot be understated.

    At the time of acceptance, it was mid-way through summer. The program did not begin until the new year. Naturally, this left me with the second half of summer and the fall free. Although I was taking a slight detour, I was still expecting to pick a career path in the near future. Those glistening golden chains encouraged me to consider this to be important free time. I refused to put it to waste.

    It had been far too long since I talked to my buddy Chris from university, so I decided to give him a call. I wanted to catch up, and also wanted to let him know I was likely coming out west in the new year.
    Enthusiastically, he said, "Oh dude, that's great. You're gonna love it. I'm heading out for the ski season, you'll have to come visit me on the mountain."
    For whatever reason, this news lit a fire within me. It was definitely stoked by the looming threat that I would soon fall into a monotonous career. I thought to myself, 'Why wait?' I was filled with a resolve to move out west for the Fall. Besides, the volunteer program could easily find me somewhere in Alberta rather than all the way west in British Columbia.

Despite having dabbled in personal investment thanks to my slow work term, I was still short on funds. I was also aware that four months is a relatively short length of time. It was too long to support myself without working, but also pretty short in terms of committing myself to a job. I was a bit worried that this reality could prove a barrier to realizing my goal. Despite the self-prophesied challenge, I had plenty of experience bartending and a fresh degree to back me up, so I still thought finding a job would be attainable. Based on conversation with Chris, I knew the easiest and most affordable way to move out there would be to find one of the many tourism industry jobs that included housing. At least I thought I would be finding one of many; I grossly underestimated the added complexity of my job search requiring staff accommodations.

  I created a fantasy in which everyone who moved out to British Columbia or Alberta was magically provided a place to live, how naive. There were shockingly few options fitting my parameters, and those in existence were hard to find. I reached out to Chris again in hopes that he could recommend a place to work.
  Regrettably, he advised me, "Sorry buddy, I only know places hiring in the winter. You've just gotta keep applying to every job on every website. Something'll work out, it always does."
  I scoured them all and applied indiscriminately, housekeeping, bartending, serving, and maintenance. As long as I was half-qualified and they had housing, they would receive my resume and cover letter. It quickly got to the point where I would take anything other than a kitchen job, as I have heard too many horror stories. In my desperation, I even applied to one Retreat four different times, for each of the positions aforementioned. Eventually, there was nowhere left to apply. All I could do was close my laptop and cross my fingers.

[CHAPTER FOUR]

  The first half of that same summer was spent working as a bartender on a waterfront patio in downtown Halifax. It was at a restaurant and bar with which I was quite familiar. Years before, during my first summer break from university, they gave me my first chance as a bartender. I was eternally grateful for the opportunity. I remember being nervous at the beginning. I considered it held one of the fanciest names in the city and formed the expectation that it must be a pretty stuck-up place. There were certainly some areas where the extra mile was demanded, such as being required to say 'my pleasure' rather than 'no problem'.

I quickly found my anxiety to be unwarranted as I was happily surprised to find that it was a fun place to work. The best part of the whole gig was the provided training, a rare occurrence for bartending positions. I loved being outside on the waterfront. The sun shone, and the seagulls attacked. God forbid anyone left a plate of fries unattended. There was even a kitchen built right onto the patio. That first summer was so relaxed that I could bring a pint down to the kitchen staff in exchange for a stone oven pizza; what more could a university student want? The patio itself was relatively new, and the managers were kind. They worked in collaboration with the staff to improve the systems. If I had an idea, we would often try it out. It was a fantastic summer, and I was sad to leave.

Bartending is a strange industry; one never knows what to expect when going into a job. Having worked a few jobs, I have found that service standards are always skewed. Some places expect bartenders to put on a show, others expect them to do nothing more than make them money. Only the most malleable of people can find success, an area in which I have struggled.

Coming back to the patio a few years later, I was hoping little had changed. I quickly came to find that things had certainly changed, and in the most drastic sense of the word. The original idea that it may be a stuck-up establishment came fully to fruition. There was a new head manager who thrived on micromanagement; nothing anyone ever did was good enough. Rules were much stricter. The kitchen moved inside, and the old shell sat out like a rusted car. It was clear there would be no under-the-table pizza trades. A short-lived bonus was that my sister got hired on as a server and then eventually as a bartender. We had a great time working together; it was pretty special. Although the money was good for her, the working conditions were not. She, along with the other female workers, were held to different standards than the men. The manager was judgmental of their short skirts and would often berate them. It seemed to be a strange and sick sort of jealousy. I may not have known what I wanted to be doing post-graduation, but it sure as hell was not to be working there. The worst bit was that I still had not heard back from any of the jobs I applied to out west. I began to worry I would be stuck at the bar until my volunteer program began. I had no clue how I would get through the next five-plus months if that was the case.

[CHAPTER FIVE]

Northern Nova Scotia is a part of the Appalachian mountain range. The scenic area is formally known as Cape Breton Island. It is well regarded for having one of the most scenic roads in the world, the Cabot Trail. The oddly-shaped island is often said to be reminiscent of the aforementioned lobster's tail. One of my good friends is from there, and the boys and I were long planning a visit. It is a place known for its rugged terrain and Celtic music. Our adventure would be both a hiking trip and a pub crawl, but as with the majority of trips, it was just a good excuse to spend uninterrupted time together. We got together to set a date for the trip. To everyone's shock, all of us were available at the same time. I immediately approached my manager to get the time booked off, considering that it was weeks away, this should have been no problem.

Without a second's thought, she told me, "I'm so sorry, we're short-staffed. I can't approve any time off, especially on the weekend."

This was frustrating, especially seeing as the reason we were short-staffed was that no one wanted to work for her.

Regardless, I did not want to risk the job, and so it seemed I would have to miss the trip.

In the weeks after I finished applying to all of the jobs out west, I developed the unhealthy habit of checking my email multiple times a day. This was wrapped in the hopes I would hear back about one of my many applications. As the weekend that the boys would head up north drew closer, I grew more and more disappointed that I could not join. A few days before they were set to leave, I checked my email expecting nothing but more disappointment. This expectation was unnecessary; my hard work paid off. I finally received a job interview. It was from a place called Arbutus Falls Retreat and Spa. The name itself made it sound like a lovely place to work. Not that beggars can be choosers, I probably would have been happy were it called Rusty's Dirty Anchor and Brothel.

Funnily enough, it happened that I heard from the spot where I applied for four different positions. Not so funnily, I did not realize this. So, when the General Manager, Kevin, asked which position I was interested in, I told him bartending.

He responded with a bit of a smirk, "Oh, it says here you also applied for housekeeping, maintenance, and, let's see here, front desk."

Naturally, this came to me as a surprise. When I prepared for the interview, I found my application for bartending and stopped searching there and then.

I collected myself and responded with all the confidence I could muster, "Yes, that's right. I merely meant that bartending is my preference. Which positions do you have openings for?"

The gentleman laughed heartily, and I smiled along with him as he said, "You applied for four different positions. I think that you would fit in well here. We actually happen to have openings in all of them. Tell me about your qualifications, and we will see what we can come up with."

I was immediately flooded with relief; I felt that the job was all but mine. How could they have openings in all four positions and not hire me for one? They would have to be crazy. I did as he asked and quickly learned that bartending was the position he was most keen to fill. After some discussion, we agreed I would work the main restaurant's bar and help out in housekeeping from time to time. Despite a lack of desired knowledge, I expressed a strong interest in working maintenance. This interest was in hopes that I might gain the knowledge I so lacked. Kevin said he understood and that this would likely be a possibility.

    Having agreed upon which role suited me the best, my future boss shared a bit of information about the Retreat's location. I could hardly contain my excitement.

    He was rather businesslike in his demeanour, "I like to give a quick spiel about the island to provide a bit of information so you know what you're getting yourself into. Arbutus Falls is on Georgia Island, one of the Gulf Islands off the coast of British Columbia. It's a small island with a small population. Do you have any questions?"

    The question that was burning a hole in my pocket was about housing; I responded with it, "Well, it's not exactly about the island. I was wondering what the deal is with staff accommodations. I read that it's provided."

    Jovially, he said, "Yes, that's right. We provide accommodation, you can do staff housing for ten dollars a day or have your own camper van for fifteen."

    Those words were music to my ears. I believe that was the moment I truly knew I would be heading out west sooner rather than later.

    After getting confirmation that there was a fair bit of partying in staff housing, I said, "Let's do the camper van, I enjoy my own space."

    I could clearly see on the video call that he was taking note of this; it appeared to be quite official.

    Kevin continued, "We like our staff to work four days a week, ten hours a day. We find this provides flexibility for off-property activities."

Hearing that the place seemed to have a culture that encouraged adventure furthered the soundtrack of music to my ears. I was absolutely sold. Perhaps, were I less desperate for a job, then I would have seen the interview for what it was, a sales pitch. Although, in my defence, it was a damn good pitch.

My new boss wrapped up the call by saying, "Okay, I've got to get going. I'll send you the contract before I hop on my water plane. I've got to get home for the weekend."
I reacted exactly as he intended me to: "Water plane?"
He smiled proudly, "That's right, my house is in Vancouver, I only live on the island during the week. The water plane is quite a bit more expensive, but it sure is worth it. You should try it while you're out here." I nodded along like that was a reasonable possibility.

The call ended, and I pushed my chair out from the desk. I was so excited that I did not know what to do with myself. I wanted to run in circles and jump up and down. Reason prevailed, and I checked my email, this time expecting something. A man of his word, Kevin sent me the contract. I gave it a read through and then booked my flight to British Columbia. It was just two weeks away.

[CHAPTER SIX]

Words could not describe the feeling of receiving my flight's booking confirmation. The email, which I subsequently sent to the head manager at the bar, also brought a smile to my face. It went something like this:

Hi Evangeline,

I just wanted to let you know that I will be unavailable to work my scheduled shifts over the next three days. I will be out of town in Cape Breton. I apologize for the late notice, and I hope you have a good weekend.

Also, please accept this as my two-week notice. My final day will be August 29th. If you would like to schedule me between my trip to Cape Breton and then, please let me know. I would be happy to work.

Many thanks,

Although my manager was less than impressed, she performed a rare demonstration of humanity and accepted my decision without fuss. She even wanted me to continue working upon my return. In all fairness, it was more likely that she was simply so desperate for workers.

The boys' trip was magical. It was filled with good food and an abundance of laughter. The cottage we booked had a huge backyard that looked out over the ocean. After spending days on the trail, we would return home to refresh ourselves in the cold salt water. We would then warm up by the barbecue and play Spike Ball until the sun went down over the water. One evening was spent at the pub down the road, and we did our best to blend in with the locals. After everyone but the driver downed a couple, we discreetly ordered a tray of six beers for our resident Cape Bretoner. The server made a whole show when she came over with the pints, and soon the entire pub was cheering as he chugged one down. I am certain they would have cheered twice as loud had they known who he was. The music was cheerful, and the beer flowed freely. The trip provided my friends and me with a lovely opportunity to say 'see you later'. I returned to the city refreshed and feeling at peace.

In stark contrast to my trip, there was some shocking and rather disappointing news awaiting me back in the city. Upon my return, my sister shared with me what happened at the bar over the weekend. One of our best and sweetest servers was taking care of a table of old men when one of them sexually assaulted her. She had no intentions of letting the incident slide, so she showed her strength of character and reported it to the head manager. As I believe I have made clear, it was widely known that this particular manager was less than competent. Despite that, I had begun to think she at least possessed some humanity. Her actions in response to the assault immediately erased the idea that there may have been an ounce within her. She did not hesitate when she told the server to suck it up and keep serving the men. It got worse. The server took the reasonable step of filing a formal complaint with human resources. In response, she was put on unpaid leave and eventually fired. The last I heard, she was suing them. I hope she won. Now, I am unsure what is worse, being an old man who gets off on wielding power over young women, or supporting this pathetic behaviour. To make matters worse, the men were friends with the general manager of the bar. It is no stretch of the imagination to think their connection may have had something to do with the patio's response to the incident. We will leave it at this; it was a shitty place in a shitty industry.

    I emailed the manager and told her I heard what transpired and that I disapproved. I also let her know that I was now unavailable for any more shifts. To say the least, I was happy to get out of that hellhole, and even more grateful when my sister tendered her resignation soon after.

    I was more than ready for a fresh start. As the days ticked down, it was with great enthusiasm that I packed my bag. After five years of monotonous university and essentially a lifetime on the East Coast, any nerves I may have had were overshadowed by anticipation for this great adventure to the west. I left home feeling free.

    As you will soon see, things did not work out even close to plan. Looking back, if I knew then what I know now, I do still think that I would have gone. Regardless of life's tumultuous unpredictability, I strongly believe that we are meant to take it as it comes. Besides, why would something happen if it is not meant to? The less control we attempt the exercise, the better. Anyway, enough about me. It is time to introduce a man for whose friendship I am ever so grateful.

[CHAPTER SEVEN]

A popular saying amongst Canadians is 'worst-case Ontario'. Canada's most populous province is by no means its most popular, and for good reason. In my humble opinion, Toronto, Ontario's capital, is the province at its worst. It is a breeding ground for crime, financial disparity, and entitled pricks. It is a city where it is as difficult to find an affordable apartment as it is to find nature. It would be a waste of words to argue in the 'Six's' favour, but the rest of the province is not so bad. Take the town of Aurora, a place perched halfway between the big smoke and Lake Simcoe. Residents are blessed with relatively clean air and considerable access to weekend getaways. If you do have to go to the city, god forbid, and hopefully it is just to use the airport, then you are within reasonable reach of it. Most importantly, the people are down-to-earth, caring folk. One downside is that Aurora is a silent victim of suburban sprawl. It is for this reason that more than seventy percent of the town's households possess a minimum of two cars. In Canada's capitalistic-capital, this translates to money.

One Jared Johnston, known fondly by his employees as JJ, best known as Jared Johnston of Hyundai Aurora, capitalized on this auto-opportunity. A mechanic turned entrepreneur, he opened his first business in 1975. He teamed up with some fellow mechanics and focused on reselling used cars. He had a nose for getting good deals on vehicles that were not quite roadworthy. His entrepreneurial talent, in conjunction with a competent team of mechanics who repaired and refurbished these cars, made for a successful business. It was nothing to get filthy rich from, but he and his employees never worried about putting food on the table. His business pivoted in the direction of the filthy rich in 1983. This was when Hyundai decided that it was time to wade into the Canadian automotive industry. Through hearsay, JJ learned about the success and reliability of this Korean company's cars. Having seen with his own eyes the success of American and German car dealerships in Aurora, he reached out to Hyundai in hopes that his business could be a part of their Canadian venture.

His proactivity paid off as his used car company evolved into Hyundai Aurora. He was able to bring all of his workers along with him; some of the mechanics even travelled to Seoul to participate in Hyundai-specific training. Any humble businessman should know you need to work hard and get lucky to hit it big. JJ was no stranger to hard work, and he was also fully aware of the luck that befell him. The thing about luck is that it often runs out, more often in ways unimaginable. As fate would have it, it was at his place of business that his only child's luck would flee.

[CHAPTER EIGHT]

Jared Johnston Jr. was not a fan of the name which his father insisted he bear. In fact, there was little middle ground upon which the two Jareds stood. While the senior was a gifted entertainer with strong opinions, the junior was soft-spoken and spent more time analyzing others than weighing in on things. Despite these differences, they got on well enough. For his time, JJ was relatively emotionally intelligent and was able to begrudgingly accept that his son would walk his own path. However, this acceptance did not stop him from making many attempts to encourage his son to take over his business. These attempts came from a place of love. He wanted his son, and hopefully his son's family, to be financially stable. The son understood from where the father was coming, yet he preferred to put his heart before his pocketbook. Besides, with his father's successes, money would likely never be a problem.

The passion possessed by Jared Jr. was instilled by his late aunt. Aunt Sarah was herself a widow and moved into the Johnston family house when he was a young lad. While his mother was distant and preferred pills to playing, Sarah was a hobby photographer. She would often bring him along on day trips up to Lake Simcoe to capture nature's beauty. He took to it from the start, and they could often be spotted wandering around downtown Aurora snapping photos, attempting to extract beauty from the seemingly mundane. While developing the film was always exciting, it was the process of capturing photos that the young man fell in love with. Naturally, Aunt Sarah left him her photography gear when she passed away all too young. While Jared missed her dearly, his stoic nature allowed him to focus on gratitude for the time well spent with her.

Jared, of course, was given his own car the moment he had his license, and maybe even a few months prior to that. Any relatively free weekend, he would make the two-and-a-half-hour drive up to Algonquin Provincial Park. He had a couple of preferred places to set up camp, always doing it as quickly as possible to make more time for photography. Once settled in, he would wander through the woods for hours. Although a talented photographer, it was not so much about the pictures themselves as it was about clearing his mind. Whether conscious or not, he was always at peace as he made his way through the trees. At this point, Jared had his first DSLR camera; he was not one to hesitate when moving on from film, although his aunt's camera would always remain near and dear.

The financial status of Jared's family allowed him the unique privilege of choosing work he actually wanted to do. Without a shadow of a doubt, his father made it clear that Jared should work in sales and be groomed to inherit Hyundai Aurora. In return, the son respectfully made it clear that this was not something that would ever happen. He spent his early twenties using his privilege to travel internationally. As you can imagine, he took many pictures along the way. He visited parts of Asia and most of central Europe, but the West Coast of Canada held a special place in his heart. Its sea-to-sky mountains were a photographer's paradise. Jared's largest struggle was finding a way to get paid for his photography. He made money here and there from submitting to travel and nature magazines, but he wanted something a bit steadier. When he returned from a trip out west, he was surprised to find it was his father who came up with a solution.

    Jared was living in his father's basement unit. It was October, and they sat in his father's kitchen looking out at the newly red and yellow leaves in the yard. His father had invited him up for a coffee and a chat.

    JJ spoke like a man who knew the truth, "Son, if I understand correctly, you're quite set on monetizing this hobby of yours, right?"

    Jared took a sip of his homemade cappuccino and responded, "You know it, the only thing is that I have no damn clue how to do it."

    Jared Sr. continued, "Well, I've got an idea that I think you might like. Actually, I don't know if you'll like it, but I think it makes sense." He paused, and looking out the window, he said, "I want you to come work for me."

    Junior rolled his eyes as he prepared to reject his father for the millionth time, "Dad, I know you want me to come sell cars, I'm just not interested. Maybe if I get really stuck in the future, but not now."

    Senior smiled knowingly, "That's not what I was going to suggest."

    Junior responded impatiently with a crook in his eyebrows, "Well, do go on, please."

    Senior went on as requested, "I want to give you a job in photography. I want you to come take photos of the cars; the pictures our guys take are shit. As much as you know I hate it, a solid online presence has become crucial. You know your way around a camera like I know my way around a car, and that's what we need. It obviously wouldn't be enough work for a full-time position, but I'd say you can stretch it into a few days a week."

    This idea perked Junior up more than the coffee; he took a minute to think it over before responding, "I like it, it's steady work, and it being part-time gives me the chance to keep figuring things out."

There were a few more details to be ironed out, but that was the beginning of Jared Jr.'s first regularly paying photography gig.

All in all, the agreement between father and son worked quite well. JJ was happy to have his boy around the dealership and wasted few opportunities to attempt to recruit him to sales. Now his pitch was that it would be just two or three days a week, and he could keep taking the pictures. Junior was grateful for the chance, yet he unwaveringly rejected his dad's offers to extend his workweek to a full one. Time went on, and as it passed, the situation only got better. At this point, Jared had begun a photography company. It was in the early stages, so he was still taking essentially any job that came his way. He utilized his father's connections and landed jobs taking pictures of homes being sold and countless family photos. His dream was to make money taking pictures in nature, but he was grateful for what he had. It is a damn good thing that he was not alone in nature when he had his seizure.

[CHAPTER NINE]

It was your typical Monday for Junior, until it was not. He was at the dealership taking some photos of the 2022 Hyundai Elantra Hybrid. His dad hated the hybrid cars, but they sure did sell. JJ liked to say, 'It may only be half a car, but people sure do pay full price for them. ' Junior had just opened the car's trunk and was leaning forward with his camera to make the space look bigger. That was when he blacked out. As he began to seize, he fell forward and cracked his head perfectly on the corner of the trunk's edge. A mechanic found him no more than a minute after his fall, and by then, he was still. An ambulance came, and he was hurried to the hospital. Both an MRI and a CT scan were performed due to the extended period of time that he spent unconscious, twenty minutes altogether. Nothing was found that should have triggered the seizure, and he would never have another in his life. It was one of those freak accidents that serves as a grave reminder that our bodies are by no means perfect. The worst part of the whole ordeal was that the blow to his head left him badly concussed.

Jared spent the next months attempting to recover. It did not go well. He could hardly focus on anything without triggering a searing pain in his head. It felt as though his brain was trying to escape; this level of discomfort lasted the entire first month. Once the pain began to subside, his problems only worsened. He would focus on a task as simple as sending a text, only to find his mind wandering aimlessly. This frustrated him to the point of anger and then depression. His coping method was unhealthy but effective. Rather than feeling distraught over his misfortune, he would smoke a joint and forget it all. When he was not stoned, he was pissed off. He was a reasonable man and understood that shit happens and that he is not immune to said shit. But his reasonable philosophy provided little comfort; he was damn annoyed that his health was not improving. The most he could manage was the walk into town to a small cafe, and that was where he found salvation of a sort.

He always came to the same cafe, and he always came during off-peak hours. Eva, a friend of the family, managed the place. On his good days, he would chat with her. It was late in summer, four months after the accident, and he was having a very good day. He was as deep in conversation as possible with Eva. By now, she was quite aware of his situation, marijuana included. Being a kind and considerate woman, she wanted what was best for Jared, and in this case, she thought that best might be a change of scenery.

Eva began, "You know the fancy Retreat my daughter's been working at this summer?"

Jared interrupted jokingly, "You mean partying at?"

Eva let out an exasperated breath, "Good, so you do remember, good for you. I've been thinking about it, you should apply. Chloe told me that they have plenty of job openings and that accommodation is included. It could be great for you to get out of here for a while, and besides, the island is beautiful."

Jared thought this over carefully and responded hesitantly, "I don't know. I do need a change, but I'm not sure I'm up to it yet."

Eva's smile reached her eyes as she said, "You think it over. I'm going to send you the information regardless, so you can at least take a look."

At that moment, Jared thought very little of the conversation. Thankfully, what he thought did not matter. A seed had been planted, a strong and resilient seed.

Later that week, when he was feeling up to facing the light on his laptop's screen, he pulled up the Retreat's website that Eva had so sweetly sent his way. He was immediately taken by the Retreat and then the island's beauty. While looking at the website, he appreciated the aerial shots of the expansive bay immensely; he gave silent kudos to the photographer. Jared had experience working in a kitchen from when he was younger, and his father had insisted he get a job, which is the same role for which he applied now. His interview went well enough, although he did not think much of the Retreat's manager, Kevin. He seemed disingenuous and overexcited. Something like a hungry dog waiting for dinner. Kevin insisted he work in both the kitchen and housekeeping. Jared was not particularly ecstatic at the prospect, but he was set on experiencing island life. Besides, he told himself he would not stay more than a year, which, for his perception of time, was not too long. He told his father he was leaving and knew he would understand. Jared Senior wished him luck and agreed that the change of scenery would treat him well. He was happy not to have his almost thirty-year-old son smoking weed in his basement any longer. The following week, Jared Junior packed his bags and headed for Georgia Island. Now, back to me and my journey to the same floating rock.

[CHAPTER TEN]

Two flights and over seven hours of airtime delivered me to the Vancouver airport. Thanks to an early morning departure and the four hours I gained from the time change, I still had a few hours of daylight to work with upon arrival. I took a bus to the Tsawwassen ferry terminal and awaited my ferry's boarding time. I did not have to wait long. With an extended day's travel behind me, I stepped onto the boat that would further deliver me to my new home. Departing from southern Vancouver, the city loomed behind me in the ever-increasing distance as we chugged towards the Minor Gulf Islands. I looked around in excitement as rugged rocky coasts blended into lush rainforests. With summer at its end, the rainy season had arrived. Thanks to the increase in water, each isle was a floating mass of green. Mount Roman is the highest point in all the Gulf Islands; it sits in the middle of Georgia Island. From afar, it can be seen towering mightily above the otherwise calm landscape. I had done just enough research to know of its existence. There was no mistaking it as we drew closer.

The boat docked with a metallic shudder. As we stopped, the ramp was released. The crew looked to be a part of the machine as they swiftly prepared to unload. Being a foot passenger, I made my way off the ferry first. I failed to notice that I was the sole foot passenger disembarking. There were two short rows of cars waiting to board. I walked past them on my way up to the main road. It was easy to find my ride, a white van with a black decal, which was idling. It read, 'Arbutus Falls Retreat and Spa'.
The front passenger window rolled down, and the driver asked, "You the guy?"
I was the only guy; I smiled enthusiastically as I got into the front seat, "I must be the guy, and that makes you Brian."
I gave pleasantries to the head of maintenance, and received none in return. Briefly, a smile passed over his lips. He did not seem to be in a good mood, although it may have simply been his natural demeanour. Thankfully, no darkness could dull

my mood, and as I launched a barrage of questions, he slowly perked up.

He answered one of the many queries, "Yeah, I can tell you a bit about the island. Only about two thousand people live on Georgia, and the island is split by a small canal. You see, there's north and south Georgia, and that canal is the divide. The majority of folk live in the northern part."

We drove through what seemed to be an endless forest of towering trees. They eventually dispersed as we approached a small wooden bridge.

Brian said, "We're leaving the north for the southern part. Arbutus Falls is about as far as you can get from civilization, which here means there's next to nothing. The south has a grocery store, which we'll be stopping at. I told some people I'd pick up booze."

I was slightly taken aback by how far the Retreat seemed to be from the island's general population, especially considering that it was only a measly two thousand. This thought was quickly dispersed by the idea that it would be cool to live in the forest.

I asked, "How do people typically get around?"

He answered almost hesitantly, "Well, some folk have their own cars, I'd make friends with them, otherwise you can book the van, but it's not cheap. I'll bet Kevin even makes you pay for this ride."

I could not place what, but something about his attitude was rather off-putting. The oddity of this was compounded by the fact that his energy was rather calming. I could not decide what to make of him.

To my immense gratitude, the 'only a grocery store' was more of a town square, albeit a miniature one at that. The store was accompanied by a gas station, cafe, and restaurant. We parked at the store and walked past the restaurant's chalk sign, which advertised two-for-one wine with dinner.

Brian saw me looking and said, "That there is about the classiest place we've got."

He then led me to the tiny liquor store. Brian told me to take my time, but in every way possible, he seemed to be in a rush. I was amazed that he had already bought a couple of hundred dollars' worth of liquor and brought it back to the van before I had even found the beer section. I grabbed a couple of local tall boys and put them on the counter.

The clerk looked me up and down before saying, "Do you want these cold?"

I shrugged in response, "If you don't mind."

The clerk opened a mini fridge that was hidden behind the counter and pulled out two cans of Bud Light. I knew my buddy Owen was somewhere smiling, "Here, these ones are better."

Not knowing quite what to say, I thanked them and paid. I guess I was drinking water, in the future I would take the beer warm.

It was time for the grocery store next door. Calling it a grocery store was a generous stretch by any means; in any city, it would hardly be considered a small convenience store. Do not get me started on the prices; you would have thought the stuff was imported from Mars. I knew meals were included at the Retreat, but I was unsure of their frequency. Not having enough food was not a risk I was willing to take; better safe than sorry. I bit the bullet and broke the bank.

Our errands complete, we got back in the van. We continued through the tall trees, eventually arriving deeper in the middle of nowhere. Turning off the main road, although another suitable name would have been 'the only road', the van's headlights lit up a large white sign that professed the establishment's name, one I would soon come to loathe, Arbutus Falls Retreat and Spa.

[CHAPTER ELEVEN]

My initial introduction to the Retreat was underwhelming. Although what else could I have expected? 'Hey there, we're so happy you're here that we threw you a parade. Want some champagne?'

Brian pulled up to the main lobby. The Retreat was perched upon a hill, and we seemed to be roughly halfway up it. He was kind enough to walk me in and ensure I was settled. It was late enough in the day that my new boss had already evacuated the premises, and so it was a sweet young woman at the front desk who took care of me. The lobby itself was a large open room that managed to give the feeling that you were on a ship. A huge balcony protruded from the back; it faced the bay and managed to catch the last light dancing in the shallows.

Luck was quick to shine upon me, the front desk lady said my permanent room was not yet available. I was to be temporarily housed in a guest suite. Based on the way in which she excitedly shared this news, I could tell it was a very good thing. I said goodbye to Brian and thanked him for everything. For whatever reason, our paths would never cross again. The woman showed me to my room. She told me that if I needed anything, I should let her know. As she made her way out, she told me her name was Liz. I looked at her closely for the first time as I thanked her. She was probably a few years older than me. She wore no make-up and her hair was in a bun. She had cute freckles and a look that radiated kindness in a hometown kind of way. As the door closed behind her, I breathed a sigh of contentment and examined the room. There was a jacuzzi tub with sliding louvred windows. If you were to sit in the tub and look through the open windows, then you would see a large ocean-viewing patio. A king bed facing an electric fireplace completed my cozy accommodations.

Just as I made up my mind to settle in by running the tub and cracking a flavourless beer, I heard a knocking at the door. I could not imagine who it could be. However, in retrospect, who else could it have been? Never having been one for modesty, I opened the door as I was, shirtless. I was pleased to find my new acquaintance, Liz. I was even more pleased to see that she was holding a bottle of wine.

Unable, or uninterested, in displaying discretion, she looked me up and down and then coolly said, "Hello again, I thought you deserved a proper Arbutus Falls welcome, so I snuck you a bottle of wine from the cupboard. We can't take too many, but they haven't noticed yet."

I was incredibly grateful for her kindness, "Oh Liz, that is so sweet of you, and it's red, my favourite."

She smiled happily, "Oh, good, it's my pleasure, I just wanted to help you feel at home."

She continued in a playful tone, "Maybe you can bring that bottle up to staff accommodations later and join in on our party."

I was flattered, but exhausted, "I would love nothing more, but I've been travelling since three am, I'm headed straight to bed after my bath."

She showed nothing but understanding, "Oh yes, of course. You must be so tired. Well, I've got to get back to the front desk. It was nice meeting you. Sweet dreams."

I wished her a good night and retreated to my room. I was not entirely truthful in that conversation. I possessed very little interest in joining in on too much partying, at least since there seemed to be so much alcohol involved. I exhausted that kind of excitement back in Newfoundland.

I was quite keen to explore and would have loved to have done it then and there. Sadly, the sun had long since set; exploration would have to wait. I attempted to unwind, feeling a healthy balance of anxiety and optimism. Nerves from being alone more than 4000 kilometres from home went to war with the endless possibilities that this new life provided. I let the tug-of-war slip from my mind as I soaked in the tub and enjoyed my beverage. After pulling the plug and drying off, I climbed cozily into bed. Sleep quickly won out as exhaustion from my coast-to-coast journey cast me into a deep and dreamless slumber.

[CHAPTER TWELVE]

On my first morning of island living, I rose early to enjoy a coffee. I brewed it in my room's Keurig and then went out onto the balcony. The salty ocean breeze mixed well with my drink's aroma. The light pushing its way past tall clouds provided a means to appreciate the beauty of my new home. The balcony provided a lovely view of how the Retreat was tucked away in a snug bay, and a large marina was protected on either side by looming rock walls. As I faced the ocean, the cliffs to my right were high and stretched at least a hundred meters along the coast. The left side was not as tall, but made up for that lack of height with a waterfall that steadily poured itself onto the beach. I had been able to hear the rushing water as I slept, and the sound was beautifully amplified outside. I could see that the beach was not sand, it was made up of small stones and shells with speckles of seaweed, which looked to provide a comfortable shore. I stood at the railing, drinking my coffee and taking it all in. Most of all, I found myself mentally preparing for the day ahead.

I awoke to a message from Kevin, telling me to ask for him at the front desk any time after nine. Feeling refreshed, I went to meet the general manager. In the lobby, I was happily surprised to see that Liz was already back at the front desk. She looked good, like she had not been up late partying the night before. I could not help but wonder if her invitation to the party was more of a personal one. We greeted each other kindly, and she showed me to the office.

I was immediately put off when I saw my new boss. Kevin was by no means the man that I imagined when chatting over the video call. It goes to show just how deceiving seeing only a person's face can be. I expected someone fit and whose energy garnered natural respect. Rather, he was a short, round man, with a shiny bowling ball precariously balanced between his shoulders. I should clarify that I know people of his stature who garner and deserve natural respect; this man simply did not.

He hardly said hello before sticking a contract in my face and saying, "You'll want to sign here, here, and there."

Not enjoying his brashness, I took my time bending down to greet his French Bulldog, asking, "What's this guy's name?"

Kevin seemed to instantly change moods, he said, "That's Oscar, he's a bit annoying, but quite friendly."

He did not even take a breath before continuing, "Now, you've agreed that you're staying until late December, correct? I have that in the contract."

I stood over the desk at which he was sitting and began to feel uncomfortable with the height difference. I opted to sit down.

Now slightly unsure, I said, "That's the plan. I've just got to be home for Christmas."

I signed here, here, and there, as ordered. All the while, I was thinking about how this man seemed absolutely nothing like the one I interviewed with. If I were more on the ball or more of a cynic, then maybe it would have occurred earlier that it was indeed not the same man.

Kevin clapped his hands together, "Okay, let's go get this out of the way."

As he barged out of the room, he slammed the door shut in his dog's face. Oscar was a cute pup. I could not imagine him being any more annoying than your standard dog. I also could not help but notice that he looked rather like a smaller version of his owner. I had one other thought as I followed him out. There was something odd in the way he confirmed I was staying until December. He did not ask it like he was confirming that it was what I wanted; he asked it as though it was an obligation. I could think of no world where that was a good sign.

Once we were outside, Kevin wasted no time in beginning the much-anticipated tour.

As we headed down towards the beach, he said, "So, this is the bay, Freshwater Bay. Our marina is huge, it boasts more than one hundred slips, we house anything from sailboats to multimillion-dollar yachts".

As he said this, he motioned to a multi-story boat taking up an entire length of dock. It must have been at least 30 meters long, and it looked like you could have your entire extended family living on there comfortably. Despite its size, it was strangely quiet, and I found myself wondering who needed something that big. There was also a separate dock that was gated off and had Canada's official government signage; it looked quite out of place.

Kevin saw me looking and explained, "That's a Canadian customs office, it's used whenever a boat or water plane comes in from the States. It's rarely used, but it is always a spectacle when it is."

Guarding the entrance to the marina's docks stood a tall building that resembled a lighthouse. "Here we have the tower, the bottom has a cafe and a gift shop. The top part is converted into accommodation, and that is where I live. I only take the water plane home on weekends, although soon I'll be moving off the island permanently, and then it will be staff accommodations."

Oh fuck yeah, we love a cafe, I thought to myself. I also did not hate the idea of him leaving the island. We were standing just above the sea, level with a chain link fenced-in pool and hot tub that were below the tower.

Kevin said, "This is the lower pool; it's okay, but the upper pool is much nicer. There are also some guest laundry facilities tucked away on the bottom floor. The changing rooms and showers get pretty filthy. They're used by the people who live on their boats."

Looking up the hill while standing at the marina, the tower was on the left side of the Retreat's main road. Across the road, on the right side, was the lobby and lodge in which I was staying.

Kevin continued, "You already know the main building. On the far end by the waterfall, there is an event room and spa.

Right now, the spa is closed; we're using it as extra staff accommodation."

I pondered within my mind, what's with all this extra staff accommodation, first the tower and now the spa. Sitting below the lobby, also just above sea level, was a restaurant.

Kevin followed my gaze and said, "This is Driftwood, you'll be bartending here most of the time. I won't bother showing you around because you'll get a proper tour on your first shift."

Driftwood, the name could be of a place that was either really nice or really trashy, nowhere in between. I was gently leaning towards trashy based on how dead the place looked. It looked deader than a raccoon that failed to make it across the Trans-Canada Highway.

We made our way up the hill along the road, passing the main building and the tower. We followed the road about halfway up before turning right towards the main lobby entrance. This was the spot where Brian had brought me the night before. On the left side of the cul-de-sac that served as a lobby drop-off point was a beautiful stone staircase that led up. Set high enough on the hill to overlook the bay was indeed a much nicer pool. Most importantly, I would soon find out that it was heated. Tucked behind the pool, and in the hill itself, was the building that served it. It housed a gym that had floor-to-ceiling panoramic windows. There were also some more changing rooms with showers. It was easy to imagine myself enjoying a workout and then hopping in for a swim. This tour was making me feel really good about this move out west.

The upper pool was about halfway up the previously mentioned staircase. At its top, and in the woods, was a series of winding trails speckled with private cottages. Each had its own kitchen, barbecue, and outdoor hot tub. I would come to learn that these were the most luxurious of the guest houses. If you were to continue up the hill along the main road, rather than take the stone stairs, you would first pass the pool on your right before arriving at the largest of the cottages. There were five of them, and they were directly behind the pool. They were not as new as the cottages in the woods, but they did have an even lovelier view of the bay. All in all, I could not help but be impressed. The name Arbutus Falls Retreat and Spa certainly stood up to the test. This was no Rusty's Dirty Anchor and Brothel. Admittedly, it was not the kind of place I would likely ever stay on my own dollar, not so much because I could not afford it, but simply because this level of luxury does not appeal to me as a good use of money. I am more of a private and rustic cabin-in-the-woods kind of guy.

  You may recall that during my interview, I was asked to pick between living in the main staff building or a private camper van. You may also recall I opted for the slightly more expensive camper van in the name of privacy. I could tell the tour was wrapping up, so I asked Kevin if he would show me my van. Before the question was fully out of my mouth, I detected another change in this man's demeanour, as though he were reverting to the person whose office I originally walked into that morning. His tone quickly changed from friendly to frustrated.
  He said incredulously, "Your van? The vans are only for couples or people with pets. You'll be staying in the main staff building. Someone will show you later."
  I was puzzled by both the content of his response and the sudden change in character.
  Before I could even attempt to respond, he quickly continued along, saying, "You'll start by training on the bar and then we'll get you trained in housekeeping. I expect that your schedule may be a little packed the first couple of weeks. We're a bit short-staffed and need to get you trained up. That won't be an issue, will it?"
  Questions bounced around my mind. Short-staffed? Had he not said that the spa was being used for extra staff accommodations? How the hell could they be short of staff? Before I could utter a word or even finish my thought, he shoved a schedule into my hands. I took a quick look at it, and my confusion doubled. Once I started, it had me working nine days straight. That seemed to be a bit more than a little packed. Everything happened so quickly that I was unable to utter an intelligible sentence. I also

wanted to avoid making a bad first impression, so I accepted it awkwardly.

Hesitantly, I said, "This only has starting times listed. Will each shift be ten hours long?"

He continued his act of surprise, "No, the shifts will be about seven hours, depending on how busy we are, okay, I've got to go."

With that, my new boss was gone.

I was utterly baffled. I stumbled back to my room in a bit of a haze, subconsciously hoping to process this unwelcome, and frankly unbelievable, news. I made it back to my room and sat out on the balcony, hoping against hope that the fresh air would do me some good. I allowed my mind to run through what had occurred. During the interview, Kevin was crystal clear about the four-day, ten-hour workweeks. I literally wrote it down. I highly doubted there was a misunderstanding; it seemed he simply spat two outright lies. The first being the scheduling, and the second being my accommodations. I could not imagine the accommodation situation could be too bad, but doubts still began to swirl. They focused on my questions surrounding why there was so much extra staff housing. Was there something wrong with the normal ones? I began to spiral downward into a pit of anxiety and started to question what I had gotten myself into. More than anything, I was thinking of my family, especially my dog. I missed their unwavering support, and my dog's unwavering happiness. On this lovely note, let us meet an important woman.

[CHAPTER THIRTEEN]

As a rule, many humans do not happily embrace change. We are creatures of habit, and the interruption of these habits can be frightening. Change so often threatens the oasis that one has carefully sculpted. Thankfully, the oasis is imaginary, existing only within the mind. During difficult times, when that internal peace is unattainable, one must either sink or swim. The strongest of us refuse to accept this lack of peace and take it upon ourselves to swim, to force the hand of change. Perhaps we do this with the hope of one day rebuilding and revisiting that oasis. Perhaps it is simply natural, our nature. Around the time I was making my way down to Cape Breton with the boys, a woman was living in Victoria, Vancouver Island's capital city. She had been feeling the winds of change for some time. She would not sink; she was planning to let them carry her.

    Jennifer felt as though she was being beaten down by one thing after another. This had been going on for as long as she could subconsciously recollect. She had been settled in Victoria for more than two years. At its peak, her situation was a good one. Jen was a registered massage therapist and had joined a successful practice. More than that, she had been blessed enough to move into the backyard bungalow of said practice. The owner ran the business out of her family's house. They offered a wide variety of treatments along with massage therapy. There was a steady stream of clients, and in the world of a massage therapist, this equated to a solid income. That is assuming that one can keep their expenses within reason. She had developed a friendly relationship with her host family and joined them every Sunday for family dinner.

    After some time, she met someone, and not the kind of someone that you wanted to meet. To start, he seemed sweet as can be, as they often do. As soon as she let him in, he became a leech. He sank his teeth in and stole her wealth and energy. He insisted they eat out, and seeing as he was infinitely between jobs, it was assumed Jen would pay. The relationship quickly became a burden, both mentally and physically. As her mental health faltered, she fooled herself into thinking she needed the relationship to feel better.

    Eventually, the asshole did get a job, and thankfully, it was when she needed financial support the most. It was as though he could sense this, and so he dumped her without explanation. He performed the act of cutting off all communication, which I believe the kids nowadays call ghosting. At least he was gone. To add to her trouble, she had a kid brother. He lived back home with their mother. They lived just outside of Toronto, not so far from one Jared Johnston Jr. However, they lived in a very different financial situation from the Johnsons'. It was a situation requiring Jen to send her brother money so he could get by as well as she felt he deserved. In all fairness, he likely would have been okay without the money, but she sent it anyway. To the impartial eye, it would be apparent that Jen felt some guilt for not being there for Terry, especially considering how impulsive and unreliable their mother could be. Yet Jen knew she needed to stay away; there was no life for her at home. The age gap between the children was too much, and she knew she would end up playing mother. This was something that she was willing to do in no other way than the financial support she imparted.

    Jennifer's finances were spiralling down, and her relationship ended. What pushed her closest to her breaking point was the strain being placed upon her within the household she was living in. An unnecessary strain at that. There was a global sickness going around, and since it was affecting the Western world, it was labelled a pandemic. Her practice, combined with regular yoga, kept her in good health, and so she felt there was little to worry about. She experienced some initial fear when the P-word began to get thrown around, especially in conjunction with the media's catastrophization of the whole thing, but this fear faded. Despite being a spiritual person, Jen found comfort in rationalization. When it became apparent that the sickness seemed only to affect those with bad luck or ill health, she sent them good energy and shrugged it off like the flu. Sadly, the same was not done by her host family; they smelled doom and would not let it go. Jen thought this to be ridiculous, but would never tell them so. In their defence, the media did a damn good job of spreading and stoking the flames of fear, but that hardly justified the way they treated her. When the Canadian Government released a vaccine, she was uninterested. She had already had the illness and recovered quickly, so what was the point? A sick sort of nationalism formed among some. They saw those who refused to get the vaccine as heartless sociopaths, a cruel irony. The matriarch of the household, who was also her employer, led the witch-hunt against her. Perhaps they needed someone to blame for such an unfortunate situation. It is infinitely easier to blame external factors rather than find peace within. Regardless of reasoning, it was Jen who further suffered.

     As the months passed, it became clear to some that the Canadian government was, or had, gone crazy. Those who identified the madness for what it was were unable to prevent it from spreading to some of their compatriots until it was too late. For months, Massage Therapists were unable to practice, and the money in lieu was not enough for Jennifer. It was not enough for most. As lost time added up, her finances were irrecoverably strained and relationships bent beyond repair. Her world came crashing down, overwhelming her in the process. Change came her way in the form of a tidal wave, and she needed to run for the hills.

     Going home was not an option, and so she turned to something that had worked for her in the past. Jen began looking for a place where she could recover mentally while not having to stress financially. She started job hunting for a place that provided staff accommodations and meals. Fate seemed to be working in her favour, or maybe it was karma, as this woman had a huge heart. She managed to find a place just a forty-minute ferry ride away from Victoria. It was an island called Georgia and a Retreat called Arbutus Falls. She interviewed and learned that they wanted her immediately. She would be able to start as a server, but the Retreat also had a spa. It was closed for the time being; however, the nice man who interviewed her said she could practice there once it reopened. In reality, that never came to fruition. As you will see, the spa at Arbutus Falls Retreat and Spa would never reopen.

[CHAPTER FOURTEEN]

     Something that I have been putting off mentioning, mostly due to embarrassment, is another one of the reasons that I was so desperate to get out of Halifax. I would love nothing more than to leave it out, but there is no way around it. It is soon to be an integral part of the story. So, my city was on absolute lockdown in the months leading up to my graduation. For perspective, I was unable to even legally go for a walk with my friends; we are talking about North Korean levels of lockdown. My mum, who I was living with at the time, is a teacher, and so she was not home during the day. I was isolated from the world, only able to access it through a screen. As I sat at my desk checking boxes to receive my degree, I went down the hill of borderline depression. It was under these conditions that I formed the habit of smoking weed. I had used it recreationally in the past and enjoyed its euphoric aspects, but only socially. However, in the clutches of isolation, I began to use it to escape from reality. It got bad. For months, getting stoned became the first thing that I would do each morning. Thankfully, my usage decreased over the summer while I was working at the bar. I was happy with that, but I wanted to bring it down even more. I hoped that on Georgia I would be so busy between work and adventures that I would hardly have time to toke. I was right about being busy, but not about not having time to toke.

  I sat on my balcony, wading through the situation in which I found myself, and feelings of isolation crept back in. I was frustrated with Kevin for so blatantly lying to me, and at myself for having believed said lies. All these feelings continued to overwhelm me until I decided to put an end to them with the easiest method I knew. I travelled with a little bit of weed and a small pipe. I smoked it sneakily and was immediately filled with a sense of calm relief. I let the sensation settle for a moment and then decided to head out on a self-guided exploration of the Retreat.

  On my rather regrettable tour the day before, I noticed a trail that broke off from the main road. When Kevin and I walked up the hill, I saw it on the left, across from the main building and behind the tower. Based on its positioning, I gauged that it likely led to the base of the high cliffs, possibly even connecting to a hidden portion of the beach. Fuzzy-headed and shrouded in relaxation, thanks to my self-prescribed medication, I headed directly to it. I got there quickly and made my way through the trees following a soft path of grass. The pine trees were too thick for me to be able to see the cliffs ahead, but I could certainly feel their shadow looming. As I got further down the trail, the grass slowly widened. It expanded until it opened up into a small clearing. Now the crowded trees were only present behind me and to my right. Directly ahead was the sheer grey wall. The left side of the clearing was open and looked out upon the ocean. It felt like I was viewing a painting as I faced the water. It was beautifully framed by both the trees and the rock face. The only thing in the clearing was a battered old sign, which signalled 'No dogs, please be respectful'. I was perplexed. Was this not the perfect spot to bring your pup? The Retreat was even pet-friendly.

The clearing had all the natural ingredients to be peaceful: a towering cliff, lush grass, and the sound of waves crashing on the shore. I expected the place's aura to merge with the marijuana and cover me in calm. In reality, I could hardly enjoy it for even a moment; I was immediately put off by an eerie silence. Nothingness consumed me. Not even the sound of the waves could break the sort of painful trance in which I found myself. The longer I stayed, the more unsettled I became. It was almost a feeling of intrusion, as though I was not welcome here.

Time to leave, I thought. I quickly made my mind up to linger no more. I did not expect to find myself revisiting the place any time soon. This felt counterintuitive, considering how accessible and beautiful it was. As I made my way back along the soft grass, any strange notion was replaced by amplified hunger pangs. I walked faster as I left the funny feeling behind in search of food.

I learned from Brian, on the drive across the island, that meals were served twice daily. One at lunch and the other in the evening. An empty banquet hall directly above Driftwood served as a makeshift buffet for staff. I would later learn that the banquet hall had once upon a time been Arbutus Falls's second restaurant.

It had previously served as fine dining, at least when compared to Driftwood. Why it was being used as a staff dining hall was a mystery to me. It also raised the question of where the employee meals used to be served. I made my way there and found that a food line was loosely formed. At its head was a book which some staff seemed to be signing. I joined the queue and filled my plate. I skipped signing the book since I did not know its purpose.

  I sat with some of my soon-to-be coworkers, and for the second day in a row, struck luck. I was not in too talkative a mood, and neither was anyone else. We chatted just enough for me to learn that that evening a party would be held at staff accommodation, perfect. Liz was spot-on by saying they were frequent. The mere idea of the party was enough to light a spark that quickly burnt a hole in my feeling of isolation. I was not necessarily excited for the alcohol, but I sure was for the socialization. If I was going to survive here, then I was going to need some community. By no means was I tempted to spark up when I returned to my room after dinner, and that was a small victory. The evening's party would be the perfect opportunity to make some friends. I was also hoping to get an idea of what to expect from my soon-to-be living conditions.

[CHAPTER FIFTEEN]

  The staff accommodation building was the furthest thing up the hill; it was past the upper pool and the five large cottages. It was tucked even further to the right, almost in the woods. Leaving through the main lobby, I cut up the stone stairs and past some of the cottages. It seemed to be the most direct route, and I do love efficiency. I approached with my wine bottle in hand, and the sound of music grew. The accommodations looked rather bleak from the outside, but nonetheless, my overall hopes began to rise. I entered the building by the closest door and found myself in a living room. It was surrounded by a ring of doors. I could not help but think that it was not so different from my university dorm. I could see that a room directly ahead of me and down a hallway was packed with people, I headed for it. The busy room seemed to be the kitchen. The only thing I noticed other than all the people was a large wooden table in its centre. An army of red solo cups filled the space.

In that first moment, I felt a bit intimidated. I am a pretty friendly guy, but it had been some time since I had met new people, especially a whole room of them. I did a lap, shaking hands and exchanging soon-to-be-forgotten names as I went. There was a game of stack cup being played at the table, and I figured joining that was a safe bet. As the rounds went by, I became friendly with those at my shoulders, and the earlier feeling of isolation burnt itself out entirely. I was very grateful for my height; standing a head above the crowd forced me to socialize rather than blend in. As the drinking games rotated and expanded, no one was short on smiles, and the laughter was contagious. I was warmly reminded of my days at university. No one seemed too intoxicated, and it felt like a big group of automatic friends. I could hardly ask for a thing more.

As the night aged, a smaller group of us retreated to an outdoor hangout area. It hugged the outside of the laundry facility, which was level with the staff housing but still deeper in the woods. A concoction of mismatched couches and chairs was squeezed under an overhanging roof; the result was cozy, especially as it began to drizzle.

Amongst the shrinking group, stories and future plans were respectfully exchanged. I quickly felt comfortable and decided to share how my expectations for housing and scheduling were different from the reality I came to discover. Before I got to the end of my short story, people were already nodding their heads with understanding. It was immediately apparent that no one was shocked in the slightest. In response, some of my new friends took turns giving their opinions. The consensus was that while Kevin seemed kind, a manipulative dick lurked close to the surface. Some stories of his treachery were shared to nail the point home. Some people had been verbally abused by him for no more than arguing what was fair, and others were punished by being given shitty hours for seemingly no reason at all. The information itself was discouraging, yet that dead sense of isolation that had burnt itself out was now slowly being covered by blankets of camaraderie. If more issues were to arise, I knew I would not be facing them by my lonesome. I continued to soak in this blissful feeling as joints began to get passed around and connections were forged.

 As is so often the case, one woman in particular piqued my interest. She was garbed in flowing layers, and a soft, colourful scarf accentuated her dark hair which was pulled back in a messy bun. I noticed her throughout the night. The way she carried herself seemed to gently demand attention. Silence seemed to spread when she spoke, despite her quiet and calming voice. She came across as the kind of person who was young at heart yet possessed years of wisdom. It was easy to imagine that along with that experience had come some unwanted lessons, although is that not the universal case? As the moon rose higher, the two of us struck up a polite conversation. She held me in her eyes as we spoke, radiating a subtle beauty and care that erased any urge to look away.

 I expressed to this woman how impressed I was with the beauty of Arbutus Falls. This was met with what seemed to be an angry skepticism. I questioned this, and in response was offered an impromptu, late-night tour. Although quite stoned, and hearing the call of sleep, I felt compelled to accept. I could not resist the chance to further connect with someone, especially someone so seemingly worthwhile. I said brief goodbyes to my new friends. I wish I had known that that would be my only night spent with the majority of them. Then again, my ignorance was likely bliss. We then parted from the group, which had already begun to deplete. Not everyone could stay up too late, because the Retreat would not run itself the next day.

As my new, and much-improved, tour guide and I walked away, the sound of laughter slowly faded.

The woman solemnly said, "You haven't heard the history of this place, have you?"

I felt slightly caught off guard by the question. It seemed so serious for such a night of lightness. I knew nothing of worth concerning the place's history. Was there something I should have known?

I rolled with it and said, "No, I haven't heard much of anything yet."

She nodded as if she had expected so much and then continued, "I haven't been here much longer than you, but I've had enough time to ask some questions. From what I've gathered, this Retreat is built on the location of an ancient Indigenous village." My new acquaintance paused, as if contemplating whether or not to say more, and then added, "I've also found that the energy seems off here, and I can't help but wonder if the two are connected."

As I considered what she shared, I noticed we were being drawn down to the ocean along the main road. We had taken the longer and darker way, around the stone stairs. We walked for a little less than a minute in silence. I was over-tired and in a weird mood, and decided it was prudent to seem mysterious by delaying my response. As we drew nearer to my target, I looked to the trail that I had earlier explored. I found it rather intimidating in the dark of night.

Breaking the man-made silence, I motioned to it and said, "That's interesting. I hadn't heard a word about that. I actually think I know what you mean about the energy being off. Are you familiar with that trail?" She nodded that yes, she was, as I continued, "Well, I followed it earlier, and despite the lovely view, I couldn't stick around."

She nodded knowingly, as if she understood, and responded, "I'm not shocked that you hadn't heard anything. This doesn't strike me as the kind of place that mentions it is built on the site of an Indigenous village, especially during orientation. Also, I have an idea as to why you felt so off-put when you went down that trail. That being said, it's not something I'm willing to discuss after dark. I believe that it can be dangerous to talk about spirits when the sun is resting."

Wanting to lighten the mood, I smiled playfully and said, "Fair enough, I'm going to make a guess and say that it has something to do with spirits."

She rolled her eyes and shot me a look that I imagine could be given to a misbehaving younger brother.

Our conversation brought us down and onto the beach. Looking out at the rolling ocean, we shared silence and listened to the steady rush of the waterfall. The clear sky was lit softly by a sliver of moon. I contemplated what she said and attempted to consider the implications of the Retreat disturbing such an ancient place. The idea of some developers disregarding such rich history in the name of creating a play place for the wealthy was disturbing. I was curious to learn more.

I turned to her, and for the first time, I realized how small she was. We were inadvertently standing so close that I had to lean down to meet her eyes.

Holding her soft gaze, I asked slowly, "I have two questions. First, have you heard anything else that you feel is worth sharing? Second, what is your name?"

That got a full smile out of her, which in turn got a full smile out of me. I find that a person's true beauty is often revealed when their smile reaches their eyes. Hers was revealed, but only for a second. The smile died upon her lips as quickly as it formed, as though she was remembering something that was momentarily forgotten.

A large tree stood between the beach and the main lodge. Nodding her head and leading my eyes with her gaze, she bade me towards it. She grabbed a rusted metal ring that all but hid itself in the bark of the tree. It squeaked loudly in her hand.

With a quiver in her voice, she said, "This band has quite the story; it is another thing that I refuse to speak of at night. If you don't hear the story from me, then I'm certain that you will from someone else. It is infamous." She said with a flare.

I nodded in understanding, and then she continued, "There is one more spot I want to show you during daylight, it's protected Indigenous land. We're technically not supposed to go, but as long as you're respectful, it's okay. You strike me as someone who would be."

I had zoned out a bit while staring at her, and snapping back, I asked, "Who would what?"

She flashed another smile, this one lingering longer, and responded, "Who would respect it. You seem like someone I could show. Oh, and my name is Jennifer, you can call me Jen."

I smiled back dumbly and nodded. It was not the name that I was expecting, but it was one I would come to know well.

Feeling sleep pulling me closer, I expressed my gratitude for the tour and bid Jen a good night.

Her eyes flashed as she gave me a cheeky smile before making her way back up the hill to staff accommodations. I looked to the ocean and inhaled a deep breath of cold, fresh air before returning to my suite. I was thankful to have made a friend, especially one it seemed I could learn from. A sweet sleep quickly swept me from Georgia Island. I wish I had known to enjoy it while I could.

[CHAPTER SIXTEEN]

I awoke the following morning without a hangover. Thankfully, I am a proficient flip cup player, and I donated my full bottle of red wine to the game. I performed the same ritual as the day before, brewing and taking my coffee out onto the balcony. It was raining, a theme that would continue with increasing regularity. I was grateful the balcony was half covered by the building's overhang. As I sat there alone, I could not help but notice that the familiar feeling of isolation had slowly begun to rebuild itself within me. The pitter-patter of rain is one of my favourites, and that sound overhead helped to keep my head between my ears.

I debated while drinking my coffee, and eventually made up my mind to brave the rain to go get some genuine fresh air. I had identified on Google Maps that there was a park with some trails close by. The name that it held was cute enough, 'Fairy Forest Nature Park'. I pulled together my rain gear, which consisted of a rain jacket, rain pants, and semi-waterproof hiking shoes. Feeling prepared, I left the building and made my way up the Retreat's main road. I waved to some faces I recognized on a golf cart that whipped by, but to my disappointment, none of them were Jen. My walk took me along the island's main road. As I cruised along, the tall trees held off most of the rain. The park and its main entrance were on my left, and I also noticed some smaller trails that cut into the forest before it. I was both surprised and impressed by a huge wooden sign which declared 'Fairy Forest'. I walked beneath the grand welcome and began to explore the trails.

     Thanks to the year's rainy season having begun, the trails were quite muddy. They were rather winding, and the park was on the wild side. There were five-foot-wide gravel paths. Two plank wooden board walkways were over some of the sunken bits. My mind wandered as I went. It soon became apparent that the rain was doing nothing but increasing in volume. I began to get soaked through my gear, and decided to pause when I came to a rather big tree that rose up at an angle. I sat at its base, which was still protected from the damp. I was in a beautiful position, I smiled to myself. I waited there as the rain began to come down in buckets. I found myself utterly consumed by its power. The individual drops, landing upon leaves and ferns, collaborated to form a steady roar. Water began to run down onto my side of the tree, yet my position remained secure. It was one of those moments I wish I could bottle up. I momentarily possessed no sense of self. All I knew was that I was exactly where I was meant to be. I broke the magic with regret as I fished out my phone to check the time. It was with even more regret that I knew I must leave. I had to go get myself dried off and then to lunch. I get pretty weird when I'm feeling at one with nature, so I verbally thanked the tree before making my way out of the forest, which naturally, I thanked as well. The rain soaked me to the bone as I made my way back to my room. I would have had it no other way. It almost felt as though this was the island's way of welcoming me.

There was something stuck on my mind from the night before, so I was hoping to run into Jen at lunch. I entered the banquet hall and scanned the room. Sure enough, there she was. Even better, there was a free chair beside her. I went directly over and claimed the chair with my sweater before plating up. Once again, there was not much conversation occurring at the table, so after greeting everyone with a smile, I turned my attention to Jen.

I said lightly, "So, you left me hanging last night. What's the story with the trail?"

She responded a bit more seriously, "What are you doing right now? If you have time for a walk after lunch, then I'll tell you."

That sounded good enough to me, and I said as much. I finished my food as quickly as I could, and then we were on our way. I was grateful to find that the sky seemed to have finished emptying itself.

When we got outside, I asked Jen, "Where to?"

She began to walk off as she responded, "Where do you think? To the trail."

I forced a smile and said, "Ah, how lovely, I may or may not have told myself that I wouldn't be returning there, but I guess anything for you."

Her serious attitude continued, and I decided to cut the shit.

She said, "Do you want to hear it or not? If I've read you right, then I think you'll find it interesting."

We reached the trailhead in no time at all, and I indicated for Jen to continue.

She said, "The upper pool is quite a bit more modern than the lower pool, right?"

I agreed, "Sure", uncertain of where she was going with this.

She mirrored my response, "Sure. That's because it is a newer addition. It was only built a few years ago. I told you that the Retreat is built on an ancient Indigenous village, but I didn't mention that they also had a burial site here."

Without much hope, and a tint of sarcasm, I said, "Ah shit, I really hope that you're about to tell me about how considerate they were in leaving it be".

Jen gave me a thin smile. I had finally matched her mood, and she said, "I wish that were the case. The developers found it when they were doing the excavation for the upper pool. The workers stopped when they found bones, assuming that the dig would be delayed. The developers had no interest in waiting, so they told the crews to keep going, all the while attempting to keep it a secret. I don't know many more details than that, other than that a lot of bones were found and disturbed."

We arrived in the clearing. It was as beautiful as the day before. Even better was that being with Jen provided comfort that seemed to protect me from the bad energy.

I asked the obvious question, "I think I know where you're going with this. Where are the bones buried, assuming that they were reburied?"

Jen nodded and said, "I think you already know." She looked down and said, "Right here. It's not exactly ideal, but it's better than nothing."

I answered, "So I'm thinking that you're thinking that the energy I'm feeling here could be attributed to what's buried?"

Now she really smiled, "Like I said, I thought you may be able to understand. Now, I've got to go get back to work. Don't come yet, I want you to be here alone." With that, she turned and headed back down the trail.

'Uh, okay,' I thought, as I watched her layers billow and hips sway out of view. I understood what she was getting at, but did not know if I believed it. Then again, I had no better explanation, if it needed one at all. As could be expected, anticipation grew within me. Seeing Jen leave, I figured the feeling from the day before would take her place. The feeling that I was an unwanted intruder. I walked over to the view of the ocean, passing the 'No dogs, please be respectful' sign. As my eyes passed over the sign, I suddenly made the connection as to the reason for its existence. I could not help but think that the sign should have been in better shape. I looked out at the water and saw that it was incredibly calm after the heavy rainfall. All of the boats were in their moorings; they looked as though they were nervous that the rain might return with a vengeance. I mulled over what Jen had shared with me and continued to question what kind of place I had agreed to work for. The fact that the Retreat was built on such a sacred land did not necessarily work in its favour, but it also did not necessarily write it off as being a terrible place to work. I was very curious as to how my first few shifts would go. My mind eventually landed on something of interest. I was feeling fine, absolutely fine. No negative feelings coursed through me. I was feeling similarly to how I was earlier when I was caught in the rain. I felt as if I was accepted, as though I was now welcome to roam here in peace. Maybe Jen was onto something after all, or maybe I was crazy.

  The rest of that day passed with little of note. An unwanted message from Kevin informed me that I would be moving into staff accommodations the following day. He ordered me to report to the front desk with my bags immediately upon the completion of my first training shift on the bar. While I was not over the moon with the news, I was at the very least looking forward to being able to settle into my permanent living quarters. Alone in the lodge, I had begun to feel quite far away from my coworkers. I hoped that living and working with them would shine a healing light on the recurring feeling of isolation within me. I focused my mind on enjoying the last of my luxury and drew another bath. It felt good to be surrounded by warm water after the colder rain had soaked me through. As I sat facing my balcony, all was silent in my room. The only thing I could hear was the constant flow of the waterfall. The Retreat itself seemed to have some faults, but this place certainly had a magic to it.

[CHAPTER SEVENTEEN]

I showed up for my shift at nine in the morning. I was feeling rather well-rested, and this helped fuel my optimism. Disappointingly, it seemed that no one was expecting me. I walked into what was essentially an empty restaurant. I double-checked my schedule to confirm the time and then sat down on a barstool. It must have been about twenty minutes, but it felt much more like an hour before a server appeared out of thin air. She burst out of some double doors that led to the kitchen and began frantically preparing a breakfast buffet. Eventually, I was able to flag her down and ask if she knew any more than I did. She brusquely told me that the bartender, Joel, was late, but that he should be arriving any minute. I retook my seat at the bar and continued to wait.

I thought many thoughts while I was waiting. The majority of them were attempts to stay calm and not let my disappointment grow. It was nine thirty when Joel strolled in casually. He politely apologized for his tardiness and then disregarded me altogether. I stood awkwardly as he casually began to open the bar. My calmness that I fought so hard to keep began to leave me. I became slightly off put that he was not explaining anything to me. I steeled myself and focused on taking in as much as I could by eye. Despite being thirty minutes late, he had the bar open and ready to go with time to spare. There did not seem to be much to it, and I happily assumed that we would be paid from nine. That was the only thing that made me glad on that first day.

When Joel did finally begin teaching me, it quickly became apparent that he was expecting me to be some kind of superstar bartender. Not only was I not, but I also had no interest in becoming one. I was in the bartending business because the money was good, not because I loved to mix cocktails. Despite the day not being too busy, and that I did not make a single drink, I felt overwhelmed from start to finish. Anxiety seemed to be coursing through my veins, and I attributed this to the sheer magnitude of information I was expected to store. The reason there was so much information for me to take in was that I was expected to be working the bar by myself after just one more day of training. There were a variety of cocktail premixes to be concocted, which I was supposed to eyeball, many different garnishes to be pre-made, fifty different wines, eight beers on tap and another twenty in the fridge, ten rotating specialty cocktails that I was expected to memorize, and I was to clean all of my own dishes. On top of all that, I had my own section of the restaurant, which I was supposed to serve both drinks and food. Now, all that may have been doable if it were not that the expectation was perfection. By the end of my first training shift, I was stressed. What the hell had I gotten myself into, I kept asking myself. My last bartending job provided proper training; I only worked alone on slow days, and it was hardly a quarter as complex. This was going to be a big leap up in terms of workload.

    Joel could tell I was struggling in the mental department and told me to sit down for a free beer at the end of my shift. He told me that for training tomorrow, he would come in right at nine and we would go through everything it took to open the bar. I was grateful for his kindness and compassion, but it did little to alleviate the cloud that swirled madly in my mind.

    My beer was finished faster than I care to admit, and I headed straight to my room to pick up my pre-packed bags. I collected them and listened to the click as my suite door closed with a tinge of regret. Naturally, I arrived to find Liz working the front desk. She was absent from the party the night before, and I assumed that she was working then as well. She confirmed this hunch before calling someone in maintenance on the radio.

    I said to her, "You seem to be working all the time, do they ever give you a break?"

She gave me a pained smile, "I don't even remember what a break is, and you just wait, they'll have you double shifting soon enough. You may even end up working front desk."

I laughed this off, but could not help feeling the truth of the statement. I admired the view from the lobby as Liz clicked away on her computer. A small but sturdy man burst into the room and scooped up one of my bags that I had placed by Liz's counter.

He shouted energetically across the lobby, "Hey buddy! Let's get you to your room."

I grabbed my other bag and gave Liz a wide-eyed, knowing look.

She met my smile with equal knowledge and said, "That's Cody, he takes care of staff housing."

With that, I was on my way. Cody was waiting on the maintenance golf cart with my bag sprawled in the back seat. I threw my other in beside it and joined him in the front. I had hardly taken my second foot off the ground before he was peeling away. I could not help but like his style, an efficient man of few, but clear words. I would quickly come to learn that he was also the kind of man who found humour in everything that he said, and without fail, made you want to laugh along with him.

For instance, as we pulled up to the building, he said, "Well, it's about time we gotcha in to yer room, eh?" With a great laugh. I could do nothing but smile back at him; this response seemed satisfactory enough as he vigorously patted me on the back.

We entered through the same door that I used to come to the party. He bee-lined it for one of the rooms to the right, carrying my bag as though it weighed less than nothing.

The door was wide open, and he said, "Housekeeping was in here gettin' her ready for ya. It's a shame the girls didn't see ya before, they may have done a better job." He laughed wildly.

I could not help but like the guy; he certainly seemed like a character.

The room was slightly appalling. The door was open alright, but only about two-thirds the way, as it was caught against the side of the bed. This was something I would soon discover to be impossible to change. The bed was only a single, but it was squeezed wall to wall. I spent many hours in that room pondering how the hell they managed to get the bed and frame in there. They must have built it on the spot, but even then, it would have been tricky. To the right was a ceiling-high wooden shelf that was threatening to either collapse or topple over. The single bright spot was a window in the middle of the wall, directly above the bed. The room was bare, save for a mattress in the bed frame. It felt more like a prison cell than anything else. I turned to Cody with my eyes wide, and he read my mind.

      He said, "I know, it's not much, but that's it. I'll tell ya what, though, there's just enough space to have ladies over. Gosh, a good-looking guy like you, I bet you'll make your way through them here." He paused, as though considering these words, and then laughed heartily at what he had said. He then continued, "You'll find a blanket and sheets in the laundry room. Grab a pillow and towel, too, while you're at it. Maybe you'll get lucky and meet one of those ladies in the laundry room, sure she'll be happy to help you."

      He handed me my key, and with that, he was gone. I could hear him laughing to himself until the door shut behind him. All I could think of was that he certainly was something else; he had the strange ability to both put me on edge and at ease simultaneously. One thing I knew for sure was that his presence had lessened the blow of these bleak living quarters.

      I tucked my bags under the wobbly bed frame. Another thing I never understood was how it managed to wobble while being wedged in between two walls. I then made my way over to the laundry building. Sure as anything, one of the ladies was there. She helped me pick out what I needed and insisted I take an extra pillow. I made my bed, cracked the window, and then filled my pipe. The job was stressful, and my room was deplorable. It would be all on my roommates and coworkers to provide some solace. I was counting on them because I sure did not feel that I had the strength to do this alone. I blew smoke out of the window and once again took the easy route to forget all of my worries.

[CHAPTER EIGHTEEN]

It is immensely difficult to classify my introduction to British Columbia's west coast. To summarize in the simplest way, I was unhappy. This reality was compounded because I lacked the emotional maturity to sit with this feeling of unhappiness in an attempt to find its root. I was unable to understand or accept the suffering that plagued me; hell, I did not know that acceptance was even an option. Rather than reflecting and growing, I drifted through my first few weeks of work in a cloudy haze. It is not with pride that I say solace was found in my most alluring vice. As I had been doing for far too long at that point, I continued to choose the easy way out.

The work itself was fine; I have had much better jobs in the past and also much worse. Most mornings were spent opening the bar. My prowess as a half-assed bartender was noted by all, and I never did work the busier evening shifts. The mornings crawled by like a drunken snail. Few folks came in for our breakfast buffet, and those already strapped numbers steadily declined as the days passed. The benefit of these slow mornings came in the form of being able to eat the plentiful leftovers. It is bad to waste, you know. Driftwood would only perk up slightly through lunch. The customers, the real drinkers, typically came in for the evening as my shift was coming to its close. Whether or not I served them their first of many hinged on how early they had gotten off work and how rough their day was. During any given shift, I experienced the perfect amount of people to balance boredom with the stress of an unfamiliar drink being ordered. Due to this unfamiliarity, there were many occasions where the servers stepped behind the bar and shooed me away. The majority of my job consisted of preparing fresh fruits and brewing cocktail mixes. I never did get good at it; it is hard to do something well when you lack motivation. The buffet's lack of lustre, in conjunction with the pre-made cocktail mixes, swiftly led me to the conclusion that our restaurant fell onto the trashy end of the name Driftwood. Nothing I ever saw in my time there contradicted this early conclusion.

As the drunken snail crawled along, I passed the time by chatting with the servers. They were an older crowd who mostly owned or rented homes across the island. There was a huge disparity in the quality of life for workers who lived at the Retreat vs the ones who lived off of it. Some of the servers drank while they worked. If not while working, then they certainly did during their breaks. No matter where on the island you lived, there was a popular medication. Its name was the bottle, or the glass, or in my case, the grass. The most notable of the alcoholic bunch was a slight and sweet lady. She was the most inconspicuous person, and yet her paper coffee cup was to be consistently filled with white wine. As the bartender, it was my role to keep it full; it pained me each time I poured.

During the rare moments that the servers were busy, or if the mood was too dull for unnecessary conversation, I would read. I would read, and read some more, until I heard the mechanical beeping of an order arriving at my printer. My book of choice at the time was the Torah. I had recently been inspired during my maiden trip to Israel. Being such a holy place for the three main monotheistic religions, I became interested in understanding what religion was all about. It was a topic that had little to no influence on my life to that point, and I became puzzled as to how it could so singularly rule the lives of others. I hoped to find some sort of clue in the original Holy Book.

Work was only fine until the bar manager showed up. Thankfully, his appearances were rare. His only consistent trait was being gone whenever you actually needed him. The only thing he ever truly managed was to always have something negative to say. Whenever he arrived on the premises, word was spread between server and cook like an unstoppable blaze. We were quick to communicate, but there was never enough time to mentally prepare. I wish I could remember his name, so I may curse him. Alas, I guess my memory considers him unworthy of remembrance. All I recall with certainty is that his wife did not know about his girlfriend. For all intents and purposes, we shall call the bastard Horner. Your manager sets the standards, and his were near non-existent.

    A bright spot in the ceaseless gloom were the shifts I worked with Jen. She was, of course, a fantastic server and was often saddled with the busier evening shifts. Our mornings together were seldom, but that made them all the more enjoyable. There was an espresso machine in the kitchen, and the two of us would always make one for the other. One day, I woke up feeling particularly motivated, and I channelled that motivation into seeing how many cups of espresso it would take before I began to shake compulsively. I was on my fifth in about an hour when I mentioned my goal to Jen.

    With play in my voice, I said, "How many shots of espresso do you think I can have before I'm incapacitated? I'm at five so far and feeling good."

    She stared at me wide-eyed for a moment, processing the information, and then burst out laughing. I was being completely serious and was unprepared for this response. Sure, my goal was slightly strange, but I did not think it was worth this giggle fit.

    When she went on laughing, I asked, "What? What is it?"

    She was laughing so hard that she struggled to breathe; between gasps for air, she said, "The first thing I did this morning was fill the machine up with decaf; we didn't get any regular beans in our order." She shook her head as she said, "What a day you picked for this challenge of yours."

    What a day indeed. I shook my head too, and could not help but appreciate the humour. I never did re-attempt my challenge when the caffeinated beans were returned. At one point, management actually told us to stop drinking the coffee because they were cutting costs. Naturally, we did not stop enjoying our caffeinated beverages. But I could no longer mindlessly justify such a wasteful consumption that my experiment would have been.

Every day that I did not open the bar, I worked in housekeeping. So much for four-day, ten-hour weeks. Something to note about housekeeping is that it did not pay as well as the bar. The wage was lower, and there were very rarely tips. However, cleaning shit out of toilets proved to be much more enjoyable than taking it from people at the bar. Much, if not most, of the credit goes to the man who ran the show. The housekeeping manager was a French gentleman; he was incredibly kind and led the team with an impressive work ethic. If someone crap-bombed a toilet, he would be the first one scraping shit off the ceiling. Yes, the ceiling.

At the start of each day, he would organize us into teams and indicate where we should start. The teams worked independently of each other to get through the cottages and villas, until we were left with the lodges. It was there, in the main building, that we would come back together as one. The daily list varied; sometimes it was rather cottage-heavy, while others were dominated by a couple of villas. This variation was most enjoyable and helped to avoid the feeling of gross repetition. Internally, each cottage consisted of two bedrooms, two bathrooms, a kitchen, a dining room, and a lounge. Externally, they had a barbecue, patio set, and hot tub. The teams were typically made up of two to four people who would take turns tackling each of the components. Naturally, each person on the team had areas they preferred to clean. The most common favourite was bedrooms, making the bed was a tedious but rewarding job. The bathrooms and kitchen were despised the most, and people were split on which was worse. I quickly made it clear that I greatly preferred the bathrooms. For whatever reason, I would rather swirl poop than smell old food; something about it makes me sick to my stomach. On my second shift, I was gagging while changing an especially nasty kitchen garbage. The cottage sat dirty for a few days, and my stomach could not handle the stench. Thanks to that incident, which I may or may not have played up, I was kept away from kitchens for some time. I made up for this skill gap by specializing in floors. Once all rooms and surfaces were cleaned, we would vacuum and mop. For reasons I could not comprehend, this was another generally despised task. I took advantage of the fact that I enjoyed doing the floors, and I was always the first to step up.

The individuals who made up the housekeeping team were a rather motley crew. The team was highlighted by an ex-tank driver, a stoner who was recovering from a head injury, a young couple who were also stoners, and a plethora of hard drug users. Rounding off the team was my friend Jen. She was recruited to housekeeping because serving five or six days a week was not considered enough; it also seemed she needed the money. Our leader, Henri, had the lovely habit of blasting tech-trance music throughout the day. I often found myself yelling over it to ask him questions. It was always a pleasure to be on his team, and I found myself on it almost every day at the beginning. As we made our way through the cleaning list, all differences were put aside. Everyone worked toward the common goal of finishing as early as possible. In a way, this goal was quite ironic when one considered the implications. Not only were we being paid for fewer hours, but no one was getting off work to do anything notable, including myself. Most people drank, some smoked weed, and others smoked crack. The team would become more and more unreliable as time went on; more often than not, I would swear it was held together by nothing more than Henri's pure power of will.

Arbutus Falls, being considered a luxury retreat, meant it was common for the housekeeping team to find questionable white powder, especially when cleaning level surfaces. Some of my coworkers shared stories that were either personally experienced or were passed down by generations of staff. The ones that were passed down were the things of legend, and they made me incredibly grateful for even the worst of the messes we cleaned. There is nothing quite like being aware of the suffering of others to lessen your own. One story that stemmed from a personal experience occurred that past summer. A group of old men, allegedly wealthier than our normal clientele, showed up for the weekend with a group of women who were not their wives. Let us just say that the ladies were beyond a shadow of a doubt paid to be there. Lurid acts were reported by neighbouring guests, many of them originating from their hot tub. When it came time for their departure, everyone at the Retreat breathed a collective sigh of relief. That is, everyone other than the housekeeping team. Someone had to clean up the mess. At best, a rolled-up Benjamin was found; at worst, a variety of bodily fluids left in indiscriminate places were cleaned. The hot tub was drained and deep-cleaned, although based on what I heard, I believe it should have been burned.

[CHAPTER NINETEEN]

My arrival at Arbutus Falls marked summer's ending and fall's beginning. In those first days, there was a mass exodus. The university students fled the Retreat to return to school. These kind kids made up the vast majority of the people that I escaped to the laundry room with during that first party at staff accommodations. Not only would I never sit at that hangout spot again, but there would not even be another party. The departure of the students sapped the energy out of temporary workers such as myself. The Retreat's lifers moved into the spotlight as the students' bright space was eclipsed.

It takes a certain kind of person to live in staff housing for years at a time. I mean that with no disrespect whatsoever, most of the people who live there are good people. Some are the kind of people who have either rejected or been rejected from mainstream society, and that is by no means a bad thing. I can say, with reserved confidence, that there were some pretty serious drug habits. The kinds that affected not just the individuals who were smoking and injecting. The kinds that affected me in more ways than one. On Georgia Island, my eyes were opened to a whole new world. One that I never expected to interact with so closely, and in many ways, I am grateful to have had the opportunity. It was apparent that the youthful energy of the summer students pumped the brakes on these habits. Sadly, with them gone, the gas steadily increased until the brake lines snapped.

     A healthy combination of garbage food, worse pay, and cloudy skies was detrimental to the general mood. Not only was the situation bleak, but we damn well knew it. Few people seemed genuinely happy, and those who did were unable to share their light with those around them. I have a good amount of experience living in less-than-ideal situations, situations in which you simply do not want to exist, and so I did what I could to get through this one as unscathed as possible. For me, this consisted of keeping my energy to myself and sharing it only with those who could reciprocate their energy to me. Despite this experience and strategy, I still struggled immensely. Some days were harder than others, and so it was in desperation that I formed a ritual to get me through the day.

     Before our coffee privileges were revoked, we received a daily ration of caffeine from the cafe on the tower's bottom floor. I would start my day by heading there to get a quadruple espresso topped with hot water. By no means was it a sexy drink, but it sure as hell got me going. On days when I was lucky, the barista would slide me a croissant on the house. On the days that I was opening the bar, I would get myself set for the day and then help myself to the half-assed, and ever-worsening, buffet. If I were in housekeeping, I would make my own luck by raiding the kitchen for fresh pastries. It was crucial to cautiously evade the chef. He was a temperamental Navy man who was regarded slightly better than the bar manager. The chef had moments of endearment, whereas Horner did not. As mentioned, the work quickly became mindless. Regardless of where I was working, I found myself floating between tasks. I would typically finish between three and four in the afternoon, which equated to a six to eight-hour workday. So despite working almost every day, the money was still not that great.

On bar days, once my relief bartender arrived and settled, or in housekeeping, once Henri gave us the go-ahead to disassemble, I would make a beeline for my room. I kept my bag pre-packed with the essentials. This stock consisted of snacks, extra layers, my smoke kit, and most importantly of all, my hammock. Years earlier, my sister gifted me one of my most prized possessions, a double hammock that could be strapped up between two trees. It played a fundamental role in my survival of Arbutus Falls Retreat and Spa. Having collected everything of importance from my room, I would don my hiking shoes and head straight to my special spot.

Most days, I found myself desperately seeking escape from a seemingly unending life on the Retreat. I had just one day off throughout the entire first month. I am not overdramatizing; I literally worked twenty-nine out of thirty days. At that, it may have even been more; I stopped counting. It became too depressing. Not only did I work every day, but on the rare days off, there was close to no adventure to be found. Especially not with my coworkers, who were too busy drowning themselves in substances. They rarely left the property at all. I am not saying I did not also drown myself in substances, but I did pride myself on at least leaving the prison during yard time.

One evening, in the first week of my sentence, I found my secret spot. I was spending my time after work exploring some of the paths that I saw next to the Fairy Forest. I was mapping out a particularly overgrown trail that seemed to run along the length of the high cliff. For perspective, this was on the right side of the bay, the opposite side from the waterfall. As I pushed branches out of my way, I was met with the warm feeling that I found something for which I did not know I was looking. What I found was the perfect spot. The large and leafy Arbutus trees were spaced just the right distance apart for optimum hammock hanging. What became apparent at a later and wetter date was that they also provided plenty of rain cover. I could listen to the water's gentle patter on the leaves for some time before feeling the first drop. A strange pile of large stones sat directly between me and the cliff's edge; no vegetation grew there. So, despite the thick and relatively overgrown woods, the place possessed an exquisite cliff-top view of Freshwater Bay. Another important factor was that I could make it from my room to the cliff in just eight minutes. Despite its close proximity to my unloving home, it was just out of earshot from the haunting sounds of the Retreat. It was rather close to the trail that I followed, mere feet from it. Thankfully, I would find that the trail itself was seldom walked, and so privacy was plentiful. In retrospect, the place could have been considered the perfect trap, one that I fell right into.

Each day, I would go to my spot. The walk up the hill flew by; it was as though I was transported directly from my room and into my hammock. I would typically spend about three hours levitating in between my trees. I would have loved to stay longer, but dinner had a time limit, and I could not afford to miss out. I would often bring a beer, and I always got stoned. As I breathed deeply, I was able to gently force the Retreat from my mind. How those precious hours of release were spent was mood-dependent. When feeling inspired, I read the Torah. I made considerable progress on the book's pages, but next to none in my understanding of religion. I began to wonder if you had to believe the stories were real to fully appreciate them. Some of the tales were certainly powerful, and there was no question that I could appreciate the lessons they contained, but to take them literally? I imagined people forming their morals based on these words, and felt myself getting close to some sort of understanding. Maybe there was something in having a 'higher power' tell you what is right or wrong, rather than feeling it for yourself. I could only imagine the internal struggle if your heart were to tell you something different than your book, which would you follow? The danger of certainty poked out its head. I eventually abandoned this reading; it seemed I would not find religion between the bound skin. On days when I was feeling less introspective, I would simply listen to music and take in the view.

As the sun dipped below the tree line, or on cloudier days, when the sky would darken, I would pack up my hammock. I had to get back for dinner. Besides, even though I was quite comfortable and knew my nook well, a strange feeling always kicked around as the sun began to sink. It was nothing as strong as the way that I felt on my first day when I found myself in the clearing, which was not so far below me, but it was persistent. I think at the time, this was a feeling I was only aware of subconsciously; had I ever stayed after dark, then maybe I would have questioned it. I never did purposely stay after dark.

[CHAPTER TWENTY]

One particularly lovely day, Horner, the bar manager, took it upon himself to ensure I knew what a lousy job I was doing as a bartender. I was naive enough to believe that if a job required no effort, it must be impossible to perform poorly. Perhaps that belief was the problem. Regardless of what I thought, he kindly and loudly berated me in front of the serving team. I believe what set him off was that he overheard me asking one of the servers if it was lemon or lime used in a particular drink. In reality, it would not have mattered which one went in, but because we were slow, I figured I should get it right.

Horner was lurking by the kitchen doors and stormed over to yell, "Are you fucking kidding me? You don't know how to make a sloppy sailor?"

That was not the drink's name, but it does sound like something trashy ol' Driftwood would sell. Anyway, I did not know how I possibly could have responded to such a useless statement, and so I was happy when he went on.

He said, "It's already been three weeks, and I'd swear you don't know how to make half the drinks. Do you even know what goes into a driftwood draught?"

I was grateful that I held little pride in being a bartender; had I, his angry words may have really gotten to me.

I could not help myself, and so responded, "You know, Horner, it's not so easy to memorize the drinks when I'm not actually making them. Hell, I'd say I've memorized more than I've made."

He was not as pleased with my response as I was, and responded, "Are you talking back to me, you little prick? Watch your mouth, or I'll be talking to Kevin."

I smiled widely at that, "Hey boss, I'm just telling it like it is, and believe me, I'd be happy to talk to Kevin. You just let me know when."

He grew red in the face and continued to bark angrily. Thankfully, by that point, I had already learned that there was absolutely no bite to him. Besides, I was one of three bartenders. What was he going to do, fire me? When an employee loses their fear of losing their job, they become a formidable opponent. That being said, I kept my mouth shut, as suggested, and nodded enthusiastically as he took out his rage. When he seemed to have finished, I told him I was grateful for the feedback and that I had to get back to work.

That was one of Jen's rare mornings in the restaurant. My scolding complete, she generously and empathetically attempted to console me. Truth be told, I was not very upset; typically, something like that only affects me if the person saying it has my respect. That considered, it still never feels great to be yelled at, unless you are into that kind of thing. No matter how you spun it, it was a lot of negative energy propelled my way. Regardless of how I felt, I was hoping to have some company after work.

I asked, "Hey Jen, we're off at the same time today, aren't we? I've been patiently waiting for you to show me that place on the private land. Why don't we go check it out once we're off?"

Her face grew tight as she responded, "Ah, sorry, I'd really love to do it, but I can't today, I already have plans."

I'm typically not one to pry, but I was a bit surprised she had plans. I had not heard of Jen getting up to much after work, and there was so little to do.

Spurred by curiosity, I said, "No worries at all, but let's do it another day soon. If you don't mind me asking, what are you up to?"

With a trickle of hesitation and a glitter of apprehension, Jen said, "I'm going to that cabin, the one on the protected land."

By no means was this what I was expecting. I heard there was a creepy cabin close to the Retreat, but it was mentioned in hushed tones. It seemed shrouded in mystery. Allegedly, it was inhabited by a local Indigenous elder, and I innocently assumed they must be taking care of the protected land. When I gently pushed Jen for more information, she clammed up and made like she had work to do. I wanted to respect her privacy, and so I left well enough alone. We ended the conversation by agreeing we would go for a walk soon to catch up. Secretly, I could not help but hope that, around less prying ears, she might be willing to share a bit about whoever lived at the cabin. Even more importantly, I was wondering what the heck she was doing there in the first place. I was curious, and you know what they say about curiosity.

Between my manager's outburst and Jen's secrets, it was a pretty damn exciting shift. I did my service for the queen by keeping my wine-loving server's cup full. I was always impressed that the paper cup never shrivelled; it was likely because she drank the cold wine so quickly. Another one of our local winos, one who lived in staff accommodations, came to buy his regular two bottles of Syrah red. He worked as a dishwasher, and soon returned with a litre and a half Tupperware container, which I was to fill to the brim with Pepsi. I was grateful when Joel came to relieve me. The day's excitement left me drained, and so I declined my after-work pint. On top of being tired from the shift, I was also exhausted from working so many days straight. At that point, it was at least twenty in a row. There were no special thoughts as I mindlessly performed my ritual of floating from the bar to my room, to the cliff. I settled myself easily into my hammock, I got the tension perfect, and could not have been more comfy. I decided to give my mom a call before reaching an even lower level of mindlessness. Service was regularly spotty, and I was distantly disappointed when my call refused to go through. In retrospect, I wonder if things would have transpired differently had the call been connected. Maybe nothing would have changed, or maybe everything. Thinking it over does nothing; it just is what it is.

[CHAPTER TWENTY ONE]

It was not until the phone call fell flat that it hit me how badly I wanted it to go through. Even from afar, a mother can provide much comfort. The sound of her voice would have warmed me like the firmest hug. Without it, I found myself feeling helplessly alone. In a continuation of my weakness, I did what I had done each day before. I solidified my loneliness. I inhaled deeply on my pipe in an attempt to leave my worries behind, not knowing that in reality, it was this very act that was stopping me from banishing them. Fully unaware of this contradiction, I relaxed temporarily as bliss settled over my body. I played the album Faces by Mac Miller, starting from Ave Maria, a silly song that never failed to bring a smile to my lips. As I listened to Mac ask if I had found a way out, I watched the sun shine upon the Pacific Ocean. No, I had not yet found a way out, but at that moment, everything in my little world was okay.

The wind softly rushed through the trees, providing a calming sound much like rain. As a relaxing instrumental titled 55 came on, I lost myself in it. I forgot any hardship from that day or week. Before the track finished, I drifted into an all-consuming sleep. It was not irregular for me to slip in and out of sleep while tucked away in my hammock, but something about this was different. This was more than slipping; it was a full slide.

I awoke without a start. I was unaware that my phone had stopped playing music; my mind was too cloudy. It was clouded to an extent that could not be explained by my drug consumption. Besides, I had not smoked more than a rip off the pipe, and my tolerance was certainly higher than that. It was higher than I would like to admit. As my waking brain slowly started to work its way up to a slow click, a faint recollection of what may have been a dream quickly faded from memory. My sleeping mind did not want to share, and so searchingly, I was only able to grasp the strong stench of the ocean and the feeling of standing on ground that was moving beneath my very feet. I did not consider what the dream could have been, but rather focused on the strangeness that I dreamt in the first place. I had both thought and experienced that one did not dream when regularly smoking weed. I would have struggled to tell you the last time I could remember even an inkling from a dream.

As I struggled to slide up into more of a sitting position, I noticed my stomach was strangely unsettled. It felt eerily similar to the feeling of being roughly rocked to and fro at sea. This sensation checked out with the feeling of having stood on ground that moved beneath me. The ocean smell continued to linger lightly, but it was fading. I considered my proximity to the water and my position in the hammock. I thought those two things could explain the seemingly inexplicable smell and sensation I was experiencing, or that I dreamt. Naturally, my mind did not enjoy this lack of understanding, and so it quickly accepted that my imagination had run amok. It is so much easier to believe everything can be explained, rather than considering the possibility of something outside of our understanding. It is one of the brain's strange defence mechanisms that gets us through moments of panic, particularly when reality's walls threaten to crumble. This rationalization required my ignoring that the hammock was not moving an inch. It also ignored that I had never gotten so much as a whiff of the ocean from so high up on the cliff. In fact, even standing on the beach at the Retreat, you rarely smelled that classic sea smell I was consumed by now. Yet, here I was, content to accept this as normal, my mind doing backflips to make sense of the insensible.

These thoughts came and went within the first seconds I was awake. Emerging from the fog, I noticed the sun had fully set. It was only the afterburn faintly lighting the sky. Soberly, I checked the time to confirm what I already knew. My phone screen lit up and confirmed there would be no staff dinner for me. Thankfully, I had a stockpile of overpriced instant noodles ready to go for just this occasion; they would have to do the job. Without a reason to hustle back, I took in the dark void widening beneath me. If I were to stand up and walk forward, I would chance walking right off the unforgiving cliff's edge. Despite a valiant attempt to enjoy my situation, I could not shake the oddness of my waking. As I nervously checked my phone, I became fully conscious of the urge to head home; that underlying feeling of discomfort had finally seeped in and tapped my awareness. Simultaneously, I heard an unknown rustling from further down the path. I should have gotten up and left immediately.

      I did not get up. I did not leave. The sound in the bushes was nothing out of the ordinary. There was a surplus of deer on the island. You could hardly drive anywhere without them appearing on the road. They also frequently wandered through the cottage's yards as we housekeepers cleaned. For whatever reason, I ignored the fact that it was likely just a deer and found myself disturbed by the sound. My angst was aided immensely by the now pitch-blackness in which I was surrounded. Perhaps it was that I had not heard any deer on my previous hangouts here, but it felt like more.

      Out of habit, I looked towards the sound, fully expecting to see nothing but darkness. What I found was unexpected and momentarily inexplicable. The best way I can describe it is as a small, singular light. Quickly, I rationalized and figured someone must be making their way up the trail with a flashlight. It was just another lonely soul wandering the woods. I was slightly puzzled as to why they were coming from further down the path, rather than the entrance at the road. This I explained by assuming they must have snuck by while I was snoozing, or that there was another trail making the connection deeper in the woods. Despite these justifications, I was unable to shake the strange feeling. Was it not odd that today should be the first time I saw another person explore this trail? Probably, but so it is.

My overly analytical brain judged the person to be three minutes away at most. I wanted to leave, I almost felt compelled to leave. I would have been long gone if I thought I could pack up before they were on me. Not feeling I had much of a choice, I opted to wait for the person to pass me by. Trying to stay calm, I zoned out for a minute and took in the absolute silence. Even the silence struck me as odd in itself. It took another few seconds before what was odd clicked. There was no sound of someone approaching. I made all kinds of noise on my walk-in. It had not rained in a couple of days, and so I should have been able to hear the sound of leaves and twigs crunching underfoot.

    I wanted to investigate the strange silence. I did this by re-examining the light. Initially, I was avoiding looking in its direction as I wanted to avoid staring at the person who made their approach. I peered towards it and saw that it had come closer, but considering the speed of someone who was walking, the light had barely moved. I stared in that direction, paying much closer attention. In the same way I noticed an absence of sound, I now noticed the light was not bobbing up and down as a human-carried torch or headlamp would most certainly be expected to. Rather than bounce or shake, it floated slowly and evenly along the path. I questioned if it was even going down the path, and then questioned if it did not seem to be coming directly for me. What the fuck was it? To my dismay, I was unable to rationalize this series of questions. Believe me when I say there was nothing I wanted more than to do just that.

    In awe, I continued to stare towards the light. I was frozen. Feebly, I attempted to calculate how much time I had before it was upon me. I grew quite certain it was indeed headed in my direction. The trajectory was difficult to gauge since it seemed to be coming straight for me. It seemed uninhibited by the path. Further, I wondered why no shadows were passing in front of it. The light was blaring and unblinking.

My calculations stopped as quickly as they started. I was suddenly gripped by an inexplicable terror. It was a warm evening, and yet it was as though my very blood had run cold. Luckily, I did not freeze in this fear for long. I jumped from my hammock and hastily filled my bag with everything I brought. As I ripped down the hammock strap closest to the light, I looked up and discovered that it had vanished. This sudden disappearance provided no reprieve whatsoever; if anything, it stoked my fear. Without the light to focus on, the true darkness of the night was revealed. It was blacker than black, so black that it almost made a noise. Normally, I would carefully stuff the hammock into its bag one strap at a time, followed by the fabric, but not now. I shoved it loosely into my pack and swung it onto my back. It was time to get the fuck out of there.

As I began rushing blindly towards the trail, I looked up to see where I was going. My heart stopped. The pale light was level with my head's centre. I could see now that it was suspended in nothing but time. As my fear grew, so did the light. The darkness was being consumed by the floating entity. It was not casting light to reveal the trees, but rather, it seemed to be expanding. It was as though the light was all that existed. There were no trees, no cliff, no trail. It continued to grow until the darkness was null. Without invitation, it moved onto me.

I was unable to think of anything; I found myself entirely consumed. At that moment, there was no sense of self to grasp onto, no fear, no curiosity, nothing. Even the very concept of nothing had fled. I slowly came out of it, back to myself. Just as I began to process what I was seeing, it was gone, as though the light was but a figment of my imagination. I could easily accept my fear was real, but I would spend many evenings questioning the rest of what I saw.

Feeling completely out of it, and taking a wide berth around where the light disappeared, I began to walk home. I made it no more than a dozen steps before something clicked, and I began to run. I did not stop until I passed the white sign declaring the Retreat's title. I moved at some pace, even once I was on the property. I went straight to my room. The way my head was swirling, I knew there would be no ramen tonight.

I collapsed onto my bed, attempting and failing to reflect upon my evening. I could look past the strange feeling of seasickness and smell of the ocean; in fact, I was at peace with those things. What I could not wrap my head around at all was the light. What in God's name had I seen? I was locked in a desperate internal debate, attempting to determine if I could truly believe what my eyes saw. I heard stories of people's brains playing tricks on them. Is that all that happened? Some neurons misfiring? For instance, just the day before, I read in the Torah that Moses saw a burning bush whose branches were not on fire. He approached it, and his God presented him with direction by speaking through said burning bush. The concept of this story being legitimate was just as unbelievable as the light I saw, but I had been given no direction. Similar to the bush in which Moses' god appeared, my mind was ablaze, and all I could do was hope I would also avoid being consumed by the flames. All I was able to take from these thoughts was the importance of being curious about the light. I should examine it as Moses did the peculiar bush. He was rewarded; perhaps I would be too. As I tried to make some sense of it all and battle these semi-blasphemous thoughts, I slipped away into a restless dream.

[CHAPTER TWENTY TWO]

The theme of deep sleep continued. It was later that same night that the rank smell of the ocean filled my lungs. One summer at university, I made a day trip to an Island off the coast of Newfoundland. Bell Island is known for towering cliffs and never-ending iron mines. I parked my car along a field and walked past some Newfoundland Ponies that were grazing in a field. I was making my way to the coast. There, by the sea, I came to a small beach surrounded by high cliffs. The beach was made up of a million baseball-sized stones that shifted precariously under each step. Trying desperately to not roll an ankle, I noticed that in between these stones were hundreds of small fish. They had beached themselves and their remains had begun decomposing in the summer sun. It was a putrid smell, eerily comparable to the one present. More than the smell, the feeling of motion sickness also returned, and this time it was much stronger. It was back with such a vengeance that my stomach became upset. Thinking I may puke, I opted to make a mad dash for the bathroom. I was unable to get a foot onto the ground before pain struck my head. When I attempted to sit up, I knocked into something solid. Considering the layout of my bedroom, I cracked my head on something that should not have been there in the first place.

    This was the second time that night that I collapsed onto my bed. The first was from overwhelming exhaustion, and the second from inexplicable pain. As I lay there recovering from the surprise, I noticed some sounds that were out of place, much like whatever I had hit my head off. There were hurried steps above me, and they seemed to reverberate from many sets of feet. As I listened closer, I heard what sounded to be the crashing of waves all around. I was immediately alarmed. Staff accommodations were only one floor, how the fuck could there be so many loud footsteps on the roof? The ocean was also several hundred meters away, and I had no right to be hearing the sound of waves crashing. Maybe if I were less woozy from banging my head, then I could have rationalized these things. For instance, maybe Christmas had come early and it was Santa and his reindeer on the roof, and perhaps simultaneously my neighbours were playing incredibly loud white noise that imitated the sound of waves, but no. Between the smell, the motion sickness, and the cracking of my head, I was at a loss.

    I am embarrassed to say that my first impulse was to reach for my phone, but I must stick to the truth as closely as possible. So that is what I will do, and that is what I did. I had plugged it into charge on my shelf, which doubled as my bedside table. My reaching hand was met with nothing but empty air. As the stars cleared and my eyes adjusted to the darkness, I realized I was not in my room at all. Before I could finish processing that thought, I was standing up. This time, I stood with fluidity and familiarity, so as to not hit my head. This time, I was not in control of my body. Having successfully stood up, I began moving through what seemed to be a labyrinth of wooden planks dimly lit by lanterns. The lanterns were brass and squeaked as they swung perpetually. They looked to be the kind you would see in an old movie, like they could be found in a museum. As my sure feet moved with purpose, I gained full comprehension that I was not in control of my body. It did not strike me to wonder if I was even in my body at all. I felt like a passenger, similar to how I felt as I watched my ferry weave through the Gulf Islands on my way to Georgia.

    Stairs groaned their protest as I made my way towards sunlight. I emerged onto the deck of a ship. It was a rather large boat with multiple masts. I noticed the sails were tucked away. What a strange dream, I had become the ultimate passenger. Even more difficult to fathom was that the smells and sensations were so genuine, they felt real. I had had realistic enough dreams before, but this was an entirely different beast. When in prior dreams that mirrored reality, I found there was some inexplicable sensation or tell separating the two. So far in this dream, there was no separation from reality. I actually felt that my dream world was blending with reality, as though two strokes from the same brush were overlapping. I thought no further than the moment I tried to get out of bed and bumped my head. I genuinely felt like I had control there, even if it was fleeting. The closest I can get to explaining the inexplicable is that this dream felt more than real; it felt important. I had the feeling that every detail was being presented for a reason, and that this was a dream that I would be ill-advised to thoughtlessly file away.

    Simply being along for the ride in this body, I had lots of time to think, and so I continued to do so. I thought to myself, maybe it is not only this dream that feels so real. Maybe all dreams have this feeling of blended reality. Maybe when we awake, the memory of realism is erased, along with most of what occurred in the dream. Heck, maybe I follow this exact train of thought every damn time. As I have said, I am a firm believer that our minds pull tricks on us. I imagine they work with great care to protect the illusion that is the fabric of reality. But then, did this dream break that illusion? So far, it seemed I could handle it. I began to question the purpose of this hypothetical function of our minds, before reminding myself that any attempt for my brain to understand my brain was in vain.

    I made my way along the deck towards the bow of the ship. I was approaching a hole in the planks. A new and equally vulgar smell announced itself as I got closer to the hole. Upon arrival, I undid my trousers and began urinating. Thus answering both the question of what the hole was, and from where the smell was coming. As I re-clasped my buttons, I realized my seasickness had passed. More than that, my legs felt confident walking on this unpredictable surface. I moved with ease, despite the lurch of the boat.

    I looked around and saw that the vast majority of people on deck were dressed in old-fashioned sailors' garb. Without greeting or being greeted by anyone, I made my way to a raised deck. I was immediately hailed by a confident-looking man who wore a more dressy uniform.
    In a surprisingly gentle voice that I did not recognize, I said, "Top of the morning, Captain, what can I do for you?"
    Almost cutting me off, and abruptly answering my question with one of his own, he said, "Do you recognize where we are?"
    I began looking around in an attempt to find some sort of landmark. We were certainly not in the open ocean but were rather surrounded by land. It felt strange that such a big ship should be in this sort of place. I was unable to recognize anything specific, not that I expected to, yet I could not help but feel an air of familiarity.
    My host clearly knew where we were, and he responded hesitantly, "Yes, sir, around that corner there lies the sheltered bay

that you are looking for. Of course, I will respect the decision you make."

He cut me off, looking at me like I was a worthless swine, and scowled, "Yes, you will."

I continued, now with less confidence, "I must remind you that I am against our going. There were simply too many Indians, strongly armed ones at that."

The Captain responded dismissively, "You have made clear your particular feelings. My choice is made, it is final. Now, did you not say these Indians were friendly?"

I nodded dumbly. I was stunned by this conversation and had no clue what to make of it.

The man who seemed to be both the captain and an asshole turned to a big beefy man who was standing off to the side, "Lieutenant, ready our most accurate shots on deck, rally our best swordsmen, with them, we shall go to shore."

The large Lieutenant did not skip a beat or ask a single question; the mean-looking man moved off heavily to fulfill the Captain's orders.

I was feeling lost. Between the overwhelming smells and sounds, I had no idea what was going on. All that I knew for certain was that I felt the overwhelming urge to protest whatever was going to happen. Despite this urge, I could not even try; I truly had no control whatsoever. I felt as though I was watching an old movie play out in the first person. Who knows, give it another decade, and maybe technology will reach that point of immersion, but I hope not. My host seemed to be taking a moment for himself. He did nothing but look out at the sea, as though searching for something that was nowhere to be found.

The daydream dissolved instantaneously as he heard orders aggressively barked. He moved to look over the raised deck's railing and saw what seemed to be men of war gathering loudly on the main deck. They were responding to the meat rack of a Lieutenant's orders in rapid fashion. One man stood out; he was stoutly staring at me, waiting to catch my eye. When our eyes locked, he gave me a sad smile and a slight shrug. It was as though he was sending the message, 'Ah well, what can you do'. The Captain stood to my right; he was next to catch my eyes in his. Without uttering a word, he told me to back away from the railing and make myself scarce. I happily obeyed. I moved out of view from the deck below and watched the Captain from behind.

I could hear that the movements of men on the main deck had for the most part ceased; that was when the Captain began to address them.

He roared from the top deck, "Okay, men, you all must know the plan by now. Lieutenant Mudge will lead you to land at the beach under the guise of peace. We hope to draw out as many of their men and warriors as possible. Once the Lieutenant has gauged the time to be right, he will give the signal. The men left on board with me will take care to shoot any Indian; those on land will assume the position before drawing swords and pistols. Focus on their leaders, spare no woman or child who resists. The men manning our cannons will only fire if serious backup appears, although I doubt it will be necessary."

The men roared their approval in response to this diabolical speech.

Anxiety and anger, which were not my own, began to grow within me. The rage was directed at one man in particular, as I stared at the captain from behind, my vision flashed red. I felt as though a great fear was being realized. It seemed the overwhelming emotions of my host were seeping into my own mind. I cannot express how I came to this conclusion, but it felt right.

The boat slowed and was drifting around a corner. I could see a natural beach in the distance. As a great gust of wind came over the deck, my vision faded. Despite its receding, I was nearly certain I saw a towering cliff to the left of the beach. I was less certain, but thought it possible that to the right of the beach, sunlight was reflecting off a great waterfall. It was reminiscent of a place I knew well. I could not help but wonder.

[CHAPTER TWENTY THREE]

As though I never left, I was back in my bed at Arbutus Falls. I found myself drenched in sweat. I felt myself encapsulated by the rank smell of the dirty sea, it was stronger than ever. Once again, I made for the bathroom. This time, I hit my head on nothing. Despite the clear air, my sudden movement reinvigorated the pain in my temple. Yes, it was still aching. This time, I made it to the toilet. This time, I was sick. Due to my lack of having had dinner, there was not much to come up. This did nothing but aid the sharpness in my throat. I sat down on the toilet and began to shake uncontrollably. This was new to me. In the moment, it felt rather dramatic, but it was out of my control. I was unfazed by my sudden sickness, and my mind cast away thoughts of shaking. I was entirely consumed by the question of what the hell had just happened. Well, by what had not happened, it was nothing but an absurdly irregular dream.

My hypothesis that the feeling of reality in my dream should fade as I came back to the conscious world was immediately disproven. The whole ordeal still felt real. I would argue it felt even more real now that I was processing it in my own body. Every moment, feeling, and smell. It was as though everything I experienced in the dream had also happened to me. Did the pounding in my head literally not prove that? Or was I only imagining that, too? The anger was what stuck with me most; I could not shake this feeling of rage. In fact, prior to that moment, I had not known such rage as the one I felt for the imaginary man piloting the imaginary ship. Such a vile feeling was painful in itself.

I splashed some water on my face in hopes of resetting, and then returned to my room. Upon returning, I did the only thing that made sense, the only thing I could control. I cracked the window and smoked my pipe. I hoped to hell it would put me to sleep. A proper dreamless sleep. This hopeful thought reminded me to do a quick search on the internet. I wanted to confirm that people who consistently smoke weed do not typically dream. I found, 'regular marijuana intake significantly diminishes our REM sleep, that's when the most vivid dreams occur'. Okay, so what the fuck was that all about? Also, that sounds like a very bad thing. From what I have heard, REM sleep is very important. I reminded myself for the millionth time to lay off the weed. I found myself vehemently responding to that reminder, 'not right now'. I smoked another bowl, exhaling into the bowels of the night.

      My dance with Mary Jane was in vain; sleep would not come. It would not find me for the rest of the night. As I lay there in frustration, there were moments when I could have sworn I felt the bed lull side to side. I found the smell of the sea and the sound of the waves seemed to come and go, too. Although as soon as I focused on them, they were gone. It was nothing if not cruel that once the sun began its daily ritual, I finally cast off into the sea of sleep.

      This time, when I awoke and reached for my phone, it was there. Checking the time, I learned that it was just past noon. An excess of stress and lack of sleep made me feel hungover. Shit, I nearly exclaimed, I was supposed to be working the bar. Although it was common practice for employees to miss the beginning of their shifts due to overconsumption the night before, this was not something I had yet fallen victim to. I would not say that I necessarily take pride in it, but I do value keeping myself accountable to show up to work on time, which is why I panicked a bit. Thankfully, this panic momentarily forced any plight from my mind. I dressed as fast as I could and walked quickly down the hill.

      My heart sank as I shuffled into the restaurant. Horner was standing behind the bar, looking like all the prick that he was.

I was subconsciously hoping he would not be there, but of course, one of the few times he actually showed up was when I overslept.

Horner said with a concerning amount of cheer, "Look who finally decided to show up. You drank too much last night, didn't you?"

Wanting nothing more than to exchange as few words as possible, I responded defeatedly, "No, I'm sick, I hardly slept a minute last night."

Horner, considerate as always, did not seem to believe me, "Like hell, you sound fine to me, why the fuck didn't you give me a heads up?"

I could not help but think about how I should not have bothered coming in. I responded with a bit more life, "I would have, but I finally fell asleep before I had the chance. Besides, the bar's dead during the buffet. How many drinks have you made?"

He paused briefly, seemingly surprised by my attitude.

He considered this and then said in a strangely detached tone, "That's not the point. I'll be talking to Kevin about this." Brushing past him, I ignored his last remark.

It was at that moment that I resolutely decided I would go to the general manager myself. The bar had become another lonely place, and the bad energy was not helping my situation. I was lucky to make more than half a dozen drinks by the end of a shift. I was feeling more like a babysitter than a bartender. Sitting on top of it all, like shit on a stick, was Horner. The bar manager had severed my last nerve.

Although I was grateful to have missed half of it, the rest of my shift crawled by like an inebriated turtle. Yes, the inebriated turtle is a good friend of the drunken snail. My mind was cluttered as I attempted to digest what had happened the night before. It was difficult to do something as simple as putting events in chronological order. After having had such a dull existence for so long, it felt like I had lived an extra month in one evening. The light was an otherworldly experience in itself. To then have been seemingly dropped into another world was inconceivable.

I focused on a rough analysis of the dream. The worst dreams that I had had before were ones that felt quite real. These were the ones where I woke up in a panic, often thinking I had to make a call or feeling depressed by the despicable actions of a friend. Within minutes of banishing these mirages, I would return to reality, and the thoughts would be filed away as the bad dreams that they were. My mind seemed to be desperately attempting to do just that, only it was not working. The smells were too strong, the emotions lingered too long. It did not feel like I had woken from a dream; it felt like I had switched lives. There was also the fact that, based on my regular marijuana consumption, I should not have been dreaming in the first place. The more I failed to make sense of things, the more frustrated I became. I continued spiralling to the point of thinking I was crazy. This was hard to face because I was quite certain that I was not, and am not, crazy. Sure, the Retreat was driving me mad, but only as a figure of speech. When logic continually failed to come to my aid, I tried to remind myself that it was just a dream. Hell, it had to be a dream. As the shift schlepped along, it was as though I had a new mantra. Whenever doubts crept back in, I would repeat it to myself. 'It was just a dream.'

I was making no headway in rationally grasping the last twenty-four hours of my life, and so I decided to focus on another thing I could control. With the morning's polite greeting from Horner in mind, I sent Kevin a message. He was short in his replies, but agreed to meet with me once the other bartender came to my relief. I was thankful that Joel was not in much of a talking mood when he arrived. Unlike me, I think he actually was hungover. I arrived at the office in relatively good spirits. I was happily armed with some important knowledge. I had come to recognize a most obvious fact. The Retreat was incredibly desperate for workers, and it did not take a genius to know I was one of the good ones. This meant I was of relative value to the company; therefore, I could demand certain things. I was unsure of how far I could push this, but I thought I might as well find out.

Another mantra may as well have been, 'What are they going to do, fire me?'

The boss's French Bulldog escaped his shackles and ran to meet me. As Oscar bobbled side to side, he really looked like a smaller version of his owner. I gave him a quick and well-deserved pat as I headed into the office to take my seat.

Kevin cut right to it and, with false empathy, said, "Horner told me you were a few hours late for your shift today. What's up?"

I was slightly annoyed by the greeting, but in that moment, I believe there was nothing he could have said that would have triggered any mood but a bad one. I remembered the lies this snake had spewed, and I wanted nothing more than to cut off his head. Thankfully for both of us, patience won out, and I kept my cool.

I responded calmly, "I'm not feeling great, but that's not why I'm here." Once again, wanting to skip the bullshit, I continued, "I'm not interested in working the bar anymore. As long as you don't mind, I would like to switch to housekeeping full-time. I've already talked to Henri, and he says he has more than enough hours for me."

I had not actually talked to Henri yet, but we had struck up a friendship, and I knew he would have my back. More than that, he would be happy to have me full-time.

His response was calm and calculated, "Right, I see. Now, why exactly do you want to make this change?"

I decided I would give him one more chance to take the easy way out of this, for both our sakes.

I responded politically, "I'd rather not get into more than we need to. Let's just say that I much prefer Henri's approach to management, and I find housekeeping to be a bit more fulfilling."

To his credit, he left well enough alone, but was not fully done, "Okay, it's your choice. I won't have an issue finding another bartender; many people would be happy to have your position. You know, bartending pays so much better than housekeeping. Are you sure you want to give that up?"

Once again, my anger almost bubbled over. I thought, 'Was this stubby thumb of a man really trying to manipulate me into staying at the bar?' I knew no one else wanted to work there, and even if they did want to, they were not trained in the slightest. Were they, then I would have already been replaced. The most important factor was that I did not give a flying fuck about the money. The bar was so dead that I would hardly notice the difference.

All but ignoring his comments, and donning as sarcastic a tone as I dared, I said, "Thanks for your understanding, I'm happy to hear it won't be an issue."

With a dirty smile on his face, he said, "My pleasure, by the way, how are you liking staff accommodations?"

This brought a wide smile to my face.

I knew he was a bachelor, so as I stood up, I said, "Oh, just lovely. Remind me, when do you move off the island? Your family must be excited."

He laughed in response and told me to have a nice day. I said just the same, although as you can imagine, there was plenty more that I wanted to say. It was most definitely best to have left it at that.

Wishful thinking had me hoping this new situation would lead to my only working five or six shifts a week. I started back to my room, but paused once the fresh air hit me. I stood outside the lobby staring up at the cloudy sky. I thought to myself, aw man, what was I going to do now? I was feeling ill-prepared to go back to the cliff with my hammock, and I had no other ideas. I once again waged war with my most persistent thoughts. The dream may have been nothing more than that, but the light sure as hell was real. No way was I going back to the cliff. My room was only the length of a single bed and the width of two, but at least its tiny window looked towards the forest; it would have to do.

[CHAPTER TWENTY FOUR]

My physical body was desperately asking for marijuana when I returned to my room. Despite this craving, something told me not to smoke, and so I did not. Instead, I set a timer to wake me up. I had to catch up on sleep, and I could not afford to miss dinner two nights in a row. I lay stiffly in bed. Sleep is such a joyous occasion; who does not covet a nap? Yet, for the first time in my life, I found myself nervous to sleep. Thankfully, it was as I debated this anxiety that I fell under. A clean sleep was much needed. I slept without dreams and awoke without trouble. There were no strange smells or feelings; it was as clean as clean can be.

After the much-needed nap, I arrived for dinner. I thanked my lucky stars that it was one of the good ones. A good dinner consisted of some sort of meat and vegetables. Even the good ones were never fantastic. A bad dinner, which was served more often than not, consisted of Chef throwing some pre-made frozen shit in the oven. Oftentimes, these were chicken pies that never seemed to defrost through to the middle. Even more frequently, we ate crappy frozen hamburgers. They were okay once a month, but when you were eating them three to four times a week, they could be hard to stomach. The same could be said for the deep-fried french fries perpetually accompanying the hamburgers. The worst part about the lacklustre dinners was that we had to pay for them. That was what the book at the head of the buffet line was for. You may be wondering why my colleagues and I paid for and ate such food every day twice a day. The fact of the matter is that there was no other option. The kitchen we had in staff accommodations was an absolute pigsty. Some incredibly questionable substances covered most surfaces and cooking utensils. Once, some others and I felt inspired and decided to give it a deep clean. Within forty-eight hours of the cleaning, the place was dirtier than it had initially been. It was as though the druggies had taken offence to our cleaning and decided to spew their shit thicker and further in retribution. I had not had the time to get groceries, and never even cooked there after cleaning it. That seemingly wasted effort was hard to recover from, and it was never cleaned again. So, staff meals it was and would be.

The one consistently positive thing about staff dinner was how good an opportunity it was for socialization. After loading my plate with stir-fried beef and rice, they had forgotten the vegetables, so I sat with Jen and Jared. I had not seen either of them yet that day; they had both been working in housekeeping. Jared, in typical Arbutus Falls fashion, was passed between housekeeping and kitchen like a hand-rolled cigarette. The kitchen, specifically, had been smoking him for too long, and he was burnt down to the filter. This left him drawing harsh breath, which he alleviated with a little help from Mary Jane. He qualified as one of the stoners previously mentioned on the housekeeping team. Visually, he fit the part of a stoner like it was his profession. He had long dark hair, which was typically held back in a messy bun or tucked up under an Aurora Brewing cap. His dark eyes were framed in a pair of rectangular wire-rimmed glasses. At this point, he had a small and clean goatee. I would later learn that he looked like a completely different and much younger man without facial hair. He was Canadian through and through. You could always find him rocking blue jeans and a flannel. As it got colder, he would add a hoodie that somehow fit flawlessly beneath the same flannels. We would become good friends.

I greeted the two of them with as much enthusiasm as I could muster. Based on Jen's response, it must not have been much; she was not fooled in the slightest.
She said bluntly, but with care, "Woah, buddy, you look like you've seen a ghost. Are you okay?"
Taking what she had said literally, I thought to myself, 'I sure hope not.'
Knowing I could be honest, at least about my emotions, "I couldn't sleep a minute last night, I was three hours late to my shift, and Horner was waiting for me at the bar. I'm sure you can guess how that went."

Jen responded with emotion, "But you never show up late, he should have cut you some slack."

I smiled, "Yeah, you're right, but tell that to him. On a better, and completely related note, I finally decided to switch full-time to housekeeping. I think that it'll make a real difference on the ol' mental health front."

Jared chimed in, "You're going to have to tell me how you pulled that one off. I've taken enough shit from Chef for a lifetime. I'm seriously considering making the switch to full-time toilet swirler myself."

I laughed at this turn of phrase as I responded, "There wasn't much to it, honestly. I went to the big man's office and told him I was done at the bar, told him I wanted to swirl toilets full-time. I may or may not have fibbed and told him Henri had approved, but I'm sure he'll have my back. I was actually going to mention it to him if I saw him at dinner, but he's probably still working. Anyways, I say you do it, man, can't hurt."

It was Jared's turn to nod along, "I like it. I can't stop imagining the pleasure of telling Chef he can go fuck himself across the seven seas."

Jen said with a sarcastic smile, "Wow, that is really lovely, Jared. But seriously, you should do it. The kitchen sounds slightly sadistic." I nodded enthusiastically in agreement. She continued, shifting her gaze to me, "We're both in housekeeping tomorrow, right? I still haven't shown you that place on the protected land that I mentioned. I feel like I owe you. Why don't we go tomorrow after work?"

I smiled and said, "Not only do you owe me that, but you've also owed me a walk in general for far too long. Let's do it."

The timing could not have been better. I could use a new spot to escape from the Retreat, and I hoped this would be it. I knew I would need some time before gaining the confidence to return to the cliff, even in the daytime.

The rest of dinner was passed with empty words that filled the soul. As we cleared our plates, Jared asked me if I smoked.

I responded with a mixed laugh, "Oh, do I ever, not much else to do, eh?"

That got a laugh from him, and he said, "Why don't you come down to the tower? I've got a joint with your name on it. Well, it's got both our names on it, but you know what I mean."

I did indeed know what he meant. Not only did a joint sound much better than my pipe, which had gotten rather dirty from overuse and under-cleaning, but some human interaction after the night before would be much appreciated. I happily agreed.

[CHAPTER TWENTY FIVE]

As we walked to the tower, I learned that the reason Jared suggested it was because that was where he was now living. I had thought Kevin was still living there. I had even made the jab at him earlier that day, asking when he left. I was happily surprised that our soon-to-be ex-general manager was already living in a lodge room, and that he would be gone at the week's end. I asked Jared how long he had been living there.

He replied, "Oh, it's only been a few days. There's only two of us in there, which is pretty sweet. Although there's space for four."

I said, "Oh shit, that doesn't sound like too bad of a deal. Must be nice being out of staff accommodations."

He said passionately, "Dude, is it ever, it's literally just two bunk beds in the middle of a room, one small toilet, plus a small kitchen, which is sweet. But tell ya what, after sharing a wall with Stanley, it feels like heaven."

I cringed as I responded, "Right, I forgot you used to live beside him. You must be pumped to be out of there."

Poor Stanley. He seemed like a nice enough guy. I had never heard him say much, and he certainly kept to himself. He was the guy who would come in and buy the two bottles of Syrah at the bar, the guy who would get his Tupperware filled with Pepsi. From what I heard, he would drink the bottles every night, alone in his room. It was crucial to hold one's breath when walking past his abode. Once, when I was going by, he had left the door open. I could not resist peeking in, and I saw empty bottles literally lining all surfaces. There was nothing in the room other than a couple of garbage bags, which looked to be filled with more empty bottles. The rotten smell oozing from his room was infamous among workers; it actually seeped into the rooms that shared a wall. He ended up getting fired when he got too drunk and broke a wall. He was one of those guys who everyone wanted to know his story, but no one had the guts to ask. Or maybe some folks had asked, and it was simply not the kind of story that you go passing around. Whatever happened to him, and wherever he is, I hope he is doing okay.

      The aforementioned joint was up in the tower. I could not resist checking out the new digs, and so I made the climb up with Jared. The rubber-covered stairs were steep and plentiful. They came out into a room that Jared had only slightly understated. To the right was a very small lounge. It included a three-person couch and a TV; it looked rather cozy due to a large window. Tucked behind that was a tiny kitchen. As promised, the left side of the room was filled with two bunk beds and two dressers. There were large windows on the far wall; these were the eyes of the tower. A large sheet hung from the roof and essentially divided it into two separate 'rooms'. Opposite the staircase was a small bathroom. It already smelled like the singular bathroom that my roommates and I shared in university.

      The final, and arguably the most important thing in the room, was yet to be identified. It was the man sprawled out on the couch. He was watching one of the more mind-numbing TV shows. His name was Eric, and he was quite the character. He is a person whom I have trouble describing; he evades proper analysis. On the surface, he was a balding man just past the age of forty, but who looked well past fifty. He was on the bigger side, and other than often finding himself out of breath on the Retreat's hills, he carried the extra weight well. Eric was an Alberta boy through and through. He was always wearing some sort of Canadian Football League hat, and often a matching sweater or jersey. He was a very nice man if he liked you, but he was a bit old school in who he liked. It was a safe bet that he would take well to you if you were a white Canadian man, but if you did not fit into that niche category, then he was likely to say mean things behind your back. On special occasions, he may even speak to you as though you are slow. I do believe that he had a good heart, perhaps everyone does, but there were certainly moments where it was impossible to see past the misogyny and racism.

When I walked in, he said, "Hey buddy! How are ya?"

He worked between dishwashing and housekeeping, and I am white, so we were friendly.

I said casually, "Hey Eric, how're you enjoying the tower? It looks like you've got a nice little TV setup going."

With unbridled enthusiasm, he said, "Oh yeah, buddy, it's awesome, I'm so glad to be out of that stinkin' building. Are you moving in here with us? You really should, I'd much rather you, you know, than the new guy."

I assumed that he was referencing the new Indian guy who was working in the kitchen. If you asked me, he seemed nice enough, but you know, racism.

I was a bit taken aback, not by his outdated views, but by the idea of taking one of the two remaining spots in the tower. It had not crossed my mind at all. My first impulse was that no, I would not be moving in. Despite the size of it and the noise that my room was surrounded by, I did like the privacy it offered, at least relative to this place. I think part of why I was having such a poor time on the island was that I had unconsciously created a small world in which to isolate myself. I expect that had I moved in with Jared and Eric, it would have burst that bubble. Subconsciously, I was too scared to leave that comfort zone.

Not wanting to hurt Eric's enthusiasm, I responded politically, "That's not a bad idea. I'll sure have to think about it. Who do you guys have for other prospects?"

Jared, who was now babying the joint in his hand, responded, "Well, we're hoping to keep it to the two of us for as long as possible, but for whatever reason, management wants it filled up as quickly as possible. Eric's right, it'd be great if you wanted to join us. You should definitely think about it."

I was still rather hesitant about the idea of giving up my isolation, I mean, my privacy. But in that moment, I was feeling the warm feeling of being wanted. Here were two men I hardly knew, and they were both warmly inviting me into their home, inviting me to be one of them. It felt good.

Jared wanted to get down to business, and so he motioned down the stairs with the joint, "Shall we?"

I once again found myself happily agreeing. I said goodbye and goodnight to Eric and promised him I would consider moving into the tower. He seemed satisfied as could be, and had his eyes glued to the TV before our pleasantries were exchanged.

Jared led me down and around to the far side of the tower, away from the Retreat. There was a small patio that was likely once meant for guests, but it looked to have fallen into disuse. The patio stones were cracked, and weeds filled the crevices. There were some comfy-enough chairs that had seen better days. All in all, I was rather impressed by the sesh spot. We each settled into our respective chairs, and Jared wasted no time sparking up. We passed the precious back and forth until it was used. As we looked out over the dark bay, conversation began. We focused on the biggest thing we had in common. That is, we took turns moaning about the Retreat. Complaining only helps when there's someone there to listen, and we were both entirely there for it.

Little of much substance was said until I quietly asked him how it was living with Eric so far.

He responded frankly, "Man, so far it's fucking brutal. The guy spends thirty minutes at a time on the toilet, and if he's not there or at work, then he's on the couch watching TV with the volume cranked." He paused his rant thoughtfully and then continued, "He always has the volume cranked, even when he isn't home. Look, it's still a bit better than sharing a wall with Stanley, but not by much."

I was disappointed, but not surprised, "Aw man, that's tough. What would your, uh, genuine take be on me moving in? Taking into consideration that I don't hate my situation as much as you did."

He responded, "Best thing for me would be if you did move in with us, we're going to get roommates eventually, so it may as well be you. But, if I were you, then I think I'd stay where I was. Maybe hang out a night or two with us to get an idea of what Eric's like."

I appreciated the honesty and told Jared as much. It was really nice shooting the shit with him, I think he was feeling the same way. It seemed that a solid friendship would be possible between the two of us. It began to drizzle, and so I made my way back up the hill. Each step brought me closer to bed and reminded me of my nightmares. Thoughts of my pleasant night were quickly replaced with a desperate hope for peaceful sleep.

[CHAPTER TWENTY SIX]

The following morning, I awoke from a sound sleep. I felt refreshed, as though I had put any prying concerns behind me. I was optimistic that the cessation of my bar shifts would improve my overall quality of life. Not only would I be avoiding a narcissistic boss, but I would also likely have some days off here and there. However, the thing that concerned me the most was that I had made it through a full night's sleep without being plagued by any strange happenings. Thank God.

The housekeeping team met at the laundry room each morning. I arrived that day with some pep in my step. Henri was there, waiting with his pen and clipboard.

I smiled at him and said, "Hey boss, beautiful morning, have you heard the good news?"

He certainly had, and despite rarely smiling during work hours, mine was so contagious that he could not help but return it in full.

In his charming French accent, he said, "I don't remember us talking about you going full-time in housekeeping. Kevin mentioned this was something we discussed." My smile grew; this was going to be fun.

I feigned innocence and said, "How strange is that? I could have sworn you had given the go-ahead."

Henri laughed at that and then quickly turned serious; he said, "Well, I did. You know, as a full timer, you'll have to start helping with houseman duties. Your, so you say, free ride, ends here."

I had forgotten about this and said, "Ah, yes. Looking forward to it. Remind me how early that starts."

Henri chuckled and told me that the start time was six in the morning. Apparently, he was wasting no time at all, as he let me know I would be trained the next morning.

Each day, someone who was working in housekeeping was scheduled to be the houseman. This special position required rising long before the sun. It was for this early start time that most people dreaded their turn. The victim would start their morning by picking up a converted housekeeping golf cart, which was pre-packed with cleaning supplies. It required first heading to the lobby, where they would check all of the public bathrooms in the main building, and from there they would do the same for the upper and lower pools. Some days, the front desk folk would have a little something extra for them, like vacuuming the lobby or mopping the stairs. It was a pretty straightforward routine. It could even be enjoyable if you were not against waking up bright, or not so bright, and early.

As we got into mid-October, I reflected that I had already spent a month and a half on the West Coast. The time so far was literally anything other than what I expected. Fall was quickly fading, and the heavy rains were growing more frequent. The shrivelled beginning of Winter brought with it a lower occupancy rate. With fewer guests and fewer employees, the housekeeping team was restructured. Rather than dividing and conquering, we began working as one large unit. This brought both good and bad. The good was that it guaranteed more shifts with Jared and Jen; the bad was that it allowed certain employees to slack off with more ease.

After I talked to Henri, Jen and I confirmed our intentions to go for a walk once the day's cleaning list had been defeated. It was a rare sunny day, and I was really looking forward to some fresh air. Jared was working that day and overheard us.
He asked, "Do you guys mind if I tag along?" He looked at me and wiggled his eyebrows, "I'll bring a joint."
Jen and I responded harmoniously, "Of course not, you're more than welcome." I added, "Your joint is too."
As we wrapped up the day by preparing the houseman's cart for the following morning, Henri kindly reminded me to set an alarm; he did not want me to miss my first day of fun. I could not help but think that word of my accidental oversleeping the day before had been passed along. After saying goodbye to the rest of the team, Jen led Jared and me away. We followed her up behind the waterfall, past some of the scattered cabins that we cleaned earlier that day.

The area was heavily wooded. Walking along Retreat trails, we came to a rare grassy area that had previously caught my eye. It was behind the cabin that I believed had the nicest view of the whole Retreat. It was elevated enough that you could see most of the cove, yet close enough that you could still hear the waves crashing. A sign stating, "Protected land, do not enter," feebly reprimanded us as we made our way towards two rocks on the edge of the grass patch. The stones formed the unofficial beginning of a pine needle-laden path; they stood guard like ancient sentries. They were weathered by the years, but still made their presence felt. Twisting roots and fallen branches were cleared as we made our way into the thick forest. I flagged this indication that the trail was seldom used. We were only a couple of minutes down the path when Jen paused ahead of us. She looked to the left, away from the ocean. I followed her gaze and for the first time I laid eyes on the cabin. The three of us were silent as we took it in, its presence huge. There was not much to actually see from the trail; it was tucked in well among the trees. It gave off the impression that it was a part of the forest, one of the few structures that truly belonged. From the little I could make out, it was low, just one story. As I recognized an abundance of sun reflecting off the windows, I knew that it likely stood in a clearing. My mind initially conjured an image of trees growing out of the cabin's sides, but this faded. An old thought resurfaced. I would have to ask Jen about what brought her to the cabin.

    In silence, we continued along. After a few paces, I asked my loaded question, "Hey Jen, how was it the other day? When you said that you were going to the cabin. I've been curious ever since."

    She could not help but laugh, and then, without looking back, responded, "I knew you were going to ask. I'm actually surprised you've held off this long. It was good, there's an old Indigenous woman who lives there."

    Grateful she answered, I pushed on, "Oh, how sweet, if you don't mind me asking, what exactly was it you were doing there?"

    Jen continued without hesitation, "Well, a few weeks ago, I met her while walking this same trail. We chatted, and she invited me for tea. That's what I was doing. I've even been back a few times since. I'm not sure if either of you guys knows, but I'm actually an RMT. I've been treating her, and also helping her prepare for winter."

    Jared said, "Oh, that's cool, I didn't know that. How nice of you."

    Jen continued humbly, "I should say, I'm helping her out in exchange for stories and advice on concocting local medicines, I do love reciprocity."

    I thought to myself how the cabin did not sound so spooky after all. The mystery surrounding it must be a classic case of 'well, I don't know what's there, so it can't be good'.

I found what Jen had said to be incredibly warming, and the whole situation fit perfectly with her mystic energy.

Before I could ask a follow-up, or even think much more for that matter, Jen said, "What about you, your energy has been off ever since Horner ripped into you. I can't imagine that that would have gotten to you that much, so what's going on?"

I felt immediate anxiety as my self-fabricated emotional isolation came under attack. There was no choice but to respond. It was a great question. What was going on? Hesitantly, I looked from Jen to Jared. I had not decided how much, or what, to share with anyone. I was caught off guard and began attempting to judge how they would react to possible rhetoric. I concluded that I would have to speak about what had happened at some point; might as well start now. Besides, what was the worst that could happen? They think that I am crazy? This whole Retreat and island were crazy.

With some weight, I said, "Okay, can I share something with you guys?" Jen nodded in such a way as to say that, of course, I could. Jared came across as a bit more reserved. I do not think he was expecting any sort of deep conversation when he joined us on this walk. He still gave me the go-ahead nonetheless.

I continued with a slight shake in my voice, "Okay, this is pretty hard to put into words, but I'll do what I can. The other night something happened, you may not believe it, I'm not sure if I even believe it myself."

Jen's face showed her focus as she continued nodding, and Jared suddenly seemed much more interested. I think that his initial reaction was due to him expecting me to say something rather pedestrian. While attempting to sound as sane as possible, I recounted what happened to me at the cliff the other night. I finished my tale with the disappearance of the floating light, not even skipping over how I ran back to the Retreat.

We came to a stop two meters above a beautifully untouched beach. Was this our destination? It seemed natural that the conversation should pause to allow my friends a moment to process the strangeness of what I said. Jen led us down a steep section of rock that could hardly be considered a path, although it did lead to the beach. We continued walking under the canopy of a large maple, whose roots had long ago been exposed by the tide. We hopped from root to root, carefully avoiding the gentle sway of the tide which pushed itself up and under the intricate system. Past the tree and in the middle of the beach was a large log. We sat there to continue our conversation.

While I was talking, Jen's nodding had seldom ceased. Jared was a bit harder to read. He listened intently, but gave little reaction. I was curious as to what each of them thought.

Jen broke the silence, "Well, I understand why you've been off, that sounds pretty freaky. Encounters with spirits can be intense, especially at night. How do you feel now?"

I considered sharing the dream that followed the light, but decided I would rather just forget it. After all, it was just a dream.

I responded, "I feel okay, a bit better after telling the story. But I've got to admit, I can't help wondering what happened; it just seems so inexplicable."

Jen took a moment to consider this and then responded, "I can imagine you're curious, but honestly, I wouldn't give it much thought. I've heard of similar encounters; strange things seem to happen around here. I'm not saying I don't believe you saw something, but I just can't imagine there being much value in chasing after it. "

This immediately reminded me of the ghost stories she promised to share when the sun was up. "I hear ya, that sounds pretty reasonable. But hold on a second, you never told me what you've heard, or the story about the ring screwed into the tree." With a smile, I added, "I've been patiently waiting."

My mentioning of the metal circle seemed to cause a stir in Jared, but he stayed silent.

Jen seemed to become a bit more reserved at my words, "Hey, at least I finally brought you to this beautiful place. But yeah, I was wondering when you would remind me. The stories really aren't anything too exciting. Just your classic ethereal body spotted on a foggy night, sounds of desperate screaming, and metal clanging. The strangest thing about them is that they all seem to centre around that old tree. Yet no one seems to know why."

The stories sounded a bit more exciting to me than Jen was making them out to be. I almost felt that there was something being left unsaid. I tried and failed to come up with a question to unlock what may be hidden. We sat in silence, the only sound was the rushing of water over the tiny stones of the beach. The ocean breathed.

Jen sharing that I was not alone in my experience of strangeness on the island provided some relief. This relief was limited, since my episode occurred so far from the seemingly innocent point of power. Jared had yet to utter a word since I told my story, and he looked a bit uneasy. I gently asked what he thought about the whole thing.

He responded hesitantly, as though he would have preferred to stay quiet, "I'm not sure, man, it does sound creepy."

He took a deep breath before continuing, "Now, you've gotta understand that I don't love saying this, but I can't help but think that maybe you were just too stoned, or still half asleep? I just don't really believe in that sort of stuff. I feel like there is always another explanation."

It seemed like he felt bad about saying as much. I thought it was an honest and genuine response, and I appreciated it.

Wanting him to know I was unbothered by the contradiction, I said, "Fair enough, man, honestly, I've been asking myself the same thing. It's possible, maybe even likely, that my mind played a trick on itself. I don't blame you one bit for not believing it, it's pretty damn unbelievable."

He seemed a bit relieved at that. I was slightly shocked that he seemed to feel so bad about sharing his truth. I had not taken him as someone who would mince words. Rather than overthink it any further, I took it as a sign that he respected what I had to say, and I hoped he understood that it went both ways.

Just like that, the conversation fizzled out. The heavy seriousness that had grasped us was replaced by calm. Jen embraced it and began to explain where she had taken us.

She grandly motioned that we were here and said, "Isn't it beautiful? This used to be known as Staff Beach, where all the Retreat workers would come to make fire and party. Sadly, some party poopers ruined it for everyone else by leaving garbage, which is why they had put the sign-up."

I looked around, truly taking in its beauty for the first time. The place was perfect. The water was crystal clear. The huge maple tree that hung over the beach spouted leaves that were a fiery blend of red and yellow. A rocky finger curved into the ocean, sheltering the beach. In stark contrast to the draining feeling that the cliff after dark provided, here felt warm and light. I thought I had found my new spot, now if only I could find a place to set up my hammock.

As we sat by the water, Jared went on an impassioned rant about how overworked the kitchen staff were. He lamented that the Chef had no respect whatsoever for anyone below him. He said he was sick and tired of having to cook shitty meals for staff dinners. Apparently, they had the supplies to cook better, but Chef was lazy. He asked me how I had gone about quitting the bar, and I shared the story. I reminded him of his value as one of the better employees; this seemed to resonate with him. By the end of the rant, he was resolved to switch full-time to housekeeping.

After a period of time that could be measured by the ocean rising about two inches, Jen decided to head back to the Retreat. Jared and I stuck around. We were lured by the joint that he brought, or that had brought him. We stood at the water's edge, passing it back and forth. An eagle was spotted flying high above the island across from us. Despite the poor luck to come, I am still certain that it was not a vulture.

As it disappeared behind some pines, Jared piped up, "Yo, I heard a story about that tree you mentioned earlier. I have no clue if there is any truth to it, but it sounds like you might be interested."

I perked up and encouraged him to share, "Oh hell yeah, let's hear it."

He said, "Okay, don't get too excited, it's pretty fucked up. Apparently, when the colonizers came to Georgia, they chained up some of the Indigenous women and raped them there." He paused long enough for me to say 'Jesus' under my breath, and then continued, "When the Retreat was originally being built, the remains of a woman and a baby were found near the base of the tree. Apparently, they're still buried there."

It was gruesome, and sadly all too believable. I could not help but picture the remains buried beneath the tree, the old bones interchangeable with the roots. One with the land in the purest sense.

I said, "Damn, that is fucked up."

He agreed, "Seriously, if you ask me, there's something even worse about all the people taking their wedding photos in front of that tree. Anyway, are you ready to go eat? I'm starting to get hungry."

Jared had a good point. The most popular spot on the Retreat was right there. The tree was the centrepiece of the beautiful bay background. I told Jared that I was equally hungry, and we started the perilous climb back up to the trail. It was a small adventure in itself, hopping from root to root, and then shuffling along the skinny path up the short cliff. As we walked back in silence, I thought further of how lovely a place Staff Beach was. I found myself curious to see how it would feel to come back by myself. I learned that places have a different feeling whether you are alone or with others. This one was definitely great with others, but would it be so welcoming to the lone wanderer?

Jared and I did not see Jen at dinner. I wondered if she had gone to the cabin; she did not say where she was off to earlier. She would be happy to know that she was not missing much. It was not a good dinner. Jared asked if I wanted to join him for another joint down at the tower, and I could hardly say no. I was going to be smoking anyway, so it's much better to do it with someone outside than by yourself inside. Of course, best not to do it at all, but with where my head was, that was not an option. After the smoke, I headed home. My head was cloudy, but I still had a lot to think about. I lay in my bed mentally thumbing through what Jen and Jared had shared with me. Despite my efforts, I managed to make no more sense out of what happened the other night. Maybe this was for the best, as Jen suggested. I slept early, knowing the morning would come soon.

[CHAPTER TWENTY SEVEN]

I awoke feeling evermore grateful to have made it through another full night undisturbed. I took this as reassurance that whatever happened a couple of nights prior was in the past and not worth lingering over. Clearly, it was a one-time thing. If anything, it would likely make a neat story someday.

I am of the rare breed that prefers to be awake as early as is reasonable. There is something special about knowing everyone else is sleeping while you roam. The mist coming off the water is like a secret just for you. The birds are more active; it is as though they are putting on a show. At its core, with fewer people around, I feel closer to the universe. More at one with it, perhaps. Admittedly, there is something egotistical about that train of thought, and I can live with it. Another thing is that many people whine and complain when they have to wake up earlier than normal. I take pride in not complaining, and even more in actually enjoying the experience.

I rolled up bright-eyed and bushy-tailed to the laundry room for houseman training. I found that there was no one there. Would this be a repeat of my first bartending shift? I waited until half past six before my trainer arrived. It was Eric, Jared's roommate in the tower, who eventually showed face. He wasted no time in making it clear that he was one of the ones who complained about early mornings. The way he was talking, you would have thought he would never sleep again. More than that, he complained about everything else imaginable. From the sprays having not been topped up, to the half-assed job that the previous houseman did in the lodge's bathrooms. These complaints fell on deaf and partially annoyed ears. He did, at best, a quarter-assed job, and I knew for a fact that this guy never helped pack the carts or fill the bottles for the next morning. In my humble opinion, this man was complaining for the sake of complaining. This helped me understand Jared's stance on living with him. However, I could not blame Eric for doing the work in the laziest way possible; this was, after all, the Arbutus Falls standard. It did not matter if you did it well, just that you did it. Hell, it did not matter if you did it at all, just that you said that you did it. Eric showed me which corners I would cut and which areas I would improve upon.

    Little happened in the week following my houseman training. It rained buckets, and this kept me inside for the most part. I learned that Jen had indeed gone to the cabin when she left Jared and me at the beach. From what I gathered, she was spending more and more time there. When pressed for information, she shared nothing of interest. I still felt she was leaving something unsaid. I wondered if I would ever learn what it was. Jared and I continued to hang out most evenings. A post-dinner joint became our ritual. Some nights, we would share stories and bond; others, we sat silently and enjoyed the company. Sadly, the first spot we hung out at was uncovered. The rain drove us behind the tower, where there was an access door with a sizeable overhang. We hauled the chairs back there, and it turned out to be a pretty cozy spot. The tower backed onto a steep hill, and so very little wind got in there, so we stayed warm and dry. We would watch as the rain poured into the pine trees and the low-growing foliage incessantly.

    I finished up the last of my bar shifts without issue. Horner did not show his face on any of the days I was working; that was fine by me. There was little of the happy-light-feeling that I normally get on my last day at a job. No, 'Ah, this will be the last time I do this menial task that I have done so many times before,' there truly was little that I had enjoyed about the position. It was not even particularly difficult saying goodbye to the servers. Not to say I did not like them, but more so because I knew I would be seeing them around. It was with great joy that I folded up my black dress shirt for what I thought would be the last time. It was with slightly less joy that I remembered Henri had scheduled me to do houseman duties the following morning.

    I woke up for my first solo houseman shift feeling determined to make the most of it. It was a cold morning, and naturally, it was raining. I felt a lovely freedom and dominion over the Retreat as I whipped around in the golf cart. The pouring rain made it all the more cozy to be on the covered electric steed. I knocked off the lodge's bathrooms with ease. There was nothing extra to do in the main building, so I thought I might be able to finish with some time to spare. This hope was kept alive when the upper pool went equally as smooth. I took a moment to sit down on one of the workout benches to sip my coffee. The glass wall that looked over much of the Retreat was distorted by the heavy rain. I could have curled up and lived in that moment; it was simple yet glorious.

    I hopped back in the cart and made my way down to the lower pool. As I pulled out, a strange feeling began to knot itself in my stomach. Although it was rainy, there was little fog. It was for this reason that I was confused to find the marina below me steeped in an impenetrable mist. It must have come in incredibly quickly. I was hardly able to park the cart before I found myself transfixed by the sight. It was like a thick wall of cloud formed without warning; it blocked everything further than the beach's edge from view.

    A deep dread filled my being as any other sensation melted away. I watched helplessly as a high yellow light began to emerge from the fog. I feared that the haunting light had returned. I wish that were what it was; it would have been much easier to explain.

The lights multiplied, and I quickly saw that they were the lanterns of a towering vessel. What struck me as odd was that it was flying the Union Jack; it felt like a cruel joke. That disgusting and terrifyingly familiar all-encompassing smell of the seas overpowered me. I cringed as the deafening sound of men shouting and methodically stomping over a wooden deck filled the world. The boat rocked to and fro out in the bay. I was hypnotized by its sway in the waves. There was no rain to be seen.

    I snapped back to reality at the sound of my name. It was being repeatedly called. After a confused moment, I recognized it was buzzing from the houseman walkie-talkie. I answered in a daze. It was Henri, he was wondering why I was not at the team meeting.
    I finally answered with a stunned, "Hello."
    He responded, "Hey man, did you run into some sort of issue?"
    I sure had, but it was no issue I could properly explain.
    I sputtered, "Yes, I mean, no. Everything's fine, I'll head straight up. Sorry about that."
    I sat back in the cart and put my head into my hands. I was suddenly exhausted; the inexplicable really drains the tank. When I finally gained the confidence to look around, I found that the fog was gone. I checked the time and was shocked; not only had I imagined an old-fashioned ship, but time had also flown by. It had been at least three-quarters of an hour that had passed; had I somehow fallen asleep? I was disturbed. The ship that appeared in the bay was eerily similar to the one that I awoke on in my dream.

    The vision of the boat faded, but once again, I continued to be plagued by a boiling anger. It was with a dreadful sense of unease that I powered the cart up the hill. I thought, I guess the lower pool's change rooms would not be getting cleaned today.

I was unable to recover throughout the day, and it became a miserable one. I could not focus long enough to even half-decently make a bed. The one saving grace was that our workload was light.

After a couple of hours of feeling poorly, I talked to Henri and told him I was feeling unwell. I asked to be excused for the rest of the day. Henri obliged my request, but added that he wanted to speak to me.

I followed Henri outside the cottage that we were cleaning so that we could speak in relative privacy.
His voice full of care, he said, "So, are the houseman mornings too early for you?"
I responded quickly and with conviction, "No, not at all. I'm just having an off day today; it has nothing to do with the early morning."
Henri carefully said, "Okay, it's just that Eric told me you seemed pretty out of it when he trained you. But if you're sure, then that's good enough for me."
This caught me completely off guard. My instant internal reaction was 'That greasy bastard said what?'. What came out was not any better.
Before I could control myself, I raged, "What the fuck did he say? That fucker shows up thirty minutes late and then has the audacity to say that I seemed off? You're kidding me."
Henri waited a moment for the words to settle and for me to cool off. He gave little reaction to the strength and anger behind my rant.
He said coolly, "Look, I shouldn't have said anything about it. Go get some rest and make sure that the next time you do houseman duties, you're having a better day."
I was able to hold the many words that were fighting to pour forth. I stormed away from Henri in a cloud of anger.

 I went directly to my room, tired and frustrated. I attempted to read, hoping that the overwhelming anger would flee from my mind. The attempt failed. I could hardly focus on the words, so I loaded up my pipe and puffed away. My emotions began to subside as I slid into calm. I slid a bit deeper and lost myself in the realm of unconsciousness.

[TWENTY EIGHT]

Does the drowned man know he has drowned, as his lifeless body ceases struggle? Does the sleeping man have a concept of time? I doubt it. If he thinks he does, then I doubt his accuracy. Despite lacking time's concept, it seemed that quite quickly I was drowning in that all-too-familiar wretched smell of the sea. I thought immediately, 'Fuck! Not again.' Although it should have been impossible, my eyes opened. I was immediately thrust into action. From what I could grasp, I was following a line of men. We were moving off the deck of the main ship and into a smaller dinghy. Our movements were practiced and orderly. A rifle hung awkwardly over my shoulder. I noticed that the ugly thing was fitted with a sharply clean bayonet. Once aboard, we sat on benches lining each side of the small watercraft. I settled upon the boat and began to look around, taking in my surroundings. I could clearly see the beach, the same one that I had only gotten a glimpse of as my previous dream faded. There was no doubting it now; I was in Freshwater Bay. My prior hunch, which I had refused to entertain, had come to fruition. Arbutus Falls was nowhere to be seen, and based on the context of what was playing out around me, this made sense. The Retreat did not belong here, not yet. Despite my immediate panic at having been transported back to this surreal world, I could not help but take in how beautiful the place was. The trees were a more lustrous green. The water sparkled with unbelievable clarity. Most lovely of all was the strength with which the waterfall roared. It was roaring.

We set off once everyone took their place on the dinghy. There were about a dozen men on mine, and we were joined by another boat holding roughly the same amount. I felt a strange concoction of both nerves and confidence as we approached the shore. As we touched down and took to the land, the place felt even more familiar than I thought possible. The familiarity felt unrelated to the concept that my physical body was indeed here, somewhere, sometime. What I felt was a deeper kind of connection, an emotional one. I could not tell if it was a feeling that belonged to me, or if it belonged to the owner of the body in which I inhabited. It was no easy feat to tell the difference.

Once all twenty-four men safely made landfall, the Lieutenant gave us instructions. We formed a long line and placed our weapons on the ground in front of us, all the while behaving as non-threateningly as possible. I weakly held onto the hope that our intentions were pure, and that this was not the pitiful false peace our Captain promised. A barrage of rifles rattled on the beach's small stones. A metallic sound reverberated from the murder of bayonets. Once the last one settled, there was nothing but silence. Trees shrouded the beach in shadow; they were thick enough that little could be seen further than the shoreline. I had just enough time to think that the untouched wilderness really was all the more breathtaking. Without knowing it, we were being silently surrounded.

Our hosts, at least the ones that made themselves visible, possessed a number similar to our own. However, I found that their size and an unspoken strength made them feel larger than life, especially in comparison to the unremarkable men among whom I stood. The majority of the warriors carried spears. They held them casually, almost lazily, in an unaggressive way. Some of them had bows. On the surface, they did not look prepared to use them. However, I doubt that was the case. I found myself looking upon them with a strange familiarity, and I could have sworn I noticed some of their eyes flicker in my direction. The man, who could have been no one but their chief, seemed to materialize out of thin air. He appeared directly in front of the Lieutenant, who had clearly taken the lead of our group. A wide silence filled our world, only broken by the ocean's breath and the cries of a gull.

The locals seemed to possess an infinite calm, as though they were gods amongst mortals. Our men stood in direct contrast to this, a rank aura exuding from each.

When it seemed that no one was going to begin, the Chief looked in my direction, but motioned to all, as he said, "TÁĆEL SW SIÁM".

I both hoped and felt that these words were to impart a warm welcome. The importance of how words are said should not be understated. Reading tone and facial expression are often much more valuable than knowing the words themselves.

It was in desperation that I hoped the Chief would be able to read the deceit emanating from our party. I also found myself puzzled as to why it seemed the greeting was aimed at me. Why did everyone keep looking at me? The Lieutenant grunted something indistinguishable and not particularly warm in response. The two proceeded to engage in the age-old charade played by those who do not share a language. It is a beautiful and broken game, one that I very much enjoy playing myself. Had it not been for the context, I would have welcomed their duet. After a minute of conversation, the Lieutenant began motioning my way. The Chief locked my eyes in his with a warm, familiar smile, I found myself returning one. He motioned me forward with words that I had no right to understand, but that I did. I responded in a language that was in no way English. The Chief and I laughed in unison; it truly seemed to be a reunion between old friends. He had kind eyes that gently held you in their gaze. A gull cried out in what sounded like piercing pain; the Indigenous peoples stiffened at the sound. Many hands tensed around spears. Simultaneously, the Lieutenant dropped to the ground with a scream. The rest of the men followed suit, including me. Everyone fell onto their weapons, save me, as I had moved to greet the Chief. A barrage of shots rang out from our main ship, which, due to the naturally deep bay, was well within range.

The reactions of the Indigenous people were lightning-quick, but sadly, no speed could ever have been enough. Like a clear-cut forest, they fell where they stood. Those few who stayed standing did not do so for long. The men around me regained their footing, bayonets in hand. The cowards wasted no time in finishing off those who were not killed in the first wave. A bow was drawn, and an arrow flashed to its mark, but again, it was too little too late. Our rifles took a long time to reload, but one shot per man was enough to do the devil's job. There was no thought in my mind to move for my weapon; rather, I knelt to the Chief. It was in utter horror that I watched the mighty man part with his life's blood. His dark eyes did not leave me; a defeated look of both betrayal and anger plastered his face. The look did not last long, it was as though he made the internal decision that he would not pass on feeling those feelings. His eyes softened and he moved his eyes to the sky with a weak smile on his lips. I stayed kneeling with him until his last breath. When it came, I was rocked by the feeling of losing a good friend.

 In the first moment of calm after death's storm, I wanted very much to scream. I had seen senseless violence in movies, and even initiated it through a video game's controller. As they say, this was different. The smell of fresh blood mixed crudely with billowing gunpowder. It was a sickening concoction. The dark sound of death was one that stayed with me. It is here with me now. One thing that stuck out to me as almost funny, was that the whole mess had entirely distracted me from any contemplation of what exactly the fuck I was experiencing. Because yes, I was indeed in another one of those damn dreams. If it were possible, this one felt even more realistic than the last. Although I expect that was due to the gore that I witnessed, and the emotional connection I felt. I looked at my hands and saw that they were dripping. Without realizing it, I had vainly attempted to stem the Chief's wound. I got up from my crouched position and made for the water's edge. The ocean continued to breathe, as though nothing had happened. I rinsed the red from my palms. I scrubbed for far too long. I knew the blood must be gone, but no matter how hard I tried, I could not lose the feeling of stickiness in the cracks of my palms. My mind was reeling, but it kept coming back to one strange thought, 'this must have been what it was like to go to war'. I was feeling shell-shocked.

In the aftermath of his successful siege, the towering Lieutenant approached a sturdy tree where the forest turned to beach. A crate of supplies that was fetched from one of the dinghies sat on the ground at his feet. He took what looked to be an ancient hammer and started pounding something into the tree. As he stood back to admire his work, a shiny metal ring could be seen protruding from the tree. 'Oh god', I thought, I knew exactly what that was for. I was sick to my stomach, and had I owned the one in that body, then I most certainly would have spilled my lunch. Thankfully, at least for now, I was wrong about the ring's purpose. Rather than shackling women to it, a rope was pulled from the crate and duly secured to the circle.

One of the landing craft began to make its way back out to the main ship. It was slow progress with only two men propelling it. Those remaining on the beach were standing vigilantly around its edges. Rather, they were standing on edge; the men closest to the forest looked petrified. I found myself staring out to sea, unable to look inland. When my gaze drifted to the ship, the Captain's eyes found mine. He was smiling and laughing about his raving success. I felt my blood begin to boil. I wanted revenge. For what exactly, I was uncertain.

[CHAPTER TWENTY NINE]

The Captain's shrill laugh chased me from the dream. The dream. I was now questioning if that was what it truly was. If it was a dream, then it sure was one of the more sick and twisted ones I had ever had. The eeriest part was how directly influenced it seemed to be from where I was in real life. I had never had dreams so intricately linked to my reality, this was an absolute first. The closest I have been is dreaming I am in my childhood home, but that is only the feeling. Visually, the house is an unrealistic hodgepodge of memories and experiences.

For what seemed to be the millionth time, I asked myself what the hell was happening. As I settled down in my bed, I began to cry. The smell of the sea that welcomed me was dissipated by the bloody scenes on the beach. It was for this that I cried. For this, and the smell of blood, and the men dying from gunshots. It felt wrong that I was comfortable here in my bed when I was just on the beach, cleaning blood off my hands. I had just been privy to an absolute massacre; it all felt so wrong. Along with that was the anger. I was feeling incensed, and there was nothing to be done for it. It was blinding, I did not question from where it came.

This was all too much to keep to myself; I was going to have to tell someone. Who, or when, was unknown. I also knew that I had to move; sitting in bed at this moment was not an option. I wiped tears from my face and dressed myself drearily. Leaving my room, I knew exactly where I was heading. I went down to the beach, and sure as anything, it was there as I knew it, so was the marina. I came to the water expecting something. Maybe a feeling or a sign, perhaps my burning bush. There was nothing to be found. Feeling utterly defeated, I dropped down, sitting in the same spot where I had just watched the passing of someone who seemed dear to my heart. A thought penetrated my dark shadow, whether I wanted to admit it or not; something was going on. In that moment, I steeled myself; if possible, I was going to get to the bottom of whatever it was.

I spent the rest of the day listening to music and continuing to worsen my drug habit. I simply sat in bed until dinner, attempting to lose myself in the better parts of my mind. When it came time to eat, I went down to the buffet, filled up a to-go container, and then returned back to my room. I felt I was in no place to speak to anyone or even be around people; I did not want to be looked at. What would I say if someone asked me how I was? 'Oh, I'm great thanks, I just had an incredibly realistic dream where I witnessed the slaughter of the Indigenous people who used to live here in our bay. I can still smell the blood and hear the screaming, so naturally, I am starving.' I ate my meal in bed and continued with my nothingness. A finger of light came in to penetrate this; it was Jared sending me a message to see if I wanted to come down to the tower for a toke. I shut it out and shut him down, thanks, but no thanks.

It was with great anxiety that I fell asleep that night. I was genuinely unsure as to where and when I would be waking up. I was only slightly relieved when morning came and I found myself safe in my room. Yes, I made it through the night, but it felt like another one of those dreams was lurking to the side, just out of reach. The all-encompassing feelings of dread and anxiety had gone nowhere; if anything, they manifested themselves with growing strength. Thankfully the anger fled me, that was something.

I wasted little time, and upon waking, inhaled hopes of forgetting. There was no relief to be found. Unless you were to count my gratitude at having the day off, I took a sliver of solace from that. My hope of having a regular day off by working solely in housekeeping had worked itself out. When I say regular, I don't mean that it was always a specific day of the week; I simply mean that in every seven-day schedule, I worked only six days. This meant that I was still often working ten or eleven days straight, but if I did, then I would also have two days off in a three or four-day period. Compared to having worked the first month straight, I felt that I was the luckiest man in the world.

The funny thing about being beaten down emotionally is that eventually, enough is enough. You can feel like an absolute ball of the stinkiest shit, but not forever. I should clarify that everyone has individual amounts that they can take, they also often have different responses to it. I consider myself lucky. My shit-ball reaches a certain girth, and that stops me from pushing it up the hill any further. I get bored with being sad, so I do something else. I stand to the side, allowing it to roll back down, and move onto something else. Typically, a new ball, like I am building a snowman. I may still be able to hear the old shit rolling down the hill somewhere in the distance, but I arm myself with the knowledge that it is something I can come back to, and maybe with more strength. In this case, I knew I could lay in bed no longer. As I sidestepped this rather large ball of shit, I watched, listened, and smelt my problems shoot down the hill. I replaced them with one of my incredibly sparse options. I put my attention on hardening myself and getting dressed for the light drizzle blanketing the island. It was an awkward temperature, one where I would have liked to have had on my layers, but my rain jacket would not allow them to fit comfortably underneath. That time of year, I guess.

  I headed to Staff Beach, hoping the warm feelings it held might provide me some reprieve. The fresh air and soft bed of pine needles underfoot had a slightly soothing effect. Walking in nature is an absolute hack. I have the biased belief that if everyone would just go for a daily nature walk, then the world would be a much better place. I sat on the beach leaning against the large log, the maple tree's long arms reached out to keep most of the rain from encompassing me. I closed my eyes, listening to the waves gently crashing, as the wind blew through the leaves. I took some deep breaths, and a temporary calm settled. To my chagrin, this calm was no settling boulder, but rather a pebble massaged by the ocean's edge.

  I sat there for some time, only stirring when the cold penetrated my measly layers. Unable to rely on the sun due to the stony overcast, I checked my phone and learned that lunchtime was fast approaching. Despite a lack of hunger, this was not my first rodeo with a missing appetite, and I knew my body would need fuel. I climbed the thin and steep path up to the trail. The moment I stepped foot on it, my panic returned in a rush. I told myself I would eat in the dining area, and make a valiant attempt at small talk. It was with serious disappointment that I was unable to do even that. I packed up my lunch and headed back to my room. I was in deep, and as so often happens when you find yourself there, I could see no way out.

  I spent the rest of my measly day in my cell. I left for nothing other than dinner and the toilet. Only one reasonable thought penetrated the dark cloud which was my mind. While the thought was reasonable and maybe even helpful, it did not pan out as it could have. I leaned back against the two pillows separating my back from the wall. My lower back was beginning to ache from this extended position. The thought that prodded me gently was simple: 'I should look this up'. It is a beautiful thing, forgetting about the internet. It has happened too few times in my life, but when it has, the moment of remembering has provided me with immense joy. Some constraint will be plaguing me, I will feel that I am in a hopeless scenario, and then a lightbulb blazes. I remember that I have the immense power of the extended human consciousness, all I need is my phone or laptop to tap into it. I opted for the larger screen and banged away on my keyboard. I searched something along the lines of 'dreams where you feel like you're in a movie and it feels real'. The result turned up two main kinds of dreams that I resonated with. The first was a vivid dream, which is akin to a dream with a movie-like quality. Vivid dreams are also characterized by the dreamer's ability to recollect what occurred during their subconscious adventure. I took more interest in the second kind of dream, the one known as lucid.

 I had heard of lucid dreams before, my initial understanding was that the dreamer was able to control the dream and that they were aware of their situation. What I thought I knew was not so far from the truth that I found. The most important aspect of lucid dreaming, that I identified in my context, was that typically the dreamers are aware they are in a dream. Along with that awareness, they do not confuse it to be reality. To confuse it with reality would be closer to psychosis, it seemed. I paused when thinking about psychosis. I considered, and then quickly decided not to search it. That would have to wait for another time; I was not ready to entertain such a terrifying possibility. I halted my search in its entirety and attempted to reflect. It seemed I may be experiencing a sort of sick and twisted combination of vivid and lucid dreams. I was getting the two-for-one special, lucky me. In all seriousness, I was able to see bits of my dream experience in each of these internet definitions. The results were not enough; my situation was much more unique than what either definition covered. What stuck out the most as missing from what I found was the sheer magnitude of time I was able to think. That, and the smells and sensations following me from dream to reality. The lack of gap between my dreams and reality remained unexplained, I would have to pull harder to reveal the seam.

I accepted that while my situation was unquestionably fucked, there had to be someone else out there who had experienced something similar. I felt strongly that if I were to input the right combination of words, my search engine would deliver me there. It would simply not be today, and that was okay. It was okay, because I felt like I had something to work towards. After being stuck in stagnation for too long, I was once again moving in a direction, no matter how vague it may be.

There is one other item relevant to my research that I must mention. One of my searches turned up something rather upsetting. More than upsetting, it was sickening. It made me want to shut my laptop and pretend I had not seen the pixelated words on my screen. Admittedly, I did close the tab pretty quickly, and it was not until much later that I recalled what it was I had found. It was something dark, something to do with body control. Perhaps the reason I tuned it out so completely was that in some ways it fit the bill of what I was experiencing a little too well.

I should clarify, it only fit the bill in terms of how my dreams felt. In terms of context, it could not have been further off. The idea was developed by people who committed heinous crimes. They claimed that during these crimes, they were completely out of control of their bodies. Essentially, they claimed that their bodies were being controlled by some other deity and that any resistance was futile. I was shocked by some of the crimes and stories listed, shocked more that they should be published at all. Some things should not, and can not, be put into words, as I have certainly learned while writing this. Along with these more serious happenings were more casual ones. One person shared a detailed story of their experience that was not so far off from mine. Of course, theirs was in real life, and mine was only in the two dreams.

There was no real solution or explanation offered in relation to this strange concept that a person could lose control over their own body. There was, of course, the rather unbelievable claim of possession, the one that is so often dramatized in a variety of psychological thriller films. A much more believable explanation was that these people were insane. Perhaps they could not face what they had done, and completely disassociated from it. I swear I had heard something about that before. Or, perhaps, they are well aware of what it is they have done and simply claim that defence in an attempt to hide from the repercussions. Perhaps that is another form of insanity. The final connection that my situation shared with these stories was that, if true, their nature was essentially inexplicable.

My quest for knowledge had not necessarily calmed me, but it did do a damn good job of distracting me. That evening, there was no message from Jared to reject, which naturally made me want to hang out with him all the more. My feeling of loneliness was exasperated. Oh well, another night. Despite my noble resistance that it should stand still, the night went on. The closer I came to sleep, the more nervous I became. For the first time at Arbutus Falls, I was actually grateful for my roommates' screams. They were the sole reminder that I was not alone. As I heard the sounds of people fighting and getting high, I slipped into a deep sleep.

[CHAPTER THIRTY]

No matter how deep despair goes, be it all the way, it does not matter. Through all nine circles of hell, it does not matter. May it stem from an entire nation of people destroyed, a way of life forgotten, it does not matter. For any measure of time that we may register, life goes on as though nothing but the present moment exists. No different did the universe treat my situation; life went on.

I spent the next week completely zoned out. The majority of the time, I was stranded in my own head. Cyclically, some positive thoughts made themselves known, gently encouraging me to share my plight with another person. Despite this, my negative thoughts were too strong and they beat down the light. The dark made excuses such as, 'What is there to even say to someone else?' How will you put this into words? Besides, if you cannot make sense of it, how in God's name do you expect someone else to be able to?

The Retreat experienced a strange resurgence in bookings. I found myself relieved of my one day off per schedule. That was not the only thing that changed. My habit worsened. Trapped in my mind, I was unable to make it past lunch sober. I would take lunch with me to my room, and change states each day. Although this locked me further within my mind, the restraints were different. Rather than my fiery chains of pain, these were gentle, silky knots. Ironically, such a gentle imprisonment is all the more dangerous.

Almost every night, Jared and I would get together down at the tower. I rarely spoke a word; most of that time was spent listening to his various complaints about the Retreat, or his dreams for the future. Whenever he checked in on me and asked how I was doing, I simply echoed his complaints and made it seem the Retreat conditions were wearing me down. It was becoming that cold time of the year when seasonal depression started to seep into its victims, so he took me at my word.

I often found myself searching for the words to express my burden. I came up with nothing but empty hands. It was easier to keep it to myself than it would be to explain it to another. My loneliness was not exacerbated too much. I was able to see far enough out of my own mind to know that I was not suffering alone. Many residents of Arbutus Falls were struggling with a mental health deterioration. It was on a nightly basis that the extended screams of the fiends would resonate throughout our housing. Like clockwork, they would start around nine in the evening, about three hours after the sun went down. It was just enough time for users to feel the desperate pull. This screaming often extended for a seemingly compulsory hour. Sometimes, it sounded like fighting; other times, it was desperate, animalistic howling.

    I had suspicions about what it was that my roommates were doing. I imagined it was alcohol combined with a sad variety of choice drugs. The specifics of what exactly was consumed remained a mystery. Curiosity eventually got the better of me, and I decided to ask Jen to help fill the gaps in my knowledge. I had a feeling that there was little she did not know. She was a woman who seemed to have no trouble asking the tough questions, and I witnessed no end to her curiosity.

    Jen and I were in the housekeeping building doing laundry, folding and then stacking it neatly on endless shelves of linen. We were flowing, each holding one end of the bed sheet as we made our precise holds and folds. We were taking a short break when I asked her. I would have hardly been able to ask had we been working with the team, for the people of whom I spoke were a part of it. With an air of discretion, she poked her head out the door, smartly ensuring that no one was hiding from the rain and having a smoke. She came back in and leaned against the solid folding table. She came closer to me than I would have had the confidence to do. The two of us had never been so near; I could see the smoothness of her skin and smell the freshness of her hair.

    Leaning in closer still, she spoke with a genuine sadness in her voice, "Some of our friends have a much more serious drug habit than yours and Jared's. I couldn't tell you with certainty what it is that they fight about. But I am certain they have been smoking crack in the kitchen. Thanks to my room being so close to the kitchen, the dirty smell often seeps in."

    My immediate thoughts were rather blunt; I showed it in my face and spoke it with my words, "Well, that is absolutely fucked." Jen smiled, and I continued, "To be fair, I can't say I'm shocked, but to think they're casually smoking crack in what is supposed to be the place we cook our food is mind-boggling." I shook my head as I finished, "It's driving me crazy how much they fight, it's almost every night."

Jen responded with authority, "I imagine it is money; someone always owes someone something when hard drugs and few dollars are in the mix. I've got a hunch about who the dealer is, and I don't think they're too nice when it comes to business."

I had no interest in who the dealer was; I did not even want to think about it. I was stuck on the fact that my roommates were hitting the crack pipe on the other side of the wall from where I slept. Nothing but a couple of sheets of moldy drywall and some rotten two-by-fours separated us.

My only prior run-in with smoking crack was when one of my friends at university brought the wrong guys to an after-party. In my friend's small basement apartment, one of the visitors started by pulling out his gun and setting it on the table. He then proceeded to bring out a kit and cook up some blow before smoking the stuff on the couch. I was at their place the next day and could not believe the stale smell or the stupidity of the story. That was one of many after-parties that I am grateful to have missed.

Jen interrupted my train of thought by asking a question of her own.

She looked me right in my eyes and said with concern, "Are you okay? I don't think you are, but I've been waiting for you to come to me."

There was no way that I could lie to this woman, who clearly cared so much about me.

I answered cautiously, but truthfully, "No, I'm not. I'm not okay, but I don't think there is anything to be done about it."

She was not having it, again, with authority, and still not taking her sparkling eyes off mine, she said, "We're going for a walk after work. I'm not going to force you to talk, but we need to at least walk."

I submitted. What was I going to tell her, that I was busy? 'Oh yeah, sorry, I'm actually planning on cooking something up with our roommates later. We're going to make dinner and then boil some blow if you feel so inclined as to join in on the festivities.'

[CHAPTER THIRTY ONE]

Humans are funny in a variety of ways, objectively speaking. Many jokes could be made regarding the confusion arising from the plethora of emotions we possess. One of these strange and funny aspects is the duality of our emotions. Specifically, how we may be possessed by such opposite feelings at the exact same moment. As I pulled my rain jacket over my sweater, I was swelling with anxiety. This stress was rooted in the worry and wonder of what it was that I would say to Jen. Suppose I were to say anything at all that was. Overlapping with this worry was the warm feeling of gratitude. I was thanking my lucky stars that someone on this god-forsaken island cared about me enough to go out of their way to try and help me feel better, to be with me while I was feeling so low. Anxiety and gratitude, both of the extreme variety. Existing as a human, you think nothing of those two emotions being present simultaneously. Looking from the outside, I believe that there is something rather funny to be seen. How can one be feeling anxious about the same thing that makes them feel grateful? It is a silly concept, but then so is reality.

Having donned my jacket, I stepped into my waterproof hiking shoes. I then made my way outside of the building to where Jen and I agreed to meet. Neither of us wanted to spend any more time inside than was absolutely necessary. The rain had slowed since earlier in the day. It would often rain hard in the morning, only to dissipate by the afternoon. This was a ritual that was fine by me. Between our repellent gear and the thick pines that caught droplets, we would be fine. That was, as long as the sky did not decide to suddenly open up, something that was always a possibility. Earlier, we did not discuss where we would go on our walk. I assumed we would head to Staff Beach, considering it was so lovely and so close by.

Jen had other plans.

She shocked me immediately by asking, "Would you mind taking me to the spot where you saw the light? No pressure, but I want to see it for myself."

The shock washed over me quickly, and I responded, "I actually haven't been back there since it happened, but yeah, let's do it. I'd say I'm overdue to go back."

She smiled from below the purple hood of her rain jacket, and some black curls spilled out. I took the lead as we started making our way out of the Retreat and up the hill, in the direction of my former favourite spot. I was surprised to feel that I was excited to be returning. I had been so distracted by my dreams that I had not given this place much thought.

Marching side by side, along the side of the ever-deserted road, Jen gave me a sideways glance and began to speak.

She said, "I know that I said I wouldn't force you to speak, but I'm still going to push you. What's been going on? I'd swear I haven't heard you say a word in days. I think the only time we spoke was when you asked about our rowdy neighbours this morning. I miss your voice, and I'm worried about you."

At that moment, I knew without a doubt that I was going to attempt the impossible. I was going to attempt to share what was going on. To do it correctly, I thought I must go slowly.

I said, "Yeah, you're right, I haven't said much. Honestly, I haven't had much to say. There's a lot on my mind, and I'm not sure what to make of it." Before Jen could respond, a thought came to my mind, and I deflected, "What about you? Have you been visiting that woman at all?"

Jen seemed to have been expecting this query, and she calmly responded, "Yes, actually, I have been. She's been rather talkative, says that there's a lot going on." This last bit was said in a sort of mysterious way; it piqued my curiosity. Jen copied my move and continued, "Now, are you going to make me beg? What's happening? What is it that you can't make sense of?"

I said slowly, and with more surety than I felt, "Okay, remember what I told you about seeing the light? Well, if that was me being crazy, then this is me off my rocker and over the moon. I'm scared to try and explain it to someone else because I haven't even been able to explain it to myself."

Jen nodded with understanding, keeping silent to give me space to collect my thoughts and continue.

I did just that, "The core of the issue is that I have been having rather disturbing dreams. The strangest thing is that they don't feel like dreams at all. They feel real, as real as us walking right now. As real as the smell of the wet earth, or the sound of the rain falling. There have been smells so strong that they stick with me after I have already woken up. In the first dream, I bumped my head and then woke up with it sore. I did some research, and I haven't been able to find any information about people having dreams that are this realistic. I'm not saying I don't think they exist, but what I am saying is that these dreams I'm having are more than lucid. If it weren't for the strange setting of the dreams, then I would struggle to differentiate them from reality."

We had come to my spot along the cliff's edge, and I motioned to Jen that this was the place. We moved off the path, and I continued talking. I was so caught up in the story that I felt no particular way about where we were.

I went on, "The dreams have both been set in Arbutus Falls, well, Freshwater Bay to be specific. The Retreat itself is nowhere to be seen, as it's still more than two centuries away from existence. In the first one, I was on a ship, like an old wooden British ship. The second one was absolutely fucked. A bunch of men from the ship went ashore and slaughtered the local Indigenous peoples who came to greet them. I was right there in the group. I could smell the blood and feel the deepest anxiety imaginable. I was also struck with a deep anger. I can still feel it now. I feel like I was there last week. I feel like I saw all those people murdered in cold blood. I'm absolutely terrified to have another dream. I don't think I could handle another one."

I had been talking fast, almost manically. My friend continued to look at me with interest and care. I caught my breath before continuing.

Being close to finished, I said, "I don't know how much sense what I just said made. But that's the gist of what's going on, I'm trying to figure out why I've had these dreams, that is, if they're even dreams at all. There's so much more to it, but it's hard to put it all into words. Like the other day, I was up early for housekeeping duties. I had just pulled the cart up to the lower pool, and I looked out at the water, and rather than seeing the marina, I saw the ship that I had been on in my first dream. When I came back to the real world, almost an hour had passed, and Henri was calling me on the walkie. So, yeah, pretty fucked, eh?"

Jen responded, calm as ever, "So, are you able to control what happens in the dream at all? I'm a bit confused about that."

I shook my head, "No, and I've been the same person in each dream, at least I think. I'm this guy on the ship. It's weird because I actually seem to be taking on his emotions. Even now, when I'm not dreaming, I hope. I can feel this sadness and anger deep within me. These emotions don't feel like they're my own. It makes absolutely no sense, and when I try to think about it, my head just starts swirling. At this point, I really just don't want to have another one of those dreams. I thought that by now they would have faded from my memory, but they haven't at all."

A weight was, once again, lifted from my shoulders as I finished getting those words out. Who would have thought?

It was clear that I had finished, and so Jen said, "Wow, that's really interesting. I hope that getting to share that helped a little bit. That's a lot to be going through, especially on your own. I may not be able to understand what you're feeling, but I'm always here to lend an ear."

I smiled at her and then gave my sincere thanks.

The meat of the conversation was out of the way, so I began to take in where we were. Before I could look too far, Jen came towards me. She opened her arms and gave me a warm hug. I hugged her back fully and was flooded with emotion. I'm a big hugger, and it had been some time since I received any physical touch, let alone affection. I found tears falling from my eyes. They were not necessarily tears of sadness; possibly they were of relief. The emotions that I had kept cruelly caged began flooding out freely. Jen held me tight for just the perfect amount of time. She then released me and gave me some space to cry. She wandered around the place where my hammock used to hang, while I wet my cheeks.

After a few minutes, when I had fully collected myself from my own world, Jen brought me back to the one that we shared. She noted how lovely the view was and joked lightly about how she could hardly believe that I had kept it to myself. I, in turn, kidded about how she had kept Staff Beach under wraps for just as long. She began to look towards the cliff with more interest, seemingly noting the pile of large stones that I had grown so accustomed to.

She motioned to them and said, "These look weird; something feels off about them."

She tried to examine them closer, but did not want to get too close to the edge. It seemed as though erosion had taken some of it off in the past, and there was no need to take any unnecessary risks on this lovely evening.

Jen continued, "I see what you mean by there being some sort of energy here, although I must say that I quite enjoy it."

I smiled with some pain, "I used to enjoy it too."

I felt that I had little else to say. It had taken some serious energy for me to put my plight into palatable words. I was ready to head back and decided to ask Jen if she was ready.

Just as I began to open my mouth to communicate my intentions, Jen piped up in surprise.

She said, with a shock and tremor in her voice, "What the hell is this?"

She was looking at one of the trees from which I used to hang my hammock. I had no idea what could have surprised her so much, so I made my way over while asking her what she was going on about. There was an urgency in her voice that had put me immediately on edge.

She pointed at the tree and said, "This was this you? Oh, it must have been. Why? Why did you think that was a good idea?"

I felt my face flush red and my heart rate triple. She was motioning to a carving in the tree; it was just three letters.

'SAM'

I found myself instantly embarrassed. I had completely forgotten about that foolishness. One of the evenings that I had gotten really stoned, I decided it would be a good idea to take my knife and carve my name into one of the trees. For the record, that is absolutely not something I would normally do. Typically, when I see someone has defaced nature, I think shame on them. Now, without a doubt, I was thinking shame on me. For whatever reason, that night I felt called to do it. Maybe this is just a weak and shitty justification for my juvenile actions, but I really did feel called to make the crude cuts. Something made me want to bond deeper with this place; it made me want to leave my mark, literally. I remember that as soon as I finished carving the final letter, I felt bad. I immediately apologized to the tree and asked for forgiveness. The skin of the Arbutus tree is just so beautiful, maybe I wanted to see the tree heal around the blade of my knife. It was a sick thing I wanted, but I did it all the same.

Now, I thought to myself, how the heck do I explain all of that to Jen? She clearly disapproves, and rightfully so. I went with as much of the truth as I could.

Like a kid who has done something wrong, I said, "Oh, yeah. I forgot about that. It was really stupid. I don't know what I was thinking."

She agreed, "Yeah, it was stupid. That's incredibly disrespectful, and honestly, pretty dangerous. Especially in a place ripe with so many spirits, you may as well have been asking for trouble."

I paused. Was Jen implying that this could have had something to do with the strange things that were happening to me? I asked her nervously.

She responded, "No, realistically not. But that doesn't mean that it wasn't a dumbass move."

In a sick way, I really enjoyed her telling me off. There was something about this beautiful older woman lecturing me on the finer points of life that made me stir. I steadied myself and then hoped we would leave it at that. To my gratitude, we did.

My embarrassment was quickly extinguished, and my excitement followed suit. I took one last look at my name etched into the Arbutus as Jen and I left the cliff. I felt light. I was happy to have been able to return to such a lovely place, especially considering the expectations I associated with returning. I thought returning would be a rather scary experience, but I was proved more than wrong. There was little light penetrating the tree's thick canopy as we returned to the Retreat property. Little was said on our walk back, but there was a sort of energy passing between us that was nice. Jen suddenly looked at me and told me she wanted me to come to her room. She said she had something she wanted to give me. I could not help but think that I liked the sound of that.

[CHAPTER THIRTY TWO]

Arbutus Falls staff housing was split into two halves. Each half had roughly ten bedrooms that surrounded one small central living area. The two sides were separated by the kitchen. I spent little time in the other half, which is where Jen's room was. I knew no more of her lodgings than which door was hers. In fact, all I had seen from any other rooms was another as bare as mine, and Stanley's, the one decorated top to bottom with wine bottles. I did not appreciate that I was working with such a limited sample size. This led me to expect that Jen's room would be no different from mine. My idea was reinforced by the fact that we arrived on the island at a similar time.

A feeling of excitement grew as she opened her door and led me into her realm. As I stepped in, I was immediately shocked. She turned to me with a smile as she closed the door.
Incredulously, I said, "What the fuck is this?"
Jen's smile grew; it seemed I was not the first to be blessed with this happy surprise.
I began to smile, "What an amazing setup, it actually feels like someone lives here. And what? Your room is huge, it must be twice the size of mine."
Two of the room's walls were covered by large and bright tapestries. She had a proper wooden dresser that was covered by various crystals and other Jen-esque things. Thanks to some candles and incense, the place smelled lovely. It felt as though I had stepped out of stale staff accommodations and into an actual home. I wanted to stay forever. I wanted to lie down on the bed and allow my mind to transport itself elsewhere.
Jen watched me look around in awe, and then said, "It's not much, but I had to try to build at least a small escape."
I looked into her eyes and nodded with understanding. A candle that she had immediately lit upon our entering flickered softly.
Still looking into her eyes, I said gently, "You've done a wonderful job. It's beautiful."
Jen went to the open window and fiddled. I thought she might be closing the blinds. My anticipation inflated.

I was wrong. She came back with something in her hand, and it was a small dreamcatcher. It looked simple and sturdy, just the way I like things.
Jen handed it to me and said, "I think you should borrow this. I assume you know what it is?"
I confirmed that I did. I then assured her I would be putting it up as soon as I got back to my room, and it would be my first decoration. She seemed to roll her eyes as she imagined how

bare my room likely was. Her assumption was supported by how in awe of her room I was. Before I could say another word, she told me that she would see me at dinner. She opened her door without another word. It pained me to be leaving such a lovely place.

I passed quickly through the kitchen and within seconds was back in my room. I looked at the bare walls and shuddered. It was good to know that there were steps that one could take to liven things up. At the same time, I had no interest in changing a thing. It felt as though decorating in any sort of way would be an acceptance that this was my home. That was a step I was unwilling to take. The only thing I would add would be the dreamcatcher. I had nothing to tie it up to, and so I leaned it against my window on the sill, painfully aware that I would have to move it each time I cracked the window to smoke.

I did not end up seeing Jen at dinner that evening. To my disappointment, Jared was nowhere to be seen either. This was okay. I was feeling better overall. The chat with Jen had given me a breath of fresh air. I ate with, respectfully to the less sane, one of my more sane roommates. The ex-tank driver, whom I earlier mentioned. Typically, we enjoyed each other's company, but rarely spoke. This meal did not deviate from our regular. I wordlessly waved goodbye to him and made my way directly to my room. As I passed the upper pool, I saw some guests swimming. I watched them enjoying the heated pool and found myself with a sense of longing. How nice would a dip in there be, followed by some relaxation in the hot tub? My steps carried me quickly past, and the urge followed suit. I fulfilled my prophecy of having to move Jen's dreamcatcher to have a toke as soon as I got back to my room. I noted that I enjoyed it significantly more than normal. In retrospect, that is likely because it was the first time I had smoked for pleasure in weeks. All other times were to escape from my mind. This time, it was simply out of habit; I probably could, and should have, gone without. The rest of my early evening passed quickly. My routine was complete as I fell asleep before the screaming could begin.

In the depths of my sleep, I heard some shouting. This was not the first time that my roommate's evening fun had semi-awakened my mind, so I clocked them and then thought no more. The shouts compounded, and I drifted further from sleep. This continued until a feeling of annoyance began to take hold. I opened my eyes to check what time it was, and to help in assessing whether or not I should get up for a late-night pee. My heart sank as they opened wide. Natural light flooded my vision. Wood chips and fresh pine consumed my sense of smell. My first thought was that at least it was better than rotting fish. Can you guess where I found myself? A hint is that it was not my room. I was on the beach of Freshwater Bay. I was sitting on a log, closer to the side of the waterfall than the high cliffs. Mixed with the shouting of men was the steady rolling of the falls. I found myself looking at the cliff on the far side, particularly the top edge. I was scanning it, as though looking for something that was not there.

    I thought to myself satirically, when our last episode ended, the beach looked a lot different than it does now. At last, it was well disguised by towering trees. The trees were no more; their removal and hasty processing were what accounted for the lovely smells and my makeshift stool. As the thick forest dissipated, a small village of long houses became visible. The structures looked naked, a fitting sight considering that they were so forcibly revealed. Based on the sheer number of men on the beach, I assumed the majority of our crew had come to shore. A large fire was roaring close to the beach's centre, and men were cooking meat on makeshift spits. Based on how many deer populated the island in the modern day, I assumed that was what they were cooking.

    That immediately seemed a strange thought to me; it was the first time that I consciously linked the two worlds together chronologically. It was as though I was admitting that this truly was the past of the island, and that I was visiting from the future. Something about this felt right, as though I was being willed to this collusion, perhaps by the person whose body I inhabited. The whole idea made my head hurt. Other than this rather confusing thought, I was strangely impressed with myself. Rather than lose my cool immediately, I was doing a grand job of properly taking in my surroundings. A bit inland from the fire, the fallen trees were being put to use to make a seemingly permanent structure. I could also see that the local village had been temporarily inhabited by the invaders. Despite so many people making their way to and fro on the beach, I felt incredibly alone; more alone than I had ever felt before in my life. More even than I thought was possible. I was filled with a deep yearning. As though there was something within arm's reach that I would so love to grab, rather than stay here where I was.

One man in particular stuck out on the beach. It was the Captain, and he seemed to be making his way directly to me. Another man who stuck out, like a sore thumb, was the Lieutenant. The large man intercepted the leader, who had me in his sights. They were just close enough that I could make out their conversation.

He blundered, "Captain Vancouver, sir, I require your momentary attention."

The Captain drawled, lazily, "Go on, and make it quick."

The meat rack responded, "I have a report on our progress, regarding tracking down the rest of the Indians."

With impatience, I said, "Go on, what are the men reporting?"

Almost stuttering, he said, "Well, sir, that's the issue. They're not saying anything. None of the men who have gone deep into the woods have returned. We've recovered two bodies. It appears they were both slain by arrows. The men fear the thick woods; no one wants to pursue them further."

They stood in silence as the Captain thought this over.

He then said, "I can't say I'm surprised. We're fighting on their turf after all. Well, we can't cut the whole forest down, as much as I may like to do just that. Shift the men's focus to protecting the bay. Have them maintain guard from reinforced perimeter positions. No man may enter the deep woods on their lonesome. I have an idea for how we may yet find where these worms have gone to ground." As he said this last part, he looked back in my direction, right into my eyes.

"Yes, Captain, it shall be."

The large man was dismissed, and he walked away with a pep in his step. The Captain paused, as though he was deep in thought. He nodded to himself as though he had come to some internal conclusion, and then he finished his approach.

Dread and anticipation filled me. Whatever it was that this man was to say, I knew it would be haunting. He was such pure evil, from which nothing good could come.

With more confidence than I felt, "Good day, Captain, what gives me the pleasure of your presence?"

Shortly, "Cut the shit, Freshwater. We must have a parlay."

I responded, "With regards to?"

As though confirming a well-known fact, he said, "Your surveying mission saw you stationed on this island for a few months, is that right?"

I corrected him, "Not quite, sir. It was little over a month, just enough time to confirm the bay's depth and to scout some other potential locations."

As though he had gotten what he wanted, he said, "That sounds like more than enough time to learn some of the Indian's tricks."

I responded anxiously, "I'm not sure I understand."

The Captain spoke as if I was incapable of basic understanding, "We are having issues locating where the Indians are hiding. You must have some sort of idea. You know this island better than anyone else. I can't risk the lives of any more of my crew. I'm tasking you with locating them."

I responded with more confidence than I felt, "I believe you will be disappointed. I can tell you the locals have many villages across the island. Yet it seems they are hidden close by, the way they pick off our men with ease. I can't help you any more than that. As you very well know, I was the only one who survived my expedition here."

The Captain said, "Yes, yes, I am well aware, and I have my doubts. It's awfully suspicious that the Indians would savage your two mates but leave you to come free. The Indians must have trusted you in some way or another." He continued, "Regardless of whatever you may say, this is your task. You must find the Indians."

Feeling resignation, I responded, "I see, yes, Captain, I will do what I can."

The Captain turned on the spot and marched off down the beach. My cool left me as I stared daggers at his back. If looks could kill, then this man would have been skinned alive.

I became so utterly engrossed in this world that it was as though my own thoughts were put on the back burner. As the person I was tagging along with made his way slowly along the beach, I attempted to unpack as much as I could from what I had witnessed. The thing that stuck out to me the most was the implication that I had already spent time on the island. It went a long way in explaining why the Chief had looked at me with knowing. It further explained my strange position concerning the Captain, especially the reasoning behind all of his questions. I felt like a detective connecting the strings. Another thing was that the names stuck out to me. Captain Vancouver, and his subsequent calling me Freshwater. I would have to do some more research on Georgia Island's history. I was starting to really ponder if this truly was real after all. If actually it had all happened before. More questions were naturally raised. If I had scouted out this bay myself, why was I so against the Captain and our crew coming to set up here? It was clearly a good spot. I was also wondering about what had happened to my two compatriots that I was with on the scouting mission. By the end of the conversation with the Captain, my host's emotions transformed into frustration. I felt a strong hostility to the Captain, one that had not been so prevalent before. It made my anxiety cloud to an angry red mist.

I left the beach and made my way towards the waterfall. Once there, I sat beside it on a log. No wonder this place felt so familiar; it literally was. Not only was I living here in the present, but my host had also spent more than a moon here. I could feel the pull of paths well-trodden, the one which led in the direction of Staff Beach seemed to pulsate. The burning frustration with the Captain quickly dulled; it was as though this man had resigned himself to defeat. Although he was clearly disturbed by the fate of the locals, a sense of bitter acceptance seemed to settle. The sound of rushing water was violently interrupted by screams of terror. These cut through the air. Infinitely more intense than the ones I had originally slept to avoid. These were of pain, of knowing that suffering was soon to come.

I moved to the top of the waterfall and looked out over the beach. Despite the distance, the source of the screams was immediately apparent. It seemed that not everyone was so lucky as to flee the village unharmed. Two Indigenous women were cowering at the beach's centre. Based on their posture, it was clear their arms were restrained behind their backs. The Lieutenant was cruelly dragging them along; it was obvious that any resistance was futile. My stomach dropped as I realized where they were being forced to go. I could watch no more. I turned and fled before they could be secured to the tree with the ring. I entered the woods, my only goal was to head deep enough so that the screams faded. I found myself unable to face such evil. Hell, I was the cause of the evil. I had found this place. I was unable to face myself. On top of it all, as if I had not done enough already, I was now tasked to find the rest of the locals. I would condemn them to their fate.

I found myself heading in the direction of Staff Beach. As I closed in on where I felt the cabin would have been, I was met with surprise. A figure appeared. It was a woman, the most beautiful woman imaginable. She emerged from behind a large cedar. Despite such exquisite beauty, despair plagued her features. I was further shocked when her eyes found mine. I saw a whisper of a smile. For the first time since we became intertwined, warm feelings rose to the surface of my host. His resignation and surrender gave way to thoughts of passion and will. I, on the other hand, was confused. This woman was clearly one of the locals. Why was she not killing this man who invaded her land? Should she not be taking the bow that hung from her back, stringing an arrow, and ending this man's pitiful life?

All I could think to explain it away was that they had met on the man's previous stay on the island. Did she not know that things had changed? Surely word had spread that he betrayed the Indigenous people of the island and that he deserved to be met with hostility. I was incredibly curious to see how this would play out. Sadly, I would have to wait. As this angel of a woman began to greet me, I was ripped from her world.

[CHAPTER THIRTY THREE]

After that night's adventure, I returned to a body that felt rather confused. There was even a short moment where I felt I was not yet fully in control of it. Despite this, I was rather impressed that my overall stress levels were still under control. This was the first time that I had not awoken in a full and unbridled panic. It seemed I was getting used to these out-of-body experiences being fabricated in my mind.

Rather than the trauma associated with such painful events unfolding, what stuck with me most was the aura of that woman who stepped from behind the tree. I was almost disappointed to have left, it felt as though I was ripped from the dream right as I was reaching its climax. I wanted to see her again.

My confusion quickly gave way to curiosity. I could not stop wondering why the woman smiled so fully at a man who was actively aiding and perpetrating the murder and rape of her people. I also had the feeling there was something I wanted to do, but it slipped my mind. 'Oh well,' I thought, if it was important, then it would come back to me.

I awoke from my dream about an hour before I had to prepare for my day in housekeeping. I spent the rest of it fantasizing about the woman I had so briefly met. I pondered over what her story may have been, and could not help but wonder what fate she would gleam. Would she end up helplessly chained to the raping tree? I hoped not.

The days worked were passing rather quickly, and without any major issues. Both Jen and Jared were working, and so I came as close as I possibly could to actually enjoying the work.

I hated to admit it, but it seemed that the rest of our housekeeping team was rapidly deteriorating. It was as though, as the days grew shorter, their reliance on hard drugs grew stronger. They were arriving later and later to work, and on that particular morning, I was met with a shock. One of the guys, who was nice and rather quiet normally, was even quieter. His hoodie was pulled all the way forward, and he seemed to be hiding in its shadow. It was when we almost ran into each other, him going into a bathroom, and me coming out, that I realized why. The light from the room behind me shone directly into his face; it illuminated a series of horizontal red gashes. They ran from his mouth and nose to the edge of his jaw. There were four lines that stuck out on each side; had they been any fresher, then they would have been bleeding. I had never seen anything like it before. Knowing his habits, I also knew where they were from. Or, I made an assumption that I was confident in. He must have tried to scratch his own face off. My heart sank as I processed the realization. I saw such a deep shame in his eyes as he dropped his head and pushed past me into the room. I do not like to admit it, but the truth is that I felt a rising feeling of disgust. I could not help but wonder what kind of demonic presence pushes someone to consume something that will force you to literally rip the skin from your face. There were no words.

I did not say much to Jen throughout the day, but I was hoping to chat with her that evening. I was planning to present to her my intention to figure out what was going on in my mind. I was disappointed to find she had disappeared right before we finished stocking the houseman cart after work. I still felt up for a solitary walk, and decided to retrace the steps I had taken in my most recent dream. I came to the waterfall and then strolled leisurely along the pine path toward Staff Beach. I arrived close to the place where I saw the woman, and the cabin came into view. Smoke was billowing out of its stone chimney. The place felt in no way intimidating; it looked rather cozy. In fact, it looked so lovely that I almost felt myself drawn towards it. I brought myself back to the present and turned my view to the sliver of ocean I could make out through the trees. A feeling of warmth came to me, and it was doing nothing but growing. As I watched diamonds dance upon the water's surface, I cracked my first smile in weeks. The air was fresh, and the all-important sense of purpose formed. I wanted nothing more than to soak in this moment; I needed it.

I was unable to rest there as long as I would have liked. For my peace was gently interrupted by a voice coming from behind me. I turned back in the direction of the cabin and saw a beautiful woman appearing from what I could have sworn was the same tree as in the dream. Only this was no dream, and the woman was Jen.

She said, "Hey, you."

The eerie similarity to my dream made my heart jump; however, I quickly regained my composure. I thought it was strange that she had seemingly appeared out of nowhere.

I responded as steadily as I could, "Hey Jen, funny seeing you here."

Her strangeness continued, as she said, "Would you mind coming with me? I have someone that I would like you to meet."

I knew exactly who she meant; it was as though I was waiting for this moment subconsciously.

Out of habit more than anything, I asked, "Uh, okay. Where to?"

When she did not immediately respond, I continued nervously, "You mean the cabin, don't you? She wants to meet me."

Jen nodded and then told me to follow her.

[CHAPTER THIRTY FOUR]

It was with an amplified air of mystery that Jen led me under the tall trees. We went along a path that had stayed hidden until the moment I stepped foot on it. Paths can be funny; you can walk by them a hundred times and never know they are there. Then, as soon as they are revealed, they can never be hidden again. The path becomes a part of you. As I followed Jen, you may think that a million questions formed in my mind, as had been happening so often in recent times. However, that could not be further from the truth. As we approached the cabin, I felt calm. Further, my sense of purpose was being cultivated. I felt as though I was in the right place and doing the right thing. A feeling that I had been deprived of and was craving.

The cabin was hemmed in by a low fence on all four sides. Jen held open the gate and flashed me a kind smile. With the mystery revealed, I felt that she had returned to her normal self. I passed below a vine-covered pergola that stood over the gate. Standing in the yard, I took in the cabin's unassuming beauty. Although the yard was small, it housed a thriving herb garden. Most of the plants seemed to be foreign, at least to me. Not that I am an expert. From these rose a natural assortment of aromas that flirted for attention. Some were soft and inviting, others cut sharply. The duality was lovely and added a certain allure. In that moment, I felt so far from the ocean. It was a similar sensation to when I entered Jen's room; it was like being transported to another world.

Jen was now letting me lead, and as I approached the front door, I looked back at her. She motioned reassuringly that I should head on in. I pushed gently on the old wooden door, and sure enough, it swung without resistance. The inside of the house was so dark in contrast to the outside that I was unable to see much as I entered. I was hungry to assess what was inside. I willed my eyes to adjust faster. I first noticed that the main source of light spread from the fireplace, which was burning bright. There was some natural light coming in, but most was kept out by blinds over the windows. The cabin appeared to be one large room. A high ceiling greeted me warmly. It was modestly decorated, and some herbs hung drying from a string-line that ran between crossbeams. A cedar dreamcatcher, not so dissimilar from Jen's, twisted majestically in the draft. I paused self-consciously as I took it in. I would have liked to have continued exploring with my eyes, and it was with near automation that I began to move. I was being pulled towards the fire. There was a rather cozy seating area surrounding it; this was the source of the room's life.

My host, the ancient woman who had so suddenly beckoned me to her abode, sat on a low couch. The fire burnt to her right, and she faced a large window. The blind was only half open, and I found myself wishing it was all the way up. I wondered why it was not. For the second time in quick succession, I found myself standing awkwardly. I stared expectantly at the woman. My gaze was not returned; she did not acknowledge my presence in any way. Did she even know I was there? She must have. What a strange way to greet someone whom you have invited to your home. As I stood there suspended in wonder, I was sure of only one thing. Both the cabin and its owner possessed an aura of great immensity. Despite the lack of recognition, I felt strangely honoured to be there, as though it was a great privilege.

Jen shadowed me silently. I hardly noticed her until she began to seat herself. She sat abreast the woman. I formally entered the cozy area and took my place across from them. The couch on which I sat was that perfect level of plush where you sink in comfortably without being sucked too deep. The silence now extended beyond the point of comfort. I dared not break it. I took in the rest of the room while I waited. However, I was only looking, not seeing.

It was Jen who eventually spoke.

She said, "It's nice to have someone else here with us. This is Georgia Island's Matriarch. She is regarded as one of the wisest and most respected elders among Coast Salish peoples."

I spoke to my host in hopes that she would grant me her attention, "It is both a pleasure and an honour, thank you for inviting me into your home."

I would have liked to have said welcoming me, but she had yet to do so. As I spoke to her, her eyes shifted in my direction. They were dark and warm. A small smile parted her lips. It made her look younger; it also struck me as oddly familiar.

Jen continued, "I hope you can forgive me. In my time spent here in the cabin. I have been sharing much with the Matriarch of the burden that you have so generously shared with me. Specifically, about your spiritual experience on the cliff top, and the vision-like dreams that you have been having. The Matriarch has been anxiously awaiting updates."

This did not come as a shock in the slightest. Besides, I knew that I could trust Jen, and that extended to her older friend.

I responded, "You're sweet, Jen, there's nothing to forgive. And as it is, I come bearing a rather interesting update."

Finally, the Matriarch's silence was broken; she spoke in a tired but firm voice, "I am aware. Please, share your experience."

I thought, well, at least she has spoken, and then responded, "Okay, it was just last night. This dream seemed different, or maybe it was me who was different. It was not quite as heavy; it was as though the man's emotions did not weigh so heavily upon me."

Jen spoke with glee, "Oh, that's so lovely to hear, maybe you're finally getting used to them."

I nodded in agreement and then launched into the story. I spared no detail and attempted to capture the shifts of emotion as well as I could. Everything felt important, and so everything was imparted. I shared both my wonderings and intentions. By the time my yarn was spun, I found myself as tired as the Matriarch had sounded.

      Jen seemed expectant of my exhaustion. She rose from the couch and retrieved something from the kitchen. Returning with a pot of tea, which, by the way she was holding it, had been simmering on the stove. A mug was already sitting on the table in front of me, and she filled it.

      As Jen finished pouring, she looked at me and said with a smile, "I left work a bit early to come help prepare this. I would be a liar if I said I knew exactly how it works, but it should help with any anxiety or anger you may be feeling and replenish your energy."

      I gave thanks to both Jen and the Matriarch and then began to drink. Despite how hot it was, I wasted no time getting it down. I have burnt my mouth so many times that I no longer feel much pain. When having tea with a friend, I am typically on my second cup by the time they take their first sip. It is my strange version of touching the ice. The tea was herbaceous and slightly bitter. It was not of a taste that I would drink in my spare time, but if it worked as advertised, then I would not complain. The potion wasted no time in proving itself up to the task. Almost immediately, my head cleared. I felt like my old self, the one I had been missing since I set foot on this rock, the one so full of optimism. He who was entirely unaware of the suffering to come.

      I wondered what was in the tea; the addict in me was nervous to know when the feeling would wear off. I began to look at my host. I had the irrational hope that she possessed some magical be-all answer to what I was experiencing. I could not decide exactly what to ask.

      Jen spoke before I was able to, "You may have noticed that earlier I referred to your dreams as visions. That is what the Matriarch believes them to be. As I am sure you can imagine, much of her people's past is lost. Violent colonial history has plunged it into darkness. The little that remains is peculiarly similar to what it is you have been experiencing." Jen paused to draw in a breath, and then finished, "She wants to warn you that the ending is not a happy one."

I spoke before I could stop myself, responding cynically, "Right, because it has been such a happy story so far."

Jen patiently responded, "There may be more to it. You would do well to remember that what you have seen is but a drop in the river."

I nodded with understanding, embarrassed by my haste and wondering where it came from. Jen once again rose. This signalled it was time to go. I wanted so badly to ask questions, but something stopped me. It may have simply been courtesy.

I smiled politely at the Matriarch and said, "It has been nice to meet you. Thank you very much for the tea, it was lovely."

She smiled and gave a slight nod. I was surprised she did not have more to say. I sure could have used some of the wisdom Jen raved about.

At the door, Jen said with finality, "Thanks for coming. We can chat tomorrow. I'll see you at work. Goodnight."

With a smile, I said, "Oh yes, we will, goodnight to you too."

As I walked home alone through the dark woods, I felt conflicted. I was hoping for some sort of explanation. Not only was one not provided, but I was now feeling frustrated by my host's lack of words. At the same time, I felt as though something was gained. It felt good knowing that such a seemingly connected woman held me in her thoughts. The idea reassured me. Something told me I would be seeing her again soon. I hoped that then we would converse, I had some questions.

[CHAPTER THIRTY FIVE]

Back in my room, I was struck by what I had forgotten that morning. I guess it was important enough after all. I assumed that 'Captain Vancouver' was the namesake of the city I flew into on my way to Georgia Island. I found that to be true, a good start. He first came to Georgia Island aboard the HMS Discovery; the head surveyor on the vessel was Edward Parker Freshwater. I could not find direct evidence linking Freshwater to being the namesake of Arbutus Falls' bay, but I decided I had enough to connect those dots. I was really hoping for more, but there was extremely little information on this voyage and the subsequent colonization of the island. It was just enough for me to form a sinking suspicion that the Matriarch may indeed be correct, that my dreams truly were more akin to visions.

    I lay in bed contemplating Jen's words surrounding a happy ending. Obviously, it would not end with a pot of gold, but curiosity nonetheless consumed me. I stared at the dream catcher she loaned me and willed it to protect my thoughts. Simultaneously, I found myself craving a dream. I wanted so desperately to know what would happen next. It did not take long for my wish to come true. I slipped into sleep before drifting off into another world.

    Once again, I found myself on the beach. This time, I was walking; it seemed I was leaving. For the first time in these dreams, the sun was down. The moon was nearest its pinnacle, and there was not a cloud to deter its gaze. The night's clearness meant it was far from pitch black. It took no time at all for me to recognize that I was sneaking. My host was breathing shallow and moving as quietly as his legs allowed.

    I left our makeshift camp and headed directly into the woods. It was as though I was trying to lose myself among he trees. I went in the opposite direction from last time. Rather than towards the waterfall, I was heading towards the high cliff. The thick trees blocked much of the light, and it seemed to get darker and darker the further I went. Despite the minimal light, I was confident in my footing, as though I had walked these steps many times before. After a few minutes and a bit of uphill, I came to a clearing. There, I paused. I looked around searchingly, as though expecting to find something or someone. I wondered what exactly it was that I was doing. Could it be I was attempting to find where the locals were hidden? But then why would I have crept so silently through camp? It certainly seemed I was trying to get away without being seen.

I spied a slim trail to my left, which would have been barely visible unless you knew it was there. Did I know that it was there? After waiting a couple of minutes, I began to slowly make my way along it. Recognition dawned; this was the same trail upon which I used to set up my hammock. Visually, it may not have been the trail I was so familiar with, but as each foot fell, I could feel that it was no different. Quickly, I came to an open area. This was a place that I knew beyond a shadow of a doubt. By the edge of the cliff were those strange rocks that I was so familiar with. They were not in a pile, but rather joined as one big stone. A discreet path to the giant rock's left seemed to lead down towards its front. I felt a confusion that was not my own. I stood there awkwardly staring, not sure what to do with myself. I began to panic as someone started to come up the path from the rock towards me. I thought I was in trouble. It was foolish to come here unarmed and alone. My heart fluttered and then calmed as the moon shone upon the person's face. I saw that it was the same woman as before. This time, there was no question; her smile was clear-cut, and she was happy to see me. I smiled back, feeling the same way. A cold wind came up over the cliff and chilled me to the bone. Still smiling, I went forward to embrace her. Just as I came within arm's reach of her, that angelic face contorted in terror. I winced as she let out a blood-curdling scream.

If the wind had left me chilled, then this scream left me frozen. The woman's eyes were wide. She was looking past me. As though her scream had cut the night's tension, I now heard shouting from my rear. I turned to look and found myself met with a broken heart. Countless men were running from the trees, their bayonets at the ready. The big Lieutenant led the charge. The woman reacted quicker than I; she turned and returned the way she came. I followed close behind. The path was perilous as it went so close to the cliff's edge. My heart dropped even further as we turned the corner. I was struck with a dawning realization as the rock's true form was revealed. I was face-to-face with the entrance of what seemed to be a rather large cave. It looked to be deep enough to fit many people, the perfect spot to hide. I stared dumbfounded into its mouth. I heard confident cries come from within. As Indigenous warriors emerged, spears in hand, I was rooted in place. The last thing I did on solid ground was shift my eyes to the left. There was another path from the cave that led directly into the thick woods. As I was thrown from the cliff's edge, I could just make out the figure of a woman fleeing amongst the trees. I thought, 'Please, let her live'.

Time seemed to slow as my body fell. My first thought was of the massacre which would surely be occurring at the cliff's top. I was certain that the locals would put up a good fight, but they were cornered, surprised, and outgunned. All I could do was hope that the women and children would be able to escape into the woods. Maybe they could make their way across the island to another one of their villages. For my part, I had succeeded. Yes, I would surely die, but my orders were fulfilled. I led the Captain's men directly to the locals; perhaps that is why the bay was named after me, Freshwater. At least I would not have to bear witness to the horrors above. The man whose body I inhabited deserved nothing but to perish. My only regret, as my body was bashed amongst rock and wave, was that his death was so instantaneous, so painless.

[CHAPTER THIRTY SIX]

I awoke from my latest dream as the cold of the ocean crept into my broken body. Immediately, I was back in my bed. I was wet and shivering. The day's first light was trickling through my window. I wondered why I was wet, thinking I should have left that behind in the dream. It took just another moment to gain understanding. My roof was leaking. A consistent dribble that was perfectly positioned over the middle of my bed. 'Why not?', I thought to myself, the walls in the bathroom were already mouldy, it was fitting that my ceiling should leak. Feeling surprisingly refreshed and wanting to escape the drip, I hopped out of bed and prepared for a walk.

Without making a conscious choice in terms of direction, I made my way up to the cliff. On the way, I reflected further on what Jen had said. Her words had rung true. There was no happy ending. I then questioned if that would even be the end. Now that the man whose body I inhabited had died, would I be freed from my visions? Despite having asked for the one last night, I now hoped that was the last of them. The visions had been a rather wild experience, and I was prepared to put them behind me.

I approached what was once my sacred spot. I now saw it through a completely different lens. No longer was it just a place where I came to get high. It transformed into a refuge, a forgotten battlefield. I inspected the scattered stones and found that they gave no clue to their having been a shelter that housed a people's last hope. Over the years, the edge had eroded, and so the path to its front was no more. I moved as close to the edge as I dared and looked down. Yes, that would most definitely kill a man. Looking out over the calm ocean, I became certain that I would soon be going back to see the Matriarch. Someone must have survived that final slaughter, even if just the beautiful woman. I wanted to know more about the history, so much must have transpired to get from there to here.

It seemed as though my mind had officially done a one-eighty. I had begun to genuinely believe that what I saw in the visions had actually happened. I guess there was no harm in that belief. It was as though my mind forbade me from thinking too deeply on the subject, and so it spurred another realization. 'Shit, work.' Moving with great haste, I made my way back to my room. I think I may have moved faster than the night I fled from the floating light.

I felt bad about joining the housekeeping team late. Henri was completely unbothered. It was understandable; he was just happy that I had shown up at all. It was more than one can say for most. He had texted me which cottage they were cleaning. When I walked in, he was cleaning the kitchen.

Out of breath, I said, "Good morning, boss, sorry I'm late. How are we doing today?"

In an even tone and face, he responded, "Hey man, it is okay. Now we are better since you are here."

I started to walk through the cottage in hopes of finding anything to do other than take over for him in the kitchen. Before I got far, I remembered something.

Turning back, I said, "Henri, my ceiling is leaking in staff accommodations. What do you think I should do about it?"

He processed what I said and shook his head as he responded, "I'll radio maintenance to see if I can get them to fix it. You should send them a message to their phone."

I was grateful that he was going above and beyond. Henri was such a nice guy, the best kind of manager. I thanked him and then bolted from the kitchen once again.

I cleaned the bathroom that was connected to the master bedroom. There were no windows open, and so the cleaning products did a number on me. Once finished, I made my way outside to get some fresh air. I felt no kind of rush to keep cleaning. A smile formed as I saw that Jared and Jen were on the back patio together. They had been talking intensely, but in hushed tones, as if having a secretive disagreement.

With my smile, "Hey guys, what's going on?"

Jared returned the smile and said, "Hey buddy, glad you could finally join us."

I cut him off and jabbed back with, "Of course, someone's got to clean while you run your mouth. Sorry, what were you guys saying?"

He rolled his eyes and said, "Listen to this, I figured out how much we get paid per hour, housing, food, and taxes included." Looking at Jen, who appeared rather distressed, he continued, "As you can see, Jen is not too impressed with the number."

Jen, obviously annoyed, fumed, "Yeah, I would have rather not known. Now that I do, I'm a bit pissed off. I came to this island hoping to save up some money, and that sure hasn't been happening. Now I know why."

I was aware that the pay was not great, especially considering how many days we worked. The minimum wage in British Columbia was just under seventeen dollars, and that was much more reasonable than back home in Nova Scotia, where it was fifteen. Considering that the cost of living was about twenty-five dollars nationwide, both were quite shit.

With this in mind, I asked, "So, how much are we making?"

Jared's smile grew, "We make a whopping eleven dollars an hour, twelve when we're in overtime."

With an air of disappointment, I responded, "Shit, man, that's not great. It's pretty frustrating that we have to pay for accommodations, especially considering how disgusting the place is. There's no way it's up to code. Did you hear that I woke up wet this morning?"

Jared laughed, "Woah, buddy, that is way too much information."

Laughing, I realized my poor choice of words, "I meant that my roof is leaking, you fucker. We also have to pay for the absolute garbage food, and there's no reasonable alternative. They really trap you on this island. They offer you one thing, give you another, and then pay shit all for it."

Jen, still annoyed, said, "Okay, guys, can we get back to work? We can chat about this later."

Jared, unable to contain himself, said, "Oh yeah, let's get to it, we've gotta get that money!"

Shaking my head with a smile, I headed back into the cottage.

Maintenance called me back shortly after I messaged them. It was Cody, the outspoken gentleman, who helped me move into staff accommodations in the first place. We had seldom spoken again, but he could always be heard cracking jokes and laughing loudly at staff meals. I told him the situation in as few words as possible.

He responded, "Oh fuck, bud, water coming through the roof, eh? I knew that you were going to be busy with the ladies, what were ya doing banging right up against the wall, or wha?" I was unsure of how to respond to this, so I was thankful when he continued, "Yea, buddy, no problem, I'll get that taken care of right away."

Once I got home from my shift, it was with disappointment that I found it dripping away; the bowl that was precariously placed underneath it was almost full. I sent maintenance another message, but my expectations were shattered. The kitchen was a relatively safe place during the day. I went in there to avoid my waterboarding. Jen's room was just off of it, and so I caught her cutting through. She was going for a walk. With nothing else to do, I invited myself along. Besides, I was excited to share my most recent dream.

As we strolled, Jen started, "You were in quite a good mood today. I love to see it, but I can't help wondering what's put you there."

I agreed that I had been, and smiled as I responded, "Yeah, you're right. I'm not sure. I may just be riding high following a low; either way, I'm going to enjoy it."

She said, "That's a good way to look at it. I'm happy you're happy. But you must have more than that to share?"

With some excitement, I said, "Oh, do I ever, and may I say, your prediction about the not-so-happy ending was spot on. Last night I had what I think may have been my last dream. I woke up as the man I was riding along with died."

I went to continue explaining the dream, and Jen cut me off. "Why don't we head to the cabin? That way you won't have to share the story twice?"

For some reason, I had the feeling that now was not the right time, maybe I needed to enjoy this feeling of lightness further, "Hmm, not today. I'd rather forgo deeper discussion. Hey, while we're on the subject, what was with the Matriarch hardly speaking? I found that pretty odd."

Jen nodded with understanding, but seemed a bit disappointed, "I thought you might be curious about that. Well, when it's just the two of us, she's actually quite talkative. I know it sounds cliché, but when the subject is heavier, such as yours is, she seems to speak with few words that carry great weight. For what it's worth, I think you'll find her much more talkative in the future, and she really enjoyed meeting you."

I mimicked her understanding nod, "And I, her. I have a lot of questions to ask; she better be more talkative next time."

That turned out to be the final word on the subject. Side by side, we walked slowly and in no particular direction. I felt calm and enjoyed the feeling of having nowhere to be.

After some time, Jen said, "I told Jared I'd take dinner to go and eat down at the tower with him, would you like to join? I think he wants to continue our chat from earlier."

I smiled, "I'd like nothing more."

We turned around, having gone deep into the woods. The rain clouds had dispersed, and it seemed we would be getting a final thirty minutes or so of sunlight. The sun did not reach us; it was busy drying the trees from the day's rain. I found the fresh air to be healing, and it felt good to be in the company of a friend. As we returned, the sun was shining right on the Retreat, tower included. In the direct sunlight, it was warm enough to sit outside, so we did just that.

After we finished eating, Jared offered to share a joint. I graciously declined. I suddenly realized that I had not smoked weed in almost a week. I counted that as a significant victory; it was the first sober week in many. It was strange, after what had been far too long, my reality was enjoyable as is. It had quickly become unnecessary to aid my existence with Mary Jane. I smiled to myself with the realization. The only thing that could have made the evening better would have been a good dinner. Sadly, we had to make do with some half-frozen chicken pot pies. Fuck the vegetarians, right, Chef?

Jared was not prepared to make do with the crappy food; he was sick and tired, "Guys, this sucks. The food and the accommodation suck, the pay is worse, our coworkers are addicted to crack, and one of them is the supplier for god's sake."

Jen shot back with a smirk, "Didn't I hear that you recently slept with the supplier?"

It was clear by the look on his face that Jared had not been expecting her to have known that. As far as I knew, he had only told me in the most extreme of confidences. When he looked at me accusingly, I motioned that it had not been me who spilled the beans.

Jared quickly regained his composure and continued, "That is absolutely irrelevant. You know what I heard? I heard that when the current owner bought this place, there was a stipulation that he build new staff accommodations. So not only is our housing old, but it's literally illegal, no shit, the place is mouldy and falling apart."

Jen agreed, "Yeah, apparently this is how it's been for years. Workers are drawn in by the beauty of the luxurious Retreat, only to find that the working conditions are pathetic. The only people who stay are those who literally cannot afford to leave. They make so little money and spend what they do earn on drink and drugs. It's a beautiful trap."

I chimed in, "There's no way this place would pass an inspection. Someone ought to shut it down; it's parasitic. The worst part to me is that the beauty of this place is wasted on the wealthy."

Despite our frustrations and concerns, it was an unspoken agreement that there really was nothing to be done other than complain. For my part, I was not expecting to be there for more than another month or two anyway.

Jen continued, "Have you guys heard much about how Arbutus Falls got its start? It's been a shit show right from the jump. Apparently, they violated some laws during development and then faced no substantial consequences. I'm talking even more than when they ignored the Indigenous burial ground. They poured more than forty million dollars into this place, and it's never been successful; that's why it got sold. It's quite the story, but no one seems to be aware of it."

I thought that went a long way in explaining how the Retreat had gotten to the place that it was today. I believe it can be easy to underestimate how crucial context often is. It is so much simpler to judge things when you are oblivious to their story. It is typically clear how the importance of context applies to people, but it extends so much further than that.

Jared and I nodded in response; we had been unaware, but neither of us was the slightest bit surprised. If anything, I found my curiosity piqued to learn more about the Retreat's history. I decided that it would be my next topic to research.

Jen eventually told us she was heading to the cabin. We wished her a good night. Jared and I hung out a bit longer; it felt good to shoot the shit. He offered me another joint, and this one was more difficult to decline. Eventually, he asked me how I thought Jen knew about his promiscuity.

I answered simply, "Dude, she knows everything."

[CHAPTER THIRTY EIGHT]

I sat reluctantly on the ancient woman's couch. My head was spinning relentlessly from thought to thought. I felt that in the past few days, I had finally found a sense of clarity, after more than a month of despair. I hoped deeply that having another dream would not set me back. The Matriarch said I could discover an important truth from this final dream, and I would be a liar to say I was not hoping it would provide me with some sort of closure. What an absurd hope.

The burning question of why I was having these dreams never ceased. Sure, it could be connected to the floating light that I experienced, but even if that was true, that simply shifted the location of the slippery question of 'why'. To answer one inexplicable thing with another does nothing but thicken the web of confusion. So, why me, and for God's sake, what was the cause?

I hesitantly caught the woman's eye, "Okay, how can I dream? You want me to just go home, sleep, and then come back tomorrow?"

Despite having said it, this did not sound right. The Matriarch had been talking as though she had a clearer-cut plan. I found myself reminded of the preparation Jen had earlier spoken of.

The old lady smiled knowingly, "Jen has helped me prepare a special brew, you and I will drink this tea together. I will join you as your guide."

I could not help but wonder if the tea that I had drunk last time had done more than relax and energize me. It very well may have had a hand in that last dream. The strange idea that this drink would provide me with another vision was easily overpowered by how insane it sounded that the Matriarch would be joining me. I could not imagine how that would work, so I guess it was no different from anything else that I was experiencing. Feeling nothing but skepticism, I nodded to the old lady.

Jen, who had made herself almost invisible until that point, stood and poured the tea. One cup for the Matriarch and one cup for me. As I lifted it to my lips, I noticed a rank smell. I hesitated. I looked across from me and saw that the Matriarch's cup was already empty. Peer pressure won out; I swiftly steeled my stomach and began to drink. Jen remained standing, and my partner lay down on her couch. I followed suit and made myself comfy. Anxiety got to me, and I attempted to sit back up. I realized that I wanted to ask some preparatory questions. My attempt was in vain, strength had left my body, and I dropped deeper down onto the couch. I drifted further and quickly found myself in familiar waters.

To my great relief, I was not met by the dirty smell of the sea. In its place was a gentle ocean breeze. I was in a much smaller boat than I was before. There were two men with me, and they paddled under my direction. This all but confirmed my position as a sort of leader. It took almost no time to identify that we were making way to the beach of the bay that would one day hold the name of my host.

I felt even more relieved that I was not feeling anger or stress; in their place was a sense of adventure. Freshwater was happy, even excited. It was clear that my comrades did not share my state of mind. We made land, and they dragged the boat up onto the beach. Fear was prevalent in their young faces.

In an authoritative yet kind voice, I asked, "What's going on? You two look like you'd jump at your own shadow."

They looked at each other before the shorter of the two responded, "Well, sir, to be quite blunt, we're scared. We've both heard separate accounts that this island's inhabited by dangerous Indians."

With a chuckle of experience, I responded, "Well, lads, I guess we'll see soon, won't we?"

My own bluntness, which had been intended to reassure them, seemed only to startle them further, and so I continued, "At worst, I expect they'll leave us be, at best, they may house us. Forget all the hearsay that you've heard about them being savages. If you show respect to them, then you will be met likewise."

These words of encouragement seemed to be lost on my anxious companions. They nodded in agreement, but it seemed an empty action.

My host began to walk to and fro along the beach. It seemed he was beginning an inspection. It was off to a good start; the place seemed to be fitting the bill.

Freshwater returned to the young lads, "Okay, gentleman, this is good. The bay is nicely sheltered and may very well prove a centralized location for further exploration and resource extraction."

He looked once more towards the trees surrounding the beach, and then continued, "I had expected a welcoming party to come greet us. Clearly, that has not happened, so we will head inland to see what we can find. This is the last time I will warn you, hands off your weapons at all times, don't even think about them."

The taller one piped up, "But sir, why are we heading inland? I thought we had just come to scout this beach."

I patiently responded, "I have heard of other possibilities that may be within a day's march; we will attempt to find them. Besides, I would like to meet the locals; I'm certain they will be able to help."

They looked at me incredulously, "Work with the Indians? We'll be lucky if they don't kill us on sight."

I reprimanded them harshly, "Did you not listen to a word I said? If either of you gets yourselves killed, then it will be no one's fault but your own. And don't for a minute forget who's in charge here."

We overturned our boat and left the majority of our gear below it. We then made our way into the thick woods. Almost immediately, I was happily surprised, mere meters from the tree line was what seemed to be a small village. I called out in greeting and was met with silence. It was clear that no one was there.

Turning to my companions, "This must be a seasonal village. I'm sure the locals won't mind if we make ourselves at home. Now, make yourselves useful and go back to fetch our gear."

As the two god-fearing men scurried off, I continued my exploration. One longhouse in particular caught my eye; it seemed better maintained than the others. I did a walk-around of it, and behind it, I found faint traces of a recently harvested animal. I was curious to see what the fire pit inside would reveal. I made my way back to the front of the hut and entered slowly and cautiously. It was there that I found two women taking cover in a corner. I was strangely unsurprised to find that one of them was the woman whom I recognized so well. She looked slightly younger and not a day less beautiful. I put my hands up, palms out, in an attempt to appear as unaggressive as possible. The beautiful woman met my eyes before standing and bowing deeply. I responded in turn. Through a barrage of broken communication, I shared that I was here with two others. They seemed to be alone; I assumed they had been sent ahead of the band to prepare the village for the upcoming summer.

    The women showed me to a larger longhouse and indicated that we could inhabit it. I went to the beach to alert my companions of what had occurred and showed them where to put our supplies. After the sun set, a great fire was lit. To my extreme gratitude, the women prepared dinner for five. I believe it is likely that this meal was connected to the blood I had seen behind the longhouse.

    I looked at the men who sat anxiously around the flames and said, "What did I say? Respect is met in kind. And don't either of you forget it."

    Skeptically, the shorter responded, "Who is to say they don't slit our throats while we sleep? You just wait until the men arrive. I have no fear of these women."

    With a shake of my head, "You do nothing but make unfounded assumptions. What do you know of these people? It may very well be the women who make the decisions. I strongly encourage you to be on your best behaviour."

    He rolled his eyes in response. As I sat enjoying the fire, my mind was permitted to wander.

    Okay, clearly I am once again dreaming, or having a vision. Now, what exactly is the truth that I was encouraged to find? Could it be that Freshwater is not as terrible a man as I thought? For his time, he certainly had a better-than-average understanding of Indigenous people, but so what? He eventually turns the key to unlock their demise. Could it be that I had a deeper connection with this woman? Clearly, I met her sometime before the other two visions, where she greeted me so happily. Had I really befriended her and then led her and her people to their deaths? Did this not make Freshwater even worse than I thought?

This was nothing but scattered guesses, and none of it was groundbreaking. I remembered the Matriarch and thought that my guide was nowhere to be found. I felt as alone as any other of the dreams; there was nothing to guide me but time. I looked up at the clear sky, a clearer sky than I had ever seen before. It seemed there were more stars than sky itself. As I stared at the universe, it began to disappear, transforming into the wooden beams of a cabin.

Once I awoke, I did not move an inch. I thought this final dream would have finally brought some damn clarity. It had done nothing but stir up more questions. One of those questions being: what exactly was this woman playing at? I could not help but think that she may not be quite as wise as I thought.

I sat up with my mind clouded. Jen was standing over me at the ready. She poured me another cup of tea. I eyed it suspiciously. When she noticed I was looking at it as though it might grow teeth and bite, she assured me that it was a separate concoction.

She said, "This is the one from the other night, it should give you some energy and bring you back to reality in a sort of way."

I was still hesitant; I was not entirely convinced that this one had not also had a hand in my visions. I found my trust in these women dwindling. After eventually taking a small sip, I saw that the old woman was staring at me intently. I gave her a questioning glance, still feeling perplexed.

She started, "So, perhaps now you have had a glimpse of the other side of the man with whom you have been connected. He possessed a deeper understanding of Indigenous culture than the typical white man."

I was a bit disappointed. I shrugged, "Sure, he seemed understanding, but that only gets you so far. This man brought a ship full of men who senselessly slaughtered your people. I'm not telling you how to feel, but in my book, a bit of understanding does not make up for the latter." The Matriarch looked at me with disappointment as I continued with anger, "Also, my guide, I couldn't help but notice your gaping lack of presence."

She responded with gentle reproach, "Your haste betrays you, I say again, there may have been more than meets the eye."

My frustration mounted; she seemed to be saying a whole lot of nothing.

The frustration boiled over, and I said angrily, "Look, I've tried to help you. Can you please tell me what you know? I'm losing sleep over this shit."

She ignored me and continued with what she wanted to say, "As for my guidance, I must admit that while you have been forthcoming, I have withheld. Our dreams have been connected on more nights than this. You have not been alone in the slightest. While you connect with the white man, I connect with the woman that you call beautiful."

It took a few seconds for what the Matriarch had said to melt in my brain. Once it finally did, I found myself grateful to have heard something of substance. My understanding was that this old lady was having visions from the perspective of the lovely lady. I began to run through the implications. The most glaring was that this raised the chances that she knew more about the entire situation than she had shared, which at this point was next to nothing. She must also have some sort of knowledge concerning controlling the visions. A scary thought breathed, could it have been her controlling the visions this entire time?

I thought, 'Okay, so it was more than obvious that the Matriarch knew a good amount about the visions, but why?' What mechanism gave her this ability or knowledge? She also had a level of control associated with them, once again, why? What could she possibly have to gain? Did she have some sort of goal? What did anyone have to gain? Once again, I found myself with more questions than I knew what to do with. If my head were to explode in confusion, it would be a classic case of curiosity killing the cat.

I decided to play along as though all of this was not batshit insane.

I was keen to see if she would share more, "Okay, my dreams, or visions, are connected to yours. That's cool. But why? Why are we dreaming, and how come you know so much about them?"

With a veil of mystery that frustrated me to no end, she responded, "You ask many questions. I had questions of my own. I thank you for helping me answer them."

My frustration returned two-fold, I rasped, "That's great, good for you. But why? Why did you need my help in answering them, and why have I been having these visions?"

The Matriarch continued as though I had been silent, "My requests for your good heart do not end here. I understand that you and Jen have been discussing the poor conditions at the Retreat. This place haunts my land. I hope you can help us with something. She will share more with you. As for why, it seems that you have been chosen to learn the history of this place firsthand. I hope that you will help tell the story of it in a way that may aid in returning this land to my people."

Once again, my anger fled as I was taken aback. Arbutus Falls was a multi-million dollar retreat which employed dozens of people. It had stood on the land for twenty years. How could telling the story possibly help in having the land returned to its rightful caretakers? I knew without a doubt that in this day and age, it was nearly impossible. I would have loved to help her, but she could not be serious. I once again found myself wondering if age had taken its toll on her.

Not having the heart to share the truth with this woman, I said, "I have absolutely no idea what you're talking about, but I'll do whatever I can to help. Although I must admit that I am quite unsure as to what it is that I can do."

She smiled, "There is something very important that you will do. In time, you will understand. For now, Jen will discuss with you further, and for now, I must rest my old bones. I am certain we will see each other again soon."

Jen and I left the warm herbaceous hearth and emerged into the cold night air. As we made our way out to the trail, I gave Jen a perplexed look.

If she was unable to see my face, then I'm sure my tone and words were clear: "So, what in the sweet fuck was that all about?"

Her first words in hours were, "Honestly, your guess is as good as mine. I think I may be as lost as you."

I responded a bit cynically, I did not quite believe her, "Right, well, I'm glad it's not just me. Not to be rude, but why exactly does she want the land back? Her property stretches on for several kilometres, and the entire island is designated as protected Indigenous land."

Looking a bit disappointed in me, Jen shrugged, "I'd rather not get into the why, I don't think our opinions matter. Anyway, like the Matriarch said, you and I will discuss more. Now, I don't know about you, but I think that was enough for today."

I demonstrated my agreement by staying silent.

We walked back to staff accommodations without a word. Just two minutes away from being warm and cozy at home, the sky opened up and absolutely soaked us. We huddled close together under a tree that provided momentary shelter.

I blurted out, "You know, it's times like this that I wish we could use the hot tub."

Jen started laughing, then, seeing that it was not a joke, she looked astounded and said, "Are you kidding? Follow me."

She pulled me into the downpour; it was clear that we were headed to the upper pool.

When we arrived at the gate, Jen demonstrated that any card physically inserted into the locking mechanism would unlock the gate. I had assumed it was connected to the special key cards guests and housekeeping had. She went in and led me to the family change room. It had a toilet, sink, wooden bench, and a large walk-in shower. Jen sat down on the bench and started taking off her shoes.

She looked up at me with a smile and said, "This is where I leave my clothes. Normally, I would wear a suit, but with this heavy rain, the cameras won't be able to see a thing."

By the time I had my shoes off, Jen was stripped down to her underwear. There was nothing but more smooth skin beneath her shirt. I followed suit and put my all into maintaining eye contact with her. We made our way out to the hot tub. It was glorious. The cold rain on top and the hot water below were a lovely combination. We did not speak, but rather lay back and took in the sound of rain pattering all about. Entirely consumed by the water, I was as calm as could be; not a thought ran through my mind. I opened my eyes and found Jen perched close beside me. She was looking at me intently; she seemed to be enjoying how calm I must have appeared. My heart rate doubled, and then tripled, as I failed to maintain eye contact.

She whispered in my ear, "I'm going to head back to my room. I highly recommend showering here. So you know, for the future, the pool closes to guests at eight, you can come use it any time after that."

I smiled widely and wished her a good night. Once again, I settled in and closed my eyes.

Jen had not yet left; she whispered one more thing in my ear, "Hey, you're allowed to look."

We turned in sync. My eyes followed her back out of the rain.

A few minutes later, I did just what Jen recommended. It was so nice using a shower where I did not have to fear touching the walls. The heat was higher and the pressure stronger. What a find this was. I thought about how lovely it would be to combine the hot tub with the gym and the pool. As I made my way back to my room through the pouring rain, my only regret was that I had not known about this sooner. Opening the door to my room, I was feeling glad to be clear of the water. Sadly, enough was not enough;

the hole in my ceiling had not been fixed in the slightest. I emptied out the bowl that I had been using to catch the drip and then awkwardly attempted to curve my body around it. At that moment, I was strongly regretting the size of my room, what I would have given to slide my bed over a foot or two.

As I lay there uncomfortably, my anger was prevalent. My mind wandered past the pleasure of Jen and the hot tub to the experience in the cabin. I wished the Matriarch had explained the reasoning behind my connection to Freshwater. Her playing some part in the connection and telling me that I was to learn the story did very little in the way of providing enlightenment. I was also frustrated with myself. I felt split in two, one half wished I had never experienced any of this, that I had never come to the island. The other half had a thirst for knowledge and loved the excitement. It seemed that the more I learned, the more I wanted to learn.

[CHAPTER THIRTY EIGHT]

Waking up to an alarm is unnatural and oftentimes unenjoyable. Sadly, there are other ways to wake up that make the alarm seem like a heavenly option. I was forced to fully wake before the sun rose. I was startled from sleep by the sound of my water-catching bowl crashing onto the ground. Half of the water soaked my bed and the other half drenched my floor. I refused to move, there was no way I was cleaning it up immediately. As I lay there in anguish, I found that I could not fall back to sleep. I forced myself against the wall, inhabiting the nine inches of bed that was not wet. It was in this awkwardly contorted position that I remembered my inspiration to do some digging.

I decided to begin by taking a look at the history of the Retreat at which I was living. What I found was sparse, a trending theme when it came to research. What the research lacked in length it made up for in shock factor. The ancient Indigenous village at Freshwater Bay was, relatively speaking, very well documented. Articles went back as far as 1956, it was clear that the importance of the land was by no means a secret. I learned that the land was first purchased in 1994, although the owners did not officially begin building until 2001. The reason behind the near decade-long pause was that the construction was illegal.

The investors had drastic plans, and Arbutus Falls was proof that they had come to fruition. These plans should have been deemed impossible. The legal designation of such a historic and culturally rich place should have protected the site. So what the hell happened? It took seven years of seeking official permission to build, before the group decided to go rogue. It was a year past the second millennium when they threw caution to the wind and began their illegal development. Their process disrespected and disregarded Indigenous history in the area, and as a whole. It was estimated that this first phase of development disturbed hundreds of human remains, along with countless artifacts. A local Indigenous representative for the Hul'qumi'num, visited with a group of elders. After the visit, he was quoted as saying "And as we walked we could see bones, and many fragmented bones all around the site."

Years after the excavation began, two charges were brought against the Retreat under the Ancestry Protection Act. The Retreat was charged with disturbing a burial site of historic or archeological value, and for damaging an archeological site that pre-dates 1848.

Naturally, the Retreat was found guilty. Along with he verdict, they were levied the largest fine in history under the APA Act. Sadly, this act is very rarely used, and so the amount could be conservatively described as half of a tap on the wrist. It was $35,000. More than that, the Retreat was permitted to publicly make it seem as though it was not a fine, but rather a donation to British Columbia's Archaeological Society. While I will not claim to know what could be considered justice for disturbing a shell-midden, the remains of a village, a graveyard, and violating a site alteration permit; I can tell you that a $35,000 'donation' is perhaps a millimetre of a step in the right direction.

I was disappointed. To me, this should have been a huge scandal. When considering Canada's history of Indigenous mistreatment and abuse, it is but another drop in the bucket. I found just one article each from CBC and The Globe and Mail, neither of which covered the story in detail. The Retreat's punishment was nil, and its coverup successful. The more that I read, the angrier I got. The destruction of so much history was one thing, it was another entirely that they had been allowed to get away with it. Perhaps the craziest part is that all this information was related to the original owners. The new owner had then done it all over again, and the second time there were literally no repercussions. I was practically boiling with anger as I prepared for the day. Mirroring my anger was excitement, I could hardly wait to share the discovery with Jen.

After such a full evening the night before, I was really banking on having a calm day. To my good luck, the one that followed was indeed one of the most enjoyable I had had on the island. As we crept up on winter, the Retreat had fewer and fewer rooms being filled. Naturally, this translated to a lighter workload for us housekeepers. The houseman duties essentially transformed into an excuse to drive around in the golf cart and log an extra couple hours of paid time. Getting easy money from the Retreat felt good, regardless of how measly the pay was. I typically performed houseman duties once or twice a week. On these days, I would spend the majority of my time sitting in the gym at the upper pool. I loved those cold early mornings. It felt as though the Retreat was mine, and mine alone.

This particular rainy day saw Henri off the schedule, this was surreal as he typically worked eight days a week. During my time on the island, I had not seen him take a single day off. All that I could hope was that he was well rewarded for his hard work and commitment.

Despite having been up early doing research on the Retreat, I arrived a few minutes late to the staff meeting. I was surprised to find it was only Jen there.

With mock enthusiasm, I said, "Good morning sunshine, how are we today?"

She responded likewise and said, "Oh just lovely, come take a peek at the schedule and it may brighten your day too."

I was only able to see that there was very little for us to clean, before she continued, "It's just us and Jared, he's on houseman duties. I radioed him to meet us at the first cottage."

With genuine happiness and excitement, I said, "Oh come on, let's go!"

I hopped in the cart with Jen and melted back into my seat. The sound of the rain pitter-pattering never failed to find its mark. We wound our way down the path to meet Jared. He was already there, his cart parked in front of the cabin. His feet were kicked up and he wore the biggest smile that I had ever seen on his face. We brought the fresh linens into the cottage and quickly agreed that all work would have to be put on hold until we had gotten coffee.

Jen was 'in charge' and so she stayed behind. Jared and I made our way back out to the carts.

In a mock serious voice, he said, "You know, this is probably a two-cart job."

I understood exactly what he was saying, and responded, "And you know what, we should probably race down to the cafe"

Race we did, and despite him taking off with a head start, he never had a chance. I was driving Henri's cart, and its power was unrivalled. We bounded up the steps to the cafe in a blaze of glory. The barista seemed to be pretty put off by our positive energy. It was out of place on such a dreary day, but so is the power of friendship.

On the way back, we switched carts. It was with no surprise that Jared had already parked by the time I pulled up. We were giggling like children as we made our way in the door. Jen had opened one of the back doors to the patio and she called us out. She had dried off and set up three chairs under cover. I thought to myself, now we were talking!

Seeing our unabated laughter, Jen shook her head saying, "You guys look like fools."

Jared had no shortage of quick wit, and shot back, "Would a fool clean shit for twelve dollars an hour?"

This got a laugh out of us both. As we three amigos sat there under shelter, the rain was such that we were in our own world. We sipped our coffee and began to chat.

Jared had only heard bits and pieces of what it was that Jen and I were up to. He knew enough that he was curious for more.

I began, "I'm sorry you've been out of the loop Jared, we've got a lot to catch you up on."

Jared was unbothered, he seemed more than happy to simply enjoy the moment.

I continued, "Jen, what was it that the Matriarch wanted you to discuss with me?"

Jen responded, "Okay so, as you know, she wants this land back. I've spent some time with her discussing options and we don't have many. The best we've come up with is getting the Retreat shut down, or at least putting it in a position where they need to sell it."

Like I had thought last night, it was an impossible task. It sounded even more ridiculous when put so simply. Out of the corner of my eye, I could see Jared lift an eyebrow as if to say 'What the fuck?'

I took humour in the wrong direction, and said nonchalantly, "Right, so we'll just get this forty million dollar Retreat shut down. When do we start?"

Jen rolled her eyes at my skepticism, "Look, I'm not saying it's going to work, but we should at least see what we can come up with. Even if it's just to show the Matriarch that we care.

Now, I'm not sure if you guys are aware, but the work conditions here at Arbutus Falls are pretty shit."

Yes, we were very aware, and the satire got a chuckle from Jared and I.

She continued, "I want to start keeping a record, not only of the literal laws and regulations they're breaking, but also the things which would cause public outrage. I'm thinking things like the rampant abuse of hard drugs, about which management is undoubtedly aware. Now, my cousin is a journalist in Victoria and she says she would help us to put together an expose."

I nodded, it was not much, but it was better than anything I had thought of.

Jared spoke before I could, "I may not know why you want this place shut down, but sure as shit, I'm in. Something we need to consider is that we can't underestimate the Retreat's public relations team. There was a whole shit-storm when this place was originally built, and it barely even touched the papers."

I chimed in, "That's a great point. Good timing for you to bring that up, I finally did some research this morning, and I'm now well acquainted with said shit-storm. The only solid resources that reference it are university research documents, nothing that the general public would ever just stumble across. Other than us, I guess."

Jen said, "Okay, that's a good point. Well, fingers crossed that with the change in ownership and the time that's passed, we'll be able to get something into print."

With a glance at Jen, I said, "I do think your idea is a good one. Let's collect what we can and see if we can't at least put a dent in this place. I feel like people are pretty loose with their lips around here, there will be no shortage of complaints to be found."

The conversation continued as the rain fell around us. We went back and forth describing different issues with the Retreat. Between the three of us, it already seemed there was plenty. With a bit of digging, there would certainly be an exposé's worth. It was a shame to think that it may never see the light of day. Eventually, the rain began to slow, we took that as a signal that we better start cleaning.

As we put the chairs back around the table, Jared remarked, "Damn, these things are heavy. You could so some serious damage with one of them."

Jen rolled her eyes as she responded, "This would be the first time you've ever moved one."

The music was cranked up and we began to work away. Despite the shortlist, we managed to stretch it into a full day's work. As we stocked up the houseman supplies for the next morning, Henri appeared.

With clear humour, he said, "I was wondering where you guys were, you took your time today, no?"

Winking at him and laughing, I responded, "Yeah we ran into some unexpected difficulties, you know how it is."

Shaking his head with a smile he said, "Oh yes, I do. Hey boys, the three of us have a day off together next week, want to go to Mount Roman?"

We both happily agreed, Henri was a good guy to spend time with, especially in nature, and it would be nice to momentarily escape from our prison. As we said our goodbyes, I realized I had gotten caught up in the excitement and forgot to do a full recap of the atrocious conduct of the Retreat when it first opened. I was unsure as to how much Jared actually knew. We had only scratched the surface on that conversation, it would have to wait.

[CHAPTER THIRTY NINE]

Those next days passed without much excitement, this was warmly welcomed. The lone item worth noting was actually a text message I received. It was from my friend Chris. We had not spoken since I had come out to British Columbia, and truth be told I did not have much to say to him. The message was a nice one. He wanted to let me know that he was going to be in Victoria for the next two weeks. He was visiting with a friend and said that if I wanted to hop on the ferry to spend a day or two with him, he would pick me up and have a place for me to stay. That sounded like a damn good deal, the best part of which would be hanging out with him. It had been far too long since I had seen him. The only issue was that we were far too busy at the Retreat, it would be incredibly difficult to make the visit work. I responded saying how awesome it sounded and that I would keep him updated.

The shifts were relaxed but frequent, Henri was scheduling some staff members more than others. We wanted to avoid getting a manager mixed up in our plot, so we did not explicitly share what we were up to with Henri. This effort was fruitless, he was a smart man and seemed to know there was something in the works. One positive was that the leak in my ceiling was finally plugged. There are no words to express how damn good it felt to not awake wet after a night of rain. I was even more grateful to sleep in peace. I was free to rest without fear of waking in a lost land. Everything was going as well as it could, until the day before the trip to Mount Roman. I convinced myself that there would be no more visions, and it was that day that the illusion shattered.

It was a warm evening, one of the last before winter. I felt compelled to take advantage of it, and so before sleeping, I decided to head over to Staff Beach to enjoy the moonlight. As I wandered past, I saw smoke pouring from the Matriarch's cabin. I wondered if Jen was there, and if so, what they were doing. Rather than sit in my usual spot on the log, I made my way out along the rocky finger that penetrated the ocean.

I looked back towards the beach and saw that with each crashing tide, green stars sparked in the water. It was phosphorescence revealing itself in a lime-green glow. I had heard of this but had never seen it before. As I watched in awe, I noticed there was a figure standing on the beach. I was easily within earshot and so I called out a greeting. I waited for a response and received none. Based on the non-reaction, I assumed they had simply not heard me. I was curious as to who it was that had joined me, secretly hoping it may be Jen, the silhouette looked feminine.

I made my way over and stepped onto the beach, still failing to recognize who it was. Whoever it was, they paid me no mind. I began to feel a bit strange about the way I was being ignored. I steeled my nerves and called out again. Two things happened at the same time. I got the feeling that I was in the presence of the Matriarch, and the person turned to reveal that that feeling was wrong.

I thought to myself, aw fuck here we go again. It was indeed a woman, the beautiful one. The one from my visions. There was no emotion on her face, she looked to be deep in thought, I wondered if she could even see me. My gut reaction was to look down at my hands. This was an attempt to determine if I was me, or if I was in a dream. I was flooded with momentary relief, as looking down I saw I was me. I looked back up and found myself alone on the beach. The sudden disappearance scared me shitless. I thought, well, time for me to get the fuck home. As I walked, I thought further, how lovely, who would want to enjoy an evening without a ghostly apparition coming to visit. I took some solace in the fact that this apparition was much less terrifying than the ship that had visited while I was on houseman duties. Strangely, everything I experienced up to this point prepared me for such an encounter. Just a couple months prior to this moment, I would have run home screaming to my mommy had I had this sort of experience. It is funny how quickly our normal can change.

Although it was even earlier than my typical early nights, when I got to my room, I prepared for sleep. Not only did I want to be fully rested for the hike, but I also wanted to push the vision from my mind. It did not even cross my mind that I may slip into a dream. So when I came to consciousness on the beach, my first thought was of frustration. I had placed my trust in the Matriarch. If this ancient woman was so wise, why in god's name had she led me to believe that the dreams were finished? What could this dream possibly be about, it seemed that I had seen all there was to see.

The man moved and I held on as the passenger that I was. It was the same as the dream prior, I was sneaking out of camp. Oh please, let this not be a repeat of my deathly betrayal, one watch-through had been more than enough. Having to experience it all over again would be equivalent to watching Schindler's List twice in one week. I was heading in the same direction as before, creeping among the trees. What gave it away that this was not indeed the same dream was that it was darker than before. Looking up, I saw that the moon was not half full. I thought, okay if not this again, then what?

I followed a similar route to the time before, and eventually arrived at the first clearing. Despite the dark, I could see the path to my left clear as day. Before I could take in my surroundings, someone silently launched themselves upon me. They wrapped their body around me tightly and seemed to be searching for my face. I was ready and responded in kind, hugging this body close and finding their face with mine. We parted with a lingering kiss and I saw my assailant. Who else, it was the woman whom I thought to be so beautiful. We shared a smile and once again held each other closely. After a moment of taking each other in, our smiles dimmed. They faded further as we began to converse. We spoke in a broken combination of my tongue and hers. I may not have understood each word, but I could feel the desperation. Freshwater was insisting that she and her people must flee, taking refuge in another village, or even better, with a neighbouring band. It was with regret that she refused, insisting that this was where her people belonged. It had been their home for thousands of years, and they would not relinquish it in such a way. I pleaded with her, imparting that the men were searching for their place of hiding and would not rest until her people fell by the blade. My desperate cause seemed hopeless, and seeing as I already knew the ending, I knew that any hope was futile. I told her that the captain tasked me with finding her people and that I could only continue misdirecting them for as long as luck allowed. She nodded, seemingly unaware of the danger that I was actively putting myself in. The threat was of no concern to me either, it was apparent that I loved this woman. I knew that I would give my life for her, I just hoped it would not come to that. All of our words used up, she unfurled a blanket.

We lay in each other's arms, looking up at the stars, the same way that I had on the night we met. After some time, I kissed her goodbye. It was a heavy kiss, as though I may never feel her lips again. As I stepped out of the clearing and into the dark forest, I could have sworn I saw the outline of a person in the distance. Before I could confirm or deny this, I awoke.

The sun was shining through my window as I collected myself. Well that had been nothing short of an experience, it was the most action I had seen in months. I lay in my bed with the feeling of the woman's body still fresh in my mind's eye. Just as my mind began to wander away, a realization hit me like a truck. Oh sweet god, I thought, is the Matriarch lying in her bed feeling the same way? The initial shock of the thought passed quickly. I reflected that it had probably been a while for her too and so I hoped that the pleasure had been as vivid for her as it had been for me.

My mind finally made the jump as I realized that some more of the truth was revealed in the dream. There certainly had been more to this man than I could have imagined. One question still prevailed, if he claimed to be so committed to this woman and her people's protection, why would he lead the men to their camp. It must have been an unforgivable mistake. Walking right to their doorstep was such a risk, had he truly done it unwittingly? For he did not seem a fool, yet he may have committed a fool's folly. Checking the time, I realized I had no more for reflection.

[CHAPTER FORTY]

One of the few privileges enjoyed by managers at the Retreat was that they were allowed to take out the company vans for personal use. The vans were typically used for transporting employees and guests around the island. Due to low demand, this translated to at least one always being available. For this reason, I expected Henri to roll up to staff accommodations in a white van plastered with the Arbutus Falls decal. This was not the case at all.

I had forgotten Henri was buying a car. The car that he pulled up in was indeed white, but rather than one of the ugly vans, it was an old-school Caddy. When I say white, I mean it was the whitest car I have ever seen, even the leather upholstery was pure Colombian. I complimented his new whip with excitement. His smile showed how unabashedly proud he was. It was clearly a big thing for him to have accomplished. I was happy for him and thought that he sure as hell deserved to be proud. It was a damn cool car, and to go through the process of purchasing it in a foreign country added a layer. I wondered if he had a driver's license and if the car was insured. I could imagine that on an island this small it did not really matter. Jared had come up the hill to meet us and together we hopped in. All three of us were excited to get moving. There was something special about being in a private car that was heading off of Retreat property. The Arbutus Falls shadow began to lift.

Henri leaned back in his seat, smoking as he drove. He impressed me, I did not see him light a single cigarette, and yet he never let one go out without having another already blazing. Words cannot describe how cool this guy looked, smoking cigs and driving your grandfather's car. I was blessed to witness first hand the allure of the French.

The trail for Mount Roman began from a parking lot just above the southern side of Georgia's connecting bridge. Mine and Jared's bags were brimming, we had an unhealthy amount of snacks and had made the all-important cold beer pitstop along the way. Henri was wearing his work clothes. He had a pack of smokes plus a six-pack of beer that he carried by hand. The moment we hit the trail, Jared lit up. Henri politely declined, he was not one for marijuana. I took a cheeky puff, it had been a while and I could not resist enhancing the forest's green. Besides, the hike would not be backbreaking. Mount Roman may be the oh-so-highest point in the Gulf Islands, but that translates to not much more than three hundred meters. The trail to the peak itself was short, nothing more than a straight dirt path up through the trees. The real hike would be the long and winding route back.

We arrived at the peak feeling infinitely grateful. We were blessed with a view, and at this time of year, the odds had not been in our favour. It was such a clear day that Henri managed to point out Mount Rainier, a volcano in The United States that was more than two hundred kilometres away. The parking lot had been empty, and so seemed the mountain. We plopped ourselves down, cracked some cold ones, and got a much-needed relaxation session underway. Hanging with the boys, I was expecting no kind of serious conversation. I was quite surprised when Henri spoke up immediately.

In a rather serious tone, he said, "So, are you guys really trying to get the Retreat shut down?"

I looked at Jared in disbelief, he met my eyes and shrugged. We both started laughing, there was something in how Henri had stated our goal so bluntly. It made the idea sound silly, even more so considering that he was our manager.

He continued, now chuckling himself, "You guys are not very, how do you say it... discreet. Now, what exactly do you mean to do?"

I took my time to find the words and then responded, "That is a great question. Well, the diplomatic way of saying it would be that we are in the early stages of figuring that out. The honest approach would be to say that we're going to throw shit at the wall and see if it sticks."

Jared shook his head and said, "Ignore him, he's not very optimistic about the situation. The idea is that we're going to compile violations of labor standards, as well as things like the issues with housing. Once we've collected that data, then we hope to release an expose."

I was rather curious to see how Henri would react, surely thinking that he would not be against this, he had to understand. As he nodded his head in agreement, my hope was confirmed.

He responded, "Not a bad idea. Believe it or not, I have been wanting to do something like that for some time."

I was confused by this. I thought he would understand and maybe even support what we were doing, but it seemed strange that he had had a similar idea. Jared seemed equally perplexed, he took the lead and asked what exactly Henri meant. Henri looked at us thoughtfully.

He said, "You guys really haven't heard? I've been at the Falls for more than four years, and not because I love the job. I should have had my permanent residency by now. Let's enjoy the view for now, once we get on the move I'll tell you the story."

A high layer of clouds condensed on the horizon. Mount Rainier retreated from sight. Our collective gaze shifted to Northern Georgia, upon which we overlooked. The feeling came upon us, and we knew that it was time to move on. Jared and I stood, our packs significantly lightened, Henri folded and then stuffed his turtle trap into his pocket. As we walked to the trailhead, I did not take my eyes off the view, it was mesmerizing.

This trail would take us down the far side of the mountain, deep into the rainforest. This time of year was so wet that it felt more like a jungle. The path hugged the ocean before curving back and around the far side of the mountain, eventually connecting with the main road. The path descended slowly, thick bushes were overgrown onto the trail. We went single file for much of it. The trees towered high above, blocking out any sunlight that would have fought its way through the ceiling of clouds. There was something special about trekking through the rainforest. It felt so foreign compared to what I was used to back on the East Coast. Arbutus trees surrounded us. They curved as they pleased, red bark curling on a whim. The secret of their pale green skin revealed one millimetre at a time. Each tree called for touch as we passed, I obliged many. The smoothness of their unblemished skin was hard to fathom.

  As we took great pleasure in our simple task of putting one foot in front of the other, Henri began, "So as you guys may have noticed, I'm French, from France."

  Jared and I interrupted with some polite laughter. Henri spoke in a thick accent and was easily the most French Frenchman I had ever encountered. So yes, we had noticed.

  With a smile, he continued, "I moved to Canada more than three years ago. I had the job with Arbutus Falls lined up before I came. They agreed to help me get my permanent residency. The process typically requires two years of work, something that on paper I have not yet achieved."

  Three years working at Arbutus Falls, yet not even two years on paper? That clearly did not add up, and I did not like where this was going.

  He seemed to have paused to let us do the math, before saying, "As I'm sure you can imagine, my ambitions are greater than staying here to work. I want to explore and travel, not so different from you."

  I remember my heart dropping a bit. I was faced with one of my flaws that I still struggle to accept. I have a tendency to ask far fewer questions than I answer. So, that Henri knew I had aspirations to experience different cultures around the world, and that I did not know the same of him, was upsetting. This fault of mine frustrates me as it makes me feel that other people care more about me than I do about them. I try to explain it away by telling myself that I am not good at asking questions and that when a question is put to me I answer it as thoroughly as I can. My in-depth answers often lead to further questioning, and so the cycle continues. The reality is likely that I am overthinking in these situations and that the best thing I can do is put the thoughts behind me. I know that I care, and that is enough. Regardless, I was disappointed in myself, I had genuinely thought Henri was happy at the Retreat. It was a strong reminder that you cannot know someone's heart unless you open yourself to it.

    The Frenchman continued with his explanation, "Kevin knows he can't find a manager half as motivated as me. I am quite certain that he has been fudging the books, making it seem as though I have not worked so long full-time. This has stopped my application for permanent residency from being approved. I would like to go elsewhere, but it is not so easy to find a decent place to work."

    I had forgotten all about Kevin's sorry ass. All that I had heard of him recently was that he would be back on the island to prepare a visit from the Retreat's owner. When Kevin left, there had been much hope that the new on-site manager would make some changes. While I do not doubt that he tried, what can you truly do when the ship that you captain is on fire and half sunk? To make such a vessel seaworthy it would take an army. One we did not have.

    Jared responded first, "Damn Henri, that's absolutely fucked. I've heard some horror stories, but that tops them all."

    I echoed this sentiment, "Fucked is right, I don't have another word to describe how messed up this is. Have you reached out to the Government? Surely they wouldn't let this slide."

    Henri smiled sadly, "I have, they do not respond. Why should they care? I'm here working and that's all they really want."

    Fair enough, I thought. I desperately wished there was something I could do. This was an incredible injustice, especially for such a good man.

    Some life suddenly came to Jared, "Henri, are you telling us about this for the reason I think you are?"

    Henri's smile grew, "Ah it's good to see at least one of you two has some intuition."

    Henri was walking behind me, without turning, I lifted my middle finger high in the air, he greeted it with a laugh. It clicked for me just a bit too late that he was interested in adding his story to our expose.

I looked back at Henri, matching his smile and saying, "That's a great idea. Your story will surely help the cause, and even if we don't get it shut down, there's a chance that you'll get your permanent residency anyways. Welcome to the team my friend."

Despite the warm feelings associated with Henri enlisting in our cause, we steered clear of discussing the Retreat for the rest of the hike. It was rather nice to push away our plight and disassociate from the realities of life. We bore witness to a sea lion lounging on some rocks off the coast. I was blown away by the size of the thing, this one was more like a sea-hippo. The trail eventually found its way back to the road. As we walked along it, a light drizzle began. It was refreshing, covered up in layers, we had grown warm. We came upon a fridge that was standing along the side of the road. We had driven past it many times before and so curiosity would not be denied. We were greeted with a happy surprise, someone was selling fresh fruit. Thankfully, I had cash. My change was traded for a bag of pears and plums. Gorging on fresh fruit, we could not have been happier. That was until further along the road Jared spotted a raspberry bush. When we finally made it back to the car, we were stuffed full and our hands were stained red. Berries are my preferred substance when it comes to red hands.

[CHAPTER FORTY ONE]

Henri, Jared and I returned to work the following day feeling happily refreshed. Would another day off have been nice? No question. But since when have beggars had the pleasure of choosing? I was feeling good about having Henri on our side, there was something about a manager backing us that gave our cause a sort of legitimacy. This sense of legitimacy did not equate to a sense of hope, I was still certain that our work would be in vain.

I was happy to be so bright-eyed and bushy-tailed, but it did not come without a glaring downside. Normally when I scrub toilets for below minimum wage I am out of body. As I scrubbed down a particularly vile toilet, I wished myself to be more distracted. To combat this heightened awareness, I attempted to lose myself in thoughts of our cause. Since discovering the blatant law-breaking committed during Arbutus Falls' original development, I often found myself in anger. I was angry with the developers for their deplorable actions and for thinking they were above the law. I was equally furious at the Government, who gave them a slap on the wrist, essentially confirming that they were indeed above the law. It was a dangerous precedent that the Government set. I hoped it would not lead to more ancient Indigenous sites being destroyed. A dark thought followed; many were already erased, and no one would ever know.

It was here in anger that I found inspiration. What if we came out with a second expose, one that complemented the first. The second one focusing on the Indigenous site desecration here in Freshwater Bay. I could outline the atrocities committed during the initial development of construction. When the Retreat was originally built, no one but the most attentive locals knew of the irreversible damage done. Almost all public reports were buried or non-existent. Sure, it was not technically this ownership group responsible for the majority of them, but people rarely look too closely at the details. We could also be sure to highlight the current owner's conduct when digging out the upper pool. I imagined that he must be one bad man. I thought if we could breathe some life into the old story then maybe the one-two punch of old and new could garner some sympathy. Both situations elicited a strong reaction from me, so why should they not do the same in others? I decided to share this idea with my comrades over dinner. The rest of the toilets were cleaned without a single shitty thought. The best part was that I was entirely unaware of this.

As I made my way down to lunch, I noticed a Rolls Royce parked in front of the lobby. It was not the coolest car spotted at the Retreat, but the Phantom was certainly the most expensive. There was a wood-grained PT Cruiser that easily took the cake for coolest. Hell, Henri's new car was a step above this waste of money. You cannot buy style. As we finished off our mediocre food, Henri asked Jared and I if we wanted to eat dinner later at his trailer. He had recently switched locations and gotten a makeshift fire pit installed. He wanted to take it for a test drive. We agreed, telling him we would bring Jen along too.

Later that evening, Jared, Jen, and I picked up our sub-par dinner and brought it over to Henri's. On the walk, I mentioned the expensive car that I had seen earlier. Jared was unimpressed. The dots he quickly connected for me explained his displeasure. He revealed that the car belonged to the owner of the Retreat.

Jen spoke up, "The owner of the Retreat is a fucking prick!"

Neither Jared nor I knew what to say. We were both a bit shocked. I had never heard Jen swear like that and wondered what sort of extra resentment she harboured for the man. Whatever it was, it sounded personal. Jared and I stayed quiet, neither of us having the energy to engage.

We arrived and sat down down in your classic trailer park plastic chairs. Our food was precariously balanced on our legs as we ate from styrofoam boxes.

I revealed that I had something to share, "As I was scrubbing shit earlier, I had an epiphany. I was thinking that our Arbutus Falls offensive should have a two-pronged approach. The story of how the Retreat was originally built is absolutely absurd. An abbreviated summary is that the investors originally bought the land knowing that they had no rights to make large alterations. They then applied to the government to make very minor adjustments, that proposal was accepted. By the time an agent came to inspect the site, the damage was already done. The developers completely ignored any legislation in place and performed large-scale excavations, they uncovered the remains of at least forty-two different people. The Retreat was assessed a minor fine, and even that was covered up as a donation. The local First Nations contacted the RCMP demanding an investigation, I'm sure you can imagine how that went."

Henri interrupted and asked, "Oh wow, how did they get away with that?"

I continued in rage, "That's the worst part, they got away with it easily. Next to no one even found out about it. The public relations team was so successful that upon the Retreat opening, the Head of the Islands Trust Council actually applauded Arbutus Fall's developers for "responsibly completing all required due diligence before beginning construction", like what the fuck."

I finished, apologizing for my rant, "As you guys can see, this really pisses me off, I'm hoping if we can make the story public, the anger will spread to those who can actually do something."

Jen spoke first, "Okay, I like it, what do we have to lose? Based on how passionate that speech of yours was, I'd say you can take the lead on that one."

Jared responded, "I'd be happy to help with that. It sounds like I've read the same articles as you, and I couldn't agree more. "

I was shocked at how easily we had come to agree. I guess that was the beauty in doing something with no precedent, literally no idea is a bad one. Henri fed the fire and it was burning warm. The fire pit itself was quite funny, it was an old metal barrel that Henri had cut off with a grinder. I imagined that it was a sketchy job and he said that it certainly had been.

I turned my attention to Jen, "What about you? Did something happen with the owner? You seemed pretty pissed off at him earlier."

As though on a hair trigger, she began fuming, "Oh you don't even know, everything about him was infuriating. The nerve to pull up in a car worth hundreds of thousands and yet he won't even invest in decent staff housing. I served him in the restaurant and he was incredibly disrespectful to everyone he interacted with.

He was the neediest customer I've ever had and after going above and beyond for him he didn't even tip us a cent. The worst part was that he never once looked me in the eyes, he just stared at my body whenever I came up to the table."

He certainly sounded like the kind of guy who considers himself better than his employees. He also sounded like a fucking creep. I could not blame Jen for her sentiment one bit.

Henri added, "This man is very rich. He runs the company that owns the group that owns Arbutus Falls. It's a Chinese holding group that has hundreds of millions. I checked out the company website once and the first thing you see is an image of a yellow Lamborghini on the beach, it looks very stupid."

I cannot say that I knew what the intention behind his words was, but they made me shudder. It felt as though I was hearing what we were up against for the first time. I had already thought our task impossible, but now it seemed even more daunting. This was the ultimate David versus Goliath, and I could not imagine where we would find a sling and a stone.

Jared added his two cents on the owner, "Why is it almost always the bad people who end up rich. I've heard that he parties pretty hard when he visits the Retreat and that he has an affinity for the booger sugar."

Henri confirmed this, "That's right, he and his family normally blast music and party late into the night. They typically pass out all over the cottage. I've had to clean their place many times. They sleep like the dead."

For the rest of the evening, we sat around the fire chatting happily. However, I felt that I was discreetly donning a shroud of defeat. I guess that Henri coming on board had given me more hope than I cared to admit, knowing what we were up against had ripped that away. After many laughs and some time, we said goodnight to Henri and made our way back to our respective rooms.

[CHAPTER FORTY TWO]

The walk back was short-lived. We made it no more than a few steps before Jen asked if I would accompany her to the cabin. I had yet to tell her about my most recent dream, I was unsure as to why she wanted me to go. The trigger for my invitations to the cabin had always been the sharing of my stories. I hesitantly agreed, as I had nothing better going on. Jared was still with us and asked if he could join, he said he was curious to meet the woman. It was Jen's turn to hesitate, but not for long. She responded that she thought it was a great idea. Drenched in the smell of burnt wood, we headed back past Henri's camper and into the forest. His fire was still burning bright, and I could hear him speaking as though he had new company, that was quick.

We entered the cabin, once again there was no sign of electric lighting. Despite this, there seemed to be an inexplicable brightness, as though the fire burned stronger than it had the right to. The ancient woman, with whom I now possessed some frustration, sat in her spot. She looked as though she had not moved a muscle since our last encounter. We performed our ritual. Jen sat in her usual place beside her older friend. I took my seat across from the woman, this time encouraging Jared to share my couch. He was still taking in the room as he sat down.

My eyes immediately went to the Matriarch. As soon as we made eye contact I was plagued with a sinking feeling. I had been a shortsighted fool. I knew exactly why I was called here. I did not need to tell Jen that I had a dream. The Matriarch could have just as easily told her, she had been there with me. It was one of those things that I knew that I knew, but that I had to actualize the thought to grasp the concept formally. As I was reminded of the implications of our shared adventure, I was filled with a strange feeling of both connection and confusion. I was struck with the genuine feeling that this woman and I were lovers. Like a pair who enjoyed a secret shared pleasure. I was also disappointed in myself, how I had been so slow to connect these simple dots.

Before leaning too deeply into these feelings. I relented, taking into consideration that the situation was really not so serious. There had been a lot of information to absorb, and that part just was not at the forefront of importance.

My thoughts dealt with, out of nowhere I was overtaken by an uncontrollable rage.

I raised my voice in frustration and directed it at the Matriarch, "So, the dreams are over? What the fuck was that all about? I don't know exactly what to ask, but you sure as hell know more than you've shared. So please just tell me, what the fuck is going on?"

The woman was entirely unfazed by my outburst, it was as though she had not even heard me.

While ignoring my words, she looked to the man sitting beside me, "A welcome to you Jared, it is nice to meet you. Jen has said good things about you. She says you are providing a helping hand."

Unlike the Matriarch, Jared was unable to ignore my outburst and he seemed to be questioning what he had walked into. For the first time, I saw him looking out of his depth, I was curious to see how he would recover.

Needing more time, he reverted to a stuttering politeness, "Hi, nice to finally meet you too, I have heard many things as well."

The red had not faded and so I had more to say.

Speaking quickly, I took back over, "I know you knew that wouldn't be the last vision. Now tell me, am I going to dream again? Can you at least be honest about that?"

With the patience of one who has seen many moons, she spoke slowly, "I'm not certain if this was the last. I hope that it was. Now please, can you share what it is that you saw?"

Even this half-assed, half answer seemed to fill me with calm, or maybe it was the Matriarch herself.

Feeling a bit better, I said, "You know what I saw, were you not there? Would you like to share with Jen and Jared what it was that we experienced together?"

This got a slight smile from the Matriarch, the good humour of it apparent, I smiled back. I knew what she wanted to hear, and I thought I may as well get it over with.

I said, "There really isn't much to say. At least nothing new."

I took my time and explained to the best of my abilities that it seemed the man had no ill intentions. The only thing of substance was that we were lovers. As I spoke, her face was steady, it seemed indeed that there was nothing new being imparted. I sensed some disappointment on her part. She encouraged me to share any more details that I could remember, as though she was searching for something in particular. What that could have been put me at a loss. I recalled the final detail, that it seemed there was something, or someone, in the woods. She pushed me for more about this mystery and I explained that the vision had faded.

That was enough for the Matriarch. I wanted answers desperately, and it was my turn to get them.

I asked accusatorially, "What is it that you were searching for? There's clearly something you hope to find."

I could have sworn there was a slight wince as she once again ignored me.

This time the Matriarch looked to Jen, "How comes the task you have been preparing?"

Similarly to Jared, Jen seemed a bit shaken up by our conversation, if you could even call it a conversation. She took a second to collect herself and then told the Matriarch what was going on. She shared the idea that we should publish a second article about the illegal and immoral happenings that occurred during the Retreats original development. The Matriarch nodded in approval and offered her humble thanks.

Jared seemed to have regained his footing and jumped in, "Okay, I'm obviously happy to be helping, but I'm realizing that I'm way out of the loop."

I thought that was true. I had not explicitly shared with him any of my dreams, the development that they were rather visions, or of the connection to the matriarch. He had heard almost nothing since I told him of the floating light during our walk to Staff Beach.

The Matriarch responded, "Well Jared, this one will have to decide what to share with you, maybe he will tell you the story he has uncovered. But here is not the time nor the place."

I looked at my friend, who sat beside me on the couch and gave him a reassuring nod, it said I would fill him in. I felt that he deserved to know. As I got the feeling that this woman had nothing else to say, my frustration peaked. I stood up and shot daggers at her. Without a word, I left her cabin.

I waited outside the door and could hear Jen and Jared politely saying goodbye.

Jen came out with an amused look on her face, I asked her bluntly, "What?"

She slyly responded, "What was it that you were alluding to earlier? You didn't sleep with the Matriarch, did you?"

I went red in the face, becoming grateful for the tree's shadows. What an outrageous situation.

I began to laugh almost hysterically, "Fuck me eh, I guess I did."

Jen joined me in laughter and Jared looked more puzzled than ever. We walked back for the second time that night. As we walked, I told him that in the next couple days I would take the time to explain what in the sweet heck was going on. Not that I really knew myself.

Before saying goodnight to my friends, I looked at Jen and with a smirk said, "I'll tell you what, that old lady really knows how to throw it back."

Jen's face froze as she processed what I had said. She then proceeded into uncontrollable laughter.

I returned to my room only briefly. Just long enough to collect my towel and shorts. Before I made it through the door, I decided to grab my weed bag as well. Taking advantage of the knowledge that Jen had provided, I went for a late-night workout. I swept in through the door and swiped on a dim light. I placed my towel and bag beside the entrance and blasted music from my phone. As I worked up a sweat, I held an internal debate. To smoke or not to smoke, that was the question. The argument raged as weights clanked up and down. It was not a lot of weight, but it clanked all the same. It was only settled as I cooled down with a trot on the treadmill. The winning side was of the opinion that I should indeed smoke. Did I not deserve it for coming and putting in a workout? Besides, it had been so long. I deserved it for more reasons than one. I shut off the gym's lights, returning the area to a dark gloom.

A chill ran through me as I moved over to the room with the shower. I had not realized how dark it was that evening. For some reason, it made me think of the human remains that had been dug up for me to allow this piece of luxury. These thoughts only lingered as long as it took me to pack a bowl. I cracked open the door to the family bathroom and the smoke I exhaled soon mated with the evening's mist. I tidied up before moving outside wearing just my shorts.

I stood at the pool's edge. I shivered from the cold as I leaned forward past the point of no return. Despite my open eyes, I was unable to see much more than a faint reflection off of the water's surface. My shiver turned to near convulsions as I hit the water. My breath fled my body as shock consumed it. I sank below the surface, failing to comprehend the mistake I made. Instinct took over and I clawed my way back to the surface. I scraped myself up over the rough stone edge. I was beginning to understand that the typically heated pool was currently not heated in the slightest. I told myself that that would be the first and last time that I hopped in without checking the temperature first. I moved faster than you can imagine to envelope myself in the hot tub. I thanked my lucky stars that its heat was in working order and then proceeded to look up at them. Orion's belt was just above and shining bright. My mind calmed slowly, and once it did, I quickly found the humour in what had just occurred. The jets massaged my back as I sunk deeper into relaxation. Despite my enjoyment, I could not help but feel another tinge of regret that it had taken me so long to discover this lovely ritual.

As I walked back to the shower room, the cold of the night was nothing compared to my earlier mishap. All the same, I enjoyed the warm shower immensely. I thought of the shower in staff housing, it was disgusting on its best day. Gobs of hair clogged the drain and covered the walls. They would float around as the water level rose, and it always did rise. The white shower curtain had been yellow for years, the cubicle so small that it constantly stuck to my back. On the bathroom floor, mud mixed habitually, it was constantly wet. I could go on, but I expect you get the picture. The pool's shower felt private. It had a bench for my clothes, and I possessed no fear that a molding curtain would attach itself to my skin. As I bathed in this Eden, I promised myself to never shower in staff housing ever again.

[CHAPTER FORTY THREE]

The feeling that I took on from my drug consumption was strange. I had almost forgotten that I smoked in the first place. I did not quite regret having smoked, but I did find myself questioning its necessity. Had it really done anything for me? Even if I did not need it, it felt like I did. Addiction is such a fickle beast.

Either way, the accidental cold plunge followed by the hot tub worked its magic. The cleanliness of the shower did not hurt either. I arrived back to my room towel in hand feeling absolutely refreshed. Although, as I had moved through the dark night, a certain breathlessness began to settle over me. It was a rather uncomfortable sensation to feel so refreshed and yet also be so conscious of a dark heaviness resting upon my shoulders. I got myself ready for bed and the darkness did nothing but grow. I fell asleep quickly and was not entirely shocked when a new vision began to play out. I accepted this broken reality with a tired resignation.

Once again, I was on the beach, but this time I was not creeping under the veil of darkness. The sun was sure as ever making its way down, the island enjoying the latter half of its visit. The moon, just above the tree line, was itching to take its turn to reign. The source of my before-bed darkness was immediately clear, it had not belonged to me at all, my body had simply been early to the watch party. It seemed the connection to the man called Freshwater must have been stronger than I understood it to be. Now that I understood where it was coming from, my discomfort faded. I separated myself slightly and was able to enjoy a bit more of my refreshed self. As I took in the feelings and visuals being given off by Freshwater, it was entirely obvious that this man was nervous.

I found myself approaching a man who stood at the edge of the water. His back was to me and I was unable to recognize him from behind.

The greeting he yelled without turning told me it was the Captain, "You have been absolutely useless in tracking the Indians. I wonder if you have been entirely forthcoming?"

I attempted to keep it together as I responded, "Sir, I have been risking nothing short of my very neck to discover their whereabouts. At great risk, I traveled all the way to another of their villages, only to find it abandoned. My ideas have followed suit and left me lonesome. I expect that they have fled far, for what could they possibly gain from staying in the near."

The captain said sharply, "It is of no matter, a better man has already discovered their whereabouts. We strike tomorrow at sunrise, razing them from this rock."

I failed to hide my surprise and hoped that I did better to hide my disappointment, "Oh, I see. Well, that is great news, great news indeed. And where exactly have they been hiding?"

The captain took great pleasure in slowly saying, "You are now on a need to know basis, and you do not need to know. You will not be accompanying us on the raid. Further, I question your true loyalty. I have heard you have been having some late night adventures, I wonder if you would like to share where you have gone?"

I thought to myself, he knows something, but how much, and with what surety? If he knew with certainty what I was up to, then I would already be strung from a tree or sunk to the bay's floor. At this point I had nothing to lose, so I decided to continue my charade.

I answered anxiously, "It is true that I have been wandering, I have had moments where sleep will not find me. I never go far, for fear that the Indians will strike me down."

The captain seemed unconvinced and rather indifferent, "Right, you are dismissed." And then, as if to rub it in, "Wish us luck tomorrow in our raid."

Defeated, I responded with a rather weak, "Yes sir."

I departed from the captain and retreated to my lodgings. Anxiety ran rampant as I questioned what the hell I was going to do. My options seemed nothing less than impossible. If I snuck out tonight to warn the locals then it would be obvious someone tipped them off. When their refuge was discovered empty, I would be the obvious suspect and my death would be imminent. If I did not go offer warning then more innocent people would be slaughtered. A third and rather terrifying option was that it was a bluff. Maybe the captain did not know where they were hiding and was hoping I would lead his men there. This was highly unlikely, and the thought probably only came to mind as a cowardly attempt at self-preservation. I steeled myself, knowing that my only option was to go to them that very night.

I sat hunched over, sad and lonely. I was attempting to come to terms with my fate. I awaited night fall, knowing it would allow me to escape without trace. I concluded that, once I warned the locals, I would have to hope they would allow me to flee with them. Their acceptance would be the only way I could save both them and myself. I had a less than slim chance of surviving alone on the island.

The moon eventually reclaimed its domain. I began to creep cautiously through camp. This would be the wrong time to be questioned, or worse, followed. I was so caught up in my own mind that I was entirely unaware of the unnatural silence throughout the camp. I escaped unseen and believed that I was without a tail. I made my way through the forest, creeping toward the spot where my love had awaited me so many nights. I hoped that she would be there again, I had no interest in approaching the local's place of hiding under such circumstances. I did not think that I had been followed, but there was no need to take unnecessary risks, besides, I was a surveyor, not a soldier.

I stood alone in the clearing for what felt like hours. She would never come. I steeled myself again, and then headed down the trail, directly to their refuge. I arrived at my destination. Relief flooded me as I stared into the face that I loved so deeply.

The smile that greeted me lifted all the weight from my shoulders, everything would be okay after all. Watching that smile transform to terror due to my own idiocy brought back the weight with a vengeance. She screamed and then ran from the men. I followed close behind. Her true protectors did their job well, parting me from solid ground. The only and final reprieve my heart held onto was seeing her make for the woods. I hoped desperately that my better half would survive.

I dropped like a rock, my stomach was left up at the cliff's edge. Cold water swallowed me quickly and released me even faster. This time, when I awoke, there was no water in my room. Thank goodness that the leak had been fixed. Before I was even aware that I was back in my bed, I felt a rushing feeling, a dark lightness leaving my body. I sat up almost automatically and my eyes were drawn to the window. It was darkness upon which I looked only momentarily. I could have sworn I saw an unnatural light fading into the woods. It was headed in the direction of the cabin.

So, I thought to myself, that was what the Matriarch meant by my being quick to judge. Freshwater had not been a cruel man, simply a fool. A fool who risked his life to save many others. He may very well have been a victim of his time. Hell, you could almost call him the best, the best amongst the worst. I felt as though I finally knew the story, even more, I felt at peace with it. There would be no more dreams, I was free of this inexplicable connection. Wasting no time, I began to think, what to do with the story? Why had it been told to me?

[CHAPTER FORTY FOUR]

Upon waking, there were two things that I decided. That evening, I would walk up to the cliff as I had so many times before. The second thing intertwined with the first, Jared would accompany me. It was time for him to become privy to the whole story. Besides, it could not hurt to recount it all. Maybe I could get more out of it. It was a good thing that I was rudely risen so early. It was my day for houseman duties.

I dressed quickly and made my way to the laundry. As always, the first step was to grab the cart. A happy surprise awaited me. Jared was there. His music blared as he backed Henri's cart out. I hollered for attention, his music drowned me out. Changing tactics, I began to wave my arms like a wild man. From his eyes corner, I caught his attention, he stopped reversing. My initial happiness at seeing him became clouded with the question of why he was here.

I said, "Hey buddy, what're you doing up so early? I thought it was my day for houseman duties."

His face showed that he shared my confusion, he responded, "If I were you I'd double check the schedule, I'd have sworn it was my day."

I could not help myself, and said, "Oh, believe me, dude, I know there's no chance you'd be up this early unless you were one hundred percent sure you were working."

He shook his head at my gentle jab as he took his own advice and pulled out his phone. He pulled up the schedule, and as his eyes scanned the lines, a smile formed.

The smile was followed by words, "Henri, Henri, Henri…", he looked up at me and said, "I guess we're sharing duties today my friend."

I smiled back, "Oh dude, let's fucking go!"

I cleared the distance to the cart in a few excited leaps and hopped right in. The cart squealed once from my heavy landing and then again as Jared put the pedal to the floor. I held on tight as the cart leaned around the first corner.

As we passed the tennis courts, I said in my most serious tone, "You know Jared, this is going to be a tough morning, we'll have to work real hard to get everything cleaned."

His face intensified and he matched my tone, "You're right, it's going to be no joke. We're going to need to get fuelled up if we want to get through it."

I agreed, "You're right man. Besides, I can't imagine Henri would want us working before we'd gotten some caffeine into us, it could be dangerous."

We emerged from the lobby fifteen minutes later, arms loaded with croissants and coffee. The kitchen staff were less than impressed by our jovial mood. It was as though our happiness reminded them of how unhappy they were. We headed for the upper pool. Using the gym's benches as a table, we settled in for breakfast. I wanted to waste little time and so I told Jared that I had dreamed the night before.

He responded, "Oh, seriously? Well in that case, I'm surprised you're in such a good mood."

He had a point, I said, "Yeah man, fair enough. Honestly, I guess that in a sense it was a good one. The story seems to be told, and I really think that was the last dream."

Happily, he said, "Oh hell yeah buddy, I'm happy to hear it. Okay, now please, what do you think about enlightening me? I'm dying to know what exactly this story is."

I was already nodding before he finished, "I gotchu man, I was actually planning on inviting you for a walk this evening, but it seems the fates wanted us together sooner. I don't know if we have enough time to tell all, but let's see where we get to."

I sipped my coffee thoughtfully as I considered where to begin. I am a strong and loyal supporter of chronological order, and so I opted to begin by sharing the original version of the story. As I told him, I paused periodically to share insights into my understanding of what was going on at the time each vision occurred. I hoped that by approaching it this way Jared would be able to appreciate the development of my thoughts. I shared as much detail as my memory allowed and was happy to find that it did not betray me. Jared listened intently, the skepticism he owned when I shared with him the strangeness of the floating light, so many weeks before, was a ghost.

His first question was loaded far before I finished speaking, "So, it really felt real? Like you could feel and smell, we're really talking no difference to the experience of reality." He shook his head in exaggerated disbelief as I nodded, and then continued, "That's wild man."

I could not help but agree, it had indeed been wild, "Right? It was pretty freaky at first, but eventually, I got used to it. As much as you can get used to that sort of thing."

Our rehash was cut short as Jared looked at his phone and said, "Oh fuck."

I checked my own and saw we had a missed message from Henri. We were so encompassed by the story that time had flown by. We accidentally missed the morning's meeting. Sharing a grimace, we tidied up breakfast and made our way out to the cart. We then turned on the radio that was abandoned there and let Henri know we would meet them at the first cottage.

Henri greeted us with a stern voice, "I would have thought that having two people on houseman duties would make them faster, was there a big mess?"

Fighting back a smile and once again donning his most serious voice, Jared said, "Oh Henri, you wouldn't believe it. There was so much sand in the lower pool change rooms, the drains were clogged, but don't you worry, we got it taken care of."

Henri smiled, "You're right, I don't think I would believe it. Now, in all seriousness, sorry about that boys, I didn't mean to schedule you both."

We waved him off, considering that we had done literally no work, it was us who should have been apologizing.

A couple hours later than we should have, we finally got to work. It was not a busy day and the job was relatively relaxing. Everything was going well until about twenty minutes before lunch when we received a radio from the front desk. Apparently the garbage in the main building's toilets was full. Jared and I were working on a room in the main building and looked at each other in shock. We quickly realized that our conversation stopped us from evening touching houseman duties, we broke into laughter. Henri had apparently heard the message and decided to make his way directly to us. As he approached, we brought back the shock and told him we could not believe it, but that we would be more than happy to go investigate. Henri shook his head in disapproval as we headed for the toilets. We power-cleaned the bathrooms, all the while laughing with childish joy. Henri may not have been impressed, but it was turning out to be a great day.

It was not done there, the day continued with a highly amusing pattern. Henri repeatedly tried and failed to be pissed off at Jared and I. We profusely apologized, knowing we would not be reprimanded by our friend. We continued to laugh about it over dinner before heading up to the cliff, Jared was more than happy to join me.

As we started our walk, Jared made it clear he wanted to waste no time at all.

Before we even left the Retreat he began, "Okay, I haven't been able to get the story out of my mind. Yeah, it's obviously crazy that you've been dreaming, but my mind is stuck on how absurd the story itself is. You know, we learn about colonization in school and I've heard stories over the years, but this is different, it's really sticking with me. The details that you've shared make it feel so personal. This might sound strange, but I think we can use that."

His excitement was contagious, but I did not quite understand what he meant.

I responded, "I love the energy you're bringing, but you're going to have to explain what you mean by using it?"

He shook his head and said, "Sorry, I've gotten ahead of myself. Why don't you finish up with the story and then we can get into it."

I was curious to hear what my friend had to share, I had not thought about using the story in any way. I was too busy discovering it piece by piece. Pushing the thought down, I continued. I wanted Jared to get the full picture, especially the most recent dream that I had yet to share with anyone. Other than with the Matriarch, I supposed. I explained my first meetings at the cabin, how the old woman was sharing my dreams and that she assured me they would cease. This brought context which gave him further understanding as to my anger a couple nights before. I continued, sharing how the more recent dreams provided an almost alternate version of events from the perspective of the man to whom I was bonded. I finished with the most recent dream, sharing how a light seemed to fade towards the cabin once I awoke. He seemed a bit bewildered by the concept that the Matriarch was sharing the dreams with me. I saw a whisper of his initial disbelief. He seemed to quickly push this down. Apparently he was in too deep and fully on board.

Jared showed interest in whatever it was that the woman was seeking, "I wonder if the Matriarch's curiosity will be satisfied by this dream you had last night. I'm really curious to see what she is going to have to say about your perspective."

I had not said it aloud, but I was thinking the same thing.

We came to the lookout just as the sun winked behind the tree line.

Sensing that I was done sharing the story, Jared regained his excitement, he began, "Okay, hear me out. We're going to share this story with the public. What you've told me is so insane that I can hardly believe it. Imagine if we combine it with the credibility of what the Matriarch knows, not only will that add a layer of personalization, but it will be all the more believable. I'm thinking we release it separately from our exposition about the Retreat, this deserves its own space to breathe."

As he spoke my eyes grew wide, and I responded, "You're fucking brilliant! Our best bet for getting the Retreat shut down is to elicit emotion, and if that doesn't do it then I don't know what will. Either way, this is absolutely a story that deserves to have some light shed on it."

As the day's final light faded, we went back and forth on the cliff, one idea leading to another. Our hope carried us back down to the Retreat in an optimistic haze. Jared even talked me into a celebratory joint. As we smoked, I found that my tolerance had dipped. After a couple puffs, the possibility of producing coherent thoughts went out the window. With a dumb smile on my face, I said goodnight to Jared and made my way up the hill. Almost immediately after hitting the pillow, I fell into a deep and restful sleep. There were no disturbances.

[CHAPTER FORTY FIVE]

Okay, 'no disturbances' was not a completely accurate description of the night. Something may have happened, although I do still debate that. In all likelihood, it was simply a strange dream that plagued me. No, not one of the dreams with which you and I have become so intimate, although there were technically some similarities. I may have awoken in the dark, in what seemed to be the night's middle. I pulled on my clothes. The ones that had been so unceremoniously abandoned on the floor. I donned my jacket and shoes before making my way out of staff accommodations. All of this was done without the explicit bidding of my mind to my body. It was a bit strange, sure, but I was okay with what was happening because it must have been a dream.

Fear and confusion began to creep in as I identified similarities between this experience and the ones from my visions. I was leaving the Retreat, walking up and up. It was a cold and misty night, the chill hung onto and pulled down my bones. I walked as I normally would, but without an ounce of control. I willed myself to stop, to return to my bed's warmth. I kept marching along. What was more than the lack of control was the feeling of reality. This part in particular was perfectly akin to my visions, I would have signed an affidavit testifying that this was real life. Had the possibility of this being reality not been absolutely and unequivocally impossible, then I would have been terrified.

I continued up until I reached the trail that I had frequented. The higher I climbed, the thicker the mist became. Surefooted, I emerged from the mist into a clearing. The clearing in which my hammock had so often hung. I reached into my pocket and touched something cold and hard. I expected it to be my phone. To my further confusion, it was my knife. Using my free hand, I gripped the cold blade's blunt edge and snapped it open. As it clicked into place, I approached a tree. It was one of the ones from which my hammock had hung. The one that did not have my name engraved. To my terror, I once again began carving. The wood was soft beneath the blade's pointed tip. It gave way with ease. I pushed hard and dug in deep, deeper than before. I wanted desperately to stop. If it had felt wrong the first time, then this felt like a holy disgrace. Despite fighting my hand to stop, it did not waver. It cut the Arbutus's flesh until its fresh blemish read out my name, '█████'. Thank God that this was nothing more than a strange dream.

The dream then got stranger. Once the carving was complete, control was returned. Now feeling in control, I closed my knife. Wanting to test the limits of this strange dream, I made my way to the cliffs edge. All that I could see was a light grey, it seemed to be sucking me in. I stood closer to the edge than I had ever dared before and contemplated flight. Before my feet left the ground, I decided against it and made a beeline back to bed. As I walked, I thought of how strange this was. I hoped that the dream would pass before I returned to my room. It did not. After closing my door, I reached for my phone. Just as suddenly as control was restored, it was taken away. My phone was ignored and I undressed, once again leaving my clothes in their scattered heap. I climbed into bed and possessed just enough time to remind myself that this was not real. The memory of what happened was already beginning to fade. As though it was being slowly and deliberately covered up with thick black paint. One last thought penetrated my mind; what a strange dream. I searched for something comparable. The closest that I could imagine was that it was almost like a flashback from an acid trip. I then lost consciousness.

    I awoke the following morning and carefully placed any strangeness from the night before into the deepest recesses of my mind. Like I said, there were no disturbances. One thing that stood at the forefront of my mind was that a visit to the Matriarch should happen sooner rather than later. I knew Jared would insist upon coming, hell he probably already thought it was guaranteed. I expected he would want to share that brilliant idea of his. I confirmed my suspicions with Jared as we walked over to the morning's meeting. It was there that we told Jen we had something to share and that she would not want to miss it. She was all on board. I expect she would have come regardless of our insistence. Sensing the importance, Jen suggested we go as soon as we finished work that day.

    For whatever reason, the day absolutely crawled by. I found myself filled with anticipation, and this led me to check the time on my phone more times than I care to admit. A feeling that something was going to happen or be revealed that evening filled my mind. You can call it a premonition. After what seemed to be forever, the day finally ended. We congregated and then left directly from work, this allowed us to arrive at the cabin with plenty of light left in the day. It was with a lightness that I looked upon the lovely garden. There was no way I could have known that this would be my only visit before the sun had set, other than my first. The garden was glowingly green, it had been happily soaking up the persistent rain and now twinkled in the sun. Jared paused outside, taking in the wide variety of herbs. As far as I knew, this was the first time he had seen the cabin up close during daylight. It would be his last.

    Visually, there were no changes to the cabin, yet something felt different. When we entered there was a sense of urgency in the air and the Matriarch was not a statue on the couch. Rather than sitting patiently, she turned and watched us enter. It did not show on her face, but I could sense questions bubbling below the surface, soon to overflow. She knew that I came with a fresh dream to share, she had been there. Despite her presence in the vision, it was my perspective she craved. My ego pulsated as I felt a bit of power over the woman who had deceived me on more than one occasion. It was one of those feelings that felt good in the moment but would not age well.

    I said no words of greeting and gave her a knowing smile. I would keep her waiting. What is that saying? Something about doing unto others what they have done to you. That does not sound quite right. I am more confident in the old but gold 'Don't fight fire with fire'. In this case, I was armed with napalm, and I planned to use it. What was the risk? I was already burned.

    We had barely taken our seats when the first question came. "Please have mercy, share your dream with an old woman."

    Seeing this woman so humble drove all thoughts of cruelty from my mind. Besides, I could never forget that the true saying is 'Do unto others what you would have them do unto you', and I am a fan of this one.

    I responded solemnly, "Where would you like me to begin?"

She spread her hands and smiled, this I took as indicating that I should share the story in its entirety.

Mimicking our last visits, the Matriarch listened with great intensity, she hung onto every word. Quickly after I began, tears formed in her eyes. As I continued, a new smile crept onto her face. It seemed that what she had lost was now found, and if I was one for horse races then I would bet she was happy with the result.

She took a moment after I finished before she spoke, "I owe you many thanks young man, you have answered a question which has plagued me since that day."

There was another moment of silence, and then Jared jolted violently in his seat. I looked to him and our eyes met. He wore a face of confusion. He gave the look of one in complete and utter disbelief, I wondered why.

I felt nothing of his reaction. I was merely curious as to why she was being flooded with such relief. What information had my seemingly fruitless story provided?

I responded to her thanks, "I can't say that it was my pleasure, but I'm happy you're happy. What exactly was it you were searching for, what question have you answered?"

She smiled in Jared's direction. I looked to him again and for some reason, he was now gaping beside me.

The mysterious woman said, "The question was one of trust. I have always wondered if my love betrayed my people. I never knew either way, now I know enough. I knew he was foolish, but now I know his intentions and heart were pure."

Her love? It sounded as though she may be taking our shared visions a bit too seriously. The best I could imagine was that the story had some sort of greater representation of her life than I could grasp. Perhaps this was a mystery that her people had been attempting to unravel for generations. As I mulled over the relative strangeness of her words, Jared became restless.

His eyes looking semi-crazed he spoke quickly, "I'm sorry, but are you saying what I think you're saying?"

He looked from the Matriarch to Jen. Jen had been absolutely silent, I had hardly noticed her. She was now smiling knowingly. I looked at Jared in confusion, my eyes narrowed. What was I missing, it seemed apparent that there was something?

When no one spoke, Jared shook his head and continued slowly, "I'm pretty sure this woman just implied she's hundreds of years old, that she is not just a woman, but in fact the woman. I also think our good friend Jen may have already known this."

'Oh shit, oh shit', I thought. Alarm bells went off, and then a heaviness settled upon me, it felt as though my mind was moving in molasses. I felt like a lost puppy, and yet simultaneously knew I was so close to some sort of realization.

When the silence continued, Jared broke it by saying "I think that means your visions are the Matriarch's memories."

That was the sentence that clicked in the final puzzle piece. A million thoughts formed in my mind.

All that came out of my mouth was "Oh."

Jared seemed to be right. I performed a quick reanalysis of the language she had used. Based on what the Matriarch said, she certainly seemed to be implying she was literally the beautiful woman. I considered if I could really believe such a claim. The connected dreams were pretty wild, but this seemed to be a step above what I could accept.

I looked quizzically at Jen, "Do you believe it?"

Jen's smile strayed as she demonstrated her wisdom, "Does it really matter what we believe? I don't think it changes anything."

I responded quickly, "Yes, it does. It completely changes what I know to be possible. It absolutely shatters the rules of reality. I'm not even sure it can be reality."

She was ready, "Think of it as learning something new. Is reality not shaped by the things that we know, the things that we learn. This is just another one of those things, it is just much less commonly known. Besides, whether or not you believe it, whether or not it's true, does it really matter in terms of what we are trying to accomplish here? Our goal is to get the Retreat shut down, and return that land to its rightful protectors, not to contemplate what may or may not fit into reality."

The concept that this lady sitting across from me could measure her life in centuries was unquestionably absurd. I had to admit that Jen had a point, did it really change anything in terms of what we were trying to achieve? Strangely, the next thing that came to mind was the intimate encounter I had dreamt of with the woman. The idea that I had slept with, or at least seen and felt what it was like to sleep with this woman, would normally have been near impossible to process. Yet even that lacked importance when it was considered in relativity to what our team here was working to achieve. Whatever conclusion I came to, whether to believe it or not, I knew that it would not be settled that very evening.

I responded slowly, "Okay, well I don't exactly know what to think, but I guess for now it's not too important."

I knew that I would be spending some time reflecting and thinking this over. Throughout this entire conversation, the Matriarch seemed to be lost in her own world, whichever world that was. The words seemed to pass her by, none breaking her spell.

As I studied her face, her eyes shifted to mine, "I really do thank you. I should say, you are right in your assumption, the dreams will cease. Our connection is broken."

After a few minutes of silence, I remembered the other reason Jared and I wanted to make this visit. It was his time to shine. I asked him if he wanted to share his bright idea. He surprised me with a shake of his head and a nod, implying I should share his thoughts. I was unsure if it was modesty or if he had made no headway in processing the idea of this more than ancient woman and was not yet prepared to speak any more than he already had.

I looked at Jen and smiled, "I think you're really going to like this."

I began, "So, yesterday Jared and I were working real hard on houseman duties and I caught him up on our situation. Specifically, I shared the story that the Matriarch and I have been dreaming." I looked with uncertainty at the woman, "Or I guess you've been reliving, not dreaming. Anyways, Jared came up with a fantastic idea, we should release two articles. Along with outing the development and current conditions of the Retreat, we can also share the Matriarch and her people's story."

As I spoke, Jen nodded her head and slowly sprouted a smile that grew larger and larger. I thought that the idea was perfect, and I expected Jen to be excited by the prospect. When I finished, Jen looked at the person with whom she was sharing a couch and began to snicker. I was rather taken aback. I narrowed my eyes in both annoyance and confusion.

Through her laughter, "I'm sorry, it's a great idea. It's just that that's part of what the Matriarch and I have been doing. I've been helping her write down her story, we've even been including the details you've shared with her."

My face flushed red and I looked at Jared, he merely shrugged. Any embarrassment at my slowness was quickly replaced with gratitude from the realization that the majority of work on that idea was already completed.

Recovering, I said "Okay fine, you two are miles ahead. If you have any questions about the finer details of my visions please let me know, I'd also be happy to read over what you have once it's ready."

With the strange and serious conversations complete the mood was slightly lightened. We still had some time before dinner and Jen prepared tea, it was hard to beat the fresh herbs from the garden. The beverage seemed to restore Jared's ability to speak. The fire crackling and my friends laughing brought on a serene sense of calm. I reflected on how far from expectations my time on the island had been. I was not adventuring nearly as much as I hoped, but man oh man, what an adventure it had been. You can plan all you want, life will take you where it pleases and nowhere else. The harder you fight, the more you may struggle. Accepting reality, rather than resisting it, even when reality changes, is crucial. Now that I was moving with the current, I began to wonder where it was taking me.

[CHAPTER FORTY SIX]

In a perfect world, Jared, Jen, and I would have taken a day off to refine our strategy regarding the collection of Arbutus Falls ammunition. We needed to be fully loaded to have a chance with our expose. This perfect world existed nowhere other than my mind. Since we were so catastrophically short-staffed, it was impossible. Our strategy meeting would have to take place after work hours. The most natural thing to do was get together right after a shift, this way we could take advantage of the waning sunlight. In reality, we would likely have to meet multiple times and have countless side conversations.

The Arbutus Falls expose in and of itself was no small undertaking. My brain was programmed for efficiency at university and it fired up when thinking of how to tackle the task. I thought of it as a group project and I expected that we would divide and conquer. I attempted to break down what it would take. The areas requiring the most attention were; lies told to get staff onto the island, the pathetic pay situation, the sorry state of staff accommodations, the dog-shit staff meals, our hard-drug-addicted co-workers, and last but not least, Henri's horrific permanent residency situation. That is not to mention job-specific work conditions related to the kitchen, restaurant, and housekeeping. I thought, 'Who knows, we may even be able to get some dirt on the front desk situation.' I knew they always seemed to be working day and night. As demonstrated by how infrequently I saw Liz anywhere but on the desk. The only ones who seemed to be enjoying themselves, relatively speaking, were the maintenance team. They had no one to answer to and were spared most interactions with guests. I was unsure as to what formatting the expose would take, I simply assumed that it would come together as we began to mold the pieces.

    I was having these thoughts as I sat up in bed. I was awake early, unable to sleep in. My mind had not stopped running since the strange meeting at the Matriarch's cabin the night before. A strange thought reached out and grabbed me, I would be leaving Georgia Island in no time at all. It was little more than a month at most before I would make my way back to the East Coast. I had spent little time thinking of home. The idea of returning to my dog and family fast-tracked tears to my eyes. They expanded and I had a heavy cry about everything going on in my life. I did not try to fight it, it felt good to let it all out.

    When I finally collected myself, I understood that time was of the essence and communicated this to Jen and Jared when I saw them at work. Luck, and the sun, were on our side. The three of us were able to make our way to Staff Beach at the end of the day. Despite the sun shining and birds chirping, Jen was in a mood all day. Seeing this, I thought, is it not funny that in the best of moods, a rainy day can feel friendly and familiar, yet the sunniest of days can feel like a cruel mocking when spirits are low. Count the days when weather and feelings line up, they are rare, which makes them all the more special. On this particular day, they were not too well aligned for me either. I was becoming a bit annoyed with Jens's energy. As we came to the beach, I asked Jen what was on her mind and if she would like to share.

    She sure did want to share, "I don't think I can help the Matriarch with her people's story anymore. She's becoming difficult, or I guess she has been difficult, but either way, I've run out of patience. I think you have to take over."

    I was expecting that task to be divvied my way, but I had not realized the toll it was taking on my friend.

    I responded, "I'll take that off your hands happily. I'm sorry we didn't discuss that sooner, you've had more than your fair share on your plate and honestly I thought you would have assumed I'd be taking it over."

Jens's frustration boiled over, and she said sharply, "Oh what a surprise, you, not thinking, who'd have guessed."

My anger sparked, I cut back with, "Oh fuck off with that. You have no clue what's going on in my head. Have you ever been scared to sleep?"

Before I could continue, Jared spoke over me loudly, "Okay, so we already have that sorted, good start guys. Here's what I'm thinking, let's each go around saying what we would like to be responsible for, hopefully everything is covered, but whatever isn't, we can just discuss. I'll start."

Jen and I shot daggers at each other as Jared smiled between us uneasily.

He began, "I think we can all agree that I'm best suited to chat with the kitchen staff, although I do expect they may be hesitant to discuss with me now that I'm not in the kitchen anymore. I have enough stories collected that I should have it covered. I think that pairs nicely with our not-so-scrumptious staff meal situation, which you both know I am passionately frustrated with." Jared was scarily consistent in his arguments with Chef whenever he pulled out the frozen meat pies.

He looked to Jen, who had calmed and seemed focused, "What are you thinking?"

She started, "I'd be happy to take care of the restaurant and bar." She looked at me, and without an edge said, "The bartenders and servers don't think too highly of your departure, the Retreat still hasn't found a replacement for you."

I nodded in agreement as Jen continued, "I'd like to talk to Henri and learn more about his situation. That also seems to go hand in hand with the situation in housekeeping. I have some good ideas about how to portray the lovely conditions in staff accommodation. Jared, we can work together to tie the disgusting kitchen to the staff meals."

Jared agreed, but said, "That seems like a lot Jen, are you sure you want to take all that on?" Before she could answer I jumped in, "I can help with the staff accommodation situation, it goes together nicely with the lies I was told before coming here."

Jen nodded, and added, "Besides, if it's too much, either of you can give me a hand with Henri and housekeeping." Looking at me she added, "Plus, you have some stories about the restaurant."

Sensing Jen was finished, it was my turn, "So, that leaves me with Arbutus Falls' penchant for false advertisement, and the borderline criminal pay situation which goes along with that. When I'm not helping my lady friend at the cabin, I'll focus on those. I've also been considering getting some dirt on the front desk situation, if either of you guys have any ideas for that then please let me know."

I paused, considering how to word my final piece, "I think there's room for us to discuss the situation of hard drugs at the Retreat. Personally, I don't know how to talk about it since it's such a sensitive issue, do either of you guys feel more confident about it?"

Jen spoke up, "That's a good point, I think it'd be worthwhile to mention, but we need to do it the right way. I'll think about how we can. And good idea about the front desk, I don't have any ideas now, but I'll keep you updated."

Jared smiled, happy to have things organized and to see Jen and I being friendly, "Sweet guys, let's get this started. We can check in with each other pretty easily at work, and once we've made some progress, we can meet again."

Feeling slightly more organized put everyone in a better mood. We sat together on the beach, little was said and much was thought. We knew it would be a lot of work. No one wanted to say it, but our chances of success were still scarce. Thankfully we knew there was no point in fixating on failure. We sat soaking in the company until small ripples vibrated the sea bed's ceiling. The sun continued to shine as high clouds moved overhead, rain began, it did not bother us one bit. We moved as one, first to the trail and then to dinner. I had the next day off work and planned to stay up late working away.

The rain stayed heavy for the rest of the evening. It was rather blissful to fall asleep early to its sound. Especially knowing I would be allowed the gift of sleeping in the following morning. By morning, the rain had abated, I lay peacefully in bed. I was in that lovely state where you are half awake and then drift back off to sleep a few times. I began to slip back under as a thunderous hammering began at my door. I awoke to what felt like the walls collapsing. I was filled with a dreadful feeling that I had done something wrong and was being punished. It was just as my shock began to peak that I heard my name being shouted. It was being yelled in a French accent. I thought to myself, 'What the fuck does Henri want?'

The walls were thin enough that I shouted just that, "Yeah! What do you want, man?"

Henri responded, "I need you to work."

I responded, "It's my day off."

He wasted not a second, "Please, only for the half day."

I mulled it over for just a second before saying, "Fine, but you've got to go get me a coffee."

His relief was apparent, "Meet me in the lobby once you're up."

I checked my phone and saw that it was still early. I was hoping that I had at least slept through the first hour of the work day. I had not.

I got dressed and made my way leisurely down to the lobby. Once there I asked the front desk to buzz Henri on his walkie to tell him I was waiting. He was shaking his head as he walked in to greet me. I asked him what was wrong and he launched into how two of his employees were fired without his knowing.

I stopped him as he took a breath, "What? Who was fired?"

My immediate fear was that it was Jen or Jared, or both of them. Not that there was any reason either of them should be let go, but because after being awakened in such a strange way, I was prepared to expect the worst and nothing but it. To my immense relief, it was not Jen, nor Jared.

 It was a very sweet and rather silent stoner couple that were fired. I incorrectly assumed they were infinitely capable of flying under the radar. Apparently they were not. The couple was young, both in their late teens. They both gave off the vibe that they stopped attending high school a year or two early. Whether or not they graduated said less than nothing about their intelligence. They were both sharp as a tack, albeit slightly dulled due to a persistent cloud of marijuana following them. Not that I can say anything about that. In my humble opinion, they were a bit too open about their habits of smoking while working. I once saw the girl smoking a joint just outside the restaurant while she was on dish duty. It was hard to blame her, but still, risky business. The boy often showed up to his kitchen shifts with red eyes that he struggled to keep afloat, an even riskier business.

 The couple spent the other half of their time in housekeeping. They were both okay workers. I had almost nothing to say about them, and that was a good thing. They were nice enough and did just enough work to not drive you crazy. My initial reaction to finding out that they were fired was disappointment. They were good kids, the kind that I expected to turn into good adults. I enjoyed their youth, they were nice to have around. My disappointment turned quickly to confusion and then to frustration. I began to question why they were fired in the first place? Surely it was not because of their drug habits, but if not that, then what? If the Retreat wanted to let people go who were on drugs then surely they could come up with some more deserving candidates. I asked Henri what happened. He said that he knew no more than that they were fired and moved out yesterday. I found myself feeling a rage that was similar to Henri's. How the fuck could they justify firing two decent employees when we are already working six days a week. The two of us simultaneously being angry was not a good combination. As we raged on, I do not believe either of us heard a word the other said. The two of us worked rather closely for the rest of the day and were for the most part silent. We only interrupted the angry vibrations to air another complaint or judgment on how the situation was inexplicable. We were so focused on the frustration that Henri never did get me the coffee that I had so valiantly bargained for. True to his word, I was finished by noon and rather grateful for it.

     The freedom of my half day was short-lived. I got back to my room and knew immediately that it was time to get down to business. There was important work to be done. Knowing that I write best sitting at a table, I decided to make my way down to the restaurant. It was slightly strange showing up as a customer. I say customer, but the truth is I did not get anything other than a glass of water. I would be damned if the Retreat was getting an extra penny from me. Many of the staff drank and ate away their paycheques at Driftwood. I ate out sparingly while on the island, and each time it was at a restaurant in Northern Georgia, never at Driftwood. The looks I received from the bartender and servers as I sat down and pulled out my laptop were not particularly friendly. Jen seemed to be correct about their lack of appreciation for me. I decided that I would be skipping any small talk with them. When the middle-aged server, the one whose cup of white wine I had so many times filled up, came over to take my order, she was none too impressed that I asked for a lonesome glass of water. After she delivered it, I thanked her. The words, 'you're welcome', were accompanied by ripe grapes. I took a sip and then settled into my classic pub chair.

     It took no time at all to zone out the world around me. I got right to it. Jen had added me to a shared document and I immediately possessed access to everything she and the Matriarch had written. I read through it as quick as I could and found myself impressed. Jen certainly had not made it seem like it was an easy process, and I was not expecting such a complete record of happenings. It seemed as though just about all of the story was recorded. Seeing how long it was filled me with relief that Jen dealt with that part. I could only imagine the hours she put in. I was unsure as to how I would work in the side of the story that I experienced. The things like being on the boat as it landed, seeing firsthand the underhanded actions of the initial attack on the Indigenous peoples, and knowing the vile fate of the women who were left behind. An idea struck me as I read through the document. As I read it, I would make notes where I felt that bits could be added, along with ways that I could fill in minor gaps. By the end of my review, there was less to be added than I expected, what a relief.

    As I sat there reading along and taking notes, I felt a sense of calm. It felt good to be making progress, it almost felt like the finish line was in sight. Whether or not this story along with the exposé would have any impact on anything was up for debate, but at least it was getting done, at least we were trying. I returned to the top of the document and then made my way down through the comments. The words came slowly, but after no time at all they began to pour forth. It was as though I knew exactly what to say. I quickly lost myself in a flow state. After some time, my eyes became irritated and I rubbed them. As I tore my gaze away from the laptop screen I looked out into the dark night. What had been a lovely view of the bay was no more. I checked the time and then my progress. I would have to head upstairs for dinner, I was hungry and it was time to eat. The food would have to wait another few minutes because that was all the time it would take to finish up the last bit of work. I ripped all the way through the document. The page now contained a relatively full story of an otherwise unknown history. In that moment, I felt the importance of what we had just produced. No matter the end results of our labor, this was important. The brutality and reality of this story were now recorded, it could no longer be claimed that no one knew what happened. I felt proud to be a small part of something so big.

    Feeling as though I was finished for the moment, I packed up my laptop and made my way upstairs for dinner. I waved to the server on my way out. Rather than a friendly wave back, she glared. She looked at me like I wronged her, like she had five hungry children at home who would not be eating tonight because of me. I shook my head as I made my way out the door, you cannot please everybody. As I climbed the steps, I was feeling good about this document having neared completion. All that was left to do was proofread it with the Matriarch and then check it over for grammar. I had a good idea of who I would send it to for a grammar check. It would be the same person who checked everything I had done in my entire life. My mother.

    I returned to my room after another uneventful dinner. My hunger was quenched and I was craving deep relaxation. It was a no-brainer to head to the pool. I grabbed my towel and soap before heading over. There was no way I would miss this opportunity to skip out on staff accommodation's disgusting showers. This was my first time returning since I accidentally jumped into the cold water of the pool. For this reason, I was on high alert to ensure the mistake was not repeated. I left my gear in the family bathroom and made my way out onto the pool deck. To my right, I could see the steam rising off of the hot tub, it seemed to be calling my name. I looked to the pool's shimmering depths. It gave no hint as to what its temperature may be. If it was indeed warm, then it was not warm enough to produce any vapours. The deck was a rough faux-stone that allowed for plenty of grip. It was the kind you did not want to fall on. For if you did, you would surely scrape off a layer or two of skin, more if you were unlucky. The upside of this risk was that, due to the friction, you were unlikely to slip in the first place. The pool's water was a few inches lower than the grade. I stood on one foot and dipped in a testing toe. Alarms went off immediately, and my inner voice screamed 'cold' and 'no'. My body listened to this information and began to react accordingly. Suddenly and inexplicably, it stopped reacting accordingly.

    I subconsciously instructed my body to place the testing toe, along with the rest of that foot, back onto the grippy ground. That was as far as I got before losing control. Had I gotten both feet back on solid ground, I would have walked over to the hot tub and slowly lowered myself into its warm embrace. Rather than take those literal logical steps, I began to lean forward. It was a slow lean. The way that I imagine a tree slowly and silently falls in the forest. Of course, when a tree falls, it most often has branches with which it reaches out. With these limbs it may very well land upon one of its brethren and stop its fall short. My situation was different. There were no limbs to grab ahold of, and even if there were, my arms were glued to my sides. My feet were planted to the ground, but not for much longer. The growing fear that I would soon be shocked by the oh-so-cold water almost blocked out the sensation that I lost control of my body. For better or worse, I was aware of both strange and awful occurrences. In fact, the terror that I was suddenly feeling how I felt in my forgotten dream almost overpowered the idea of the impending infinite cold.

 In seemingly slow motion, I broke the water's surface. Immediately, the pain of the cold won my mind and then consumed it. It was somehow worse than the time before, it was as though my body was buried in a block of ice. I am quite certain that I went into shock, yet that is not why I was unable to move. Believe me, had I been able to, I would have been out of that pool and into the hot tub in a heartbeat. That was not my reality, I began to sink, and as I sank, the cold was placed onto the back burner. I chanted the simple, but effective, mantra of the painfully confused 'What the fuck, what the fuck.' It has never failed me. My head started churning out thoughts at a mile a minute. What was happening? Was I about to drown? Was this a dream? I sure hoped I was dreaming. I thought to myself, 'At least I'm holding my breath.' It would be bad business inhaling mouthfuls of stale pool water.

 I sunk deep enough for my feet to touch down on the bottom. This surface was much smoother and slipperier than the pool's deck. My feet slid back as my face lowered. My nose made contact with the pool's bottom, simultaneously, I regained control of my body. I immediately messed up by taking a huge breath, well, trying to take a huge breath. I was right, a mouthful of stale pool water was anything but enjoyable. Truth be told, I was not too concerned with the minor choking hazard, my focus was on getting up and out. I pushed off with my hands and then with my feet. As promised it was no more than a heartbeat or two before I was out of the pool and into the the hot tub. My skin felt as though it was on fire, the way it does when you enter a hot tub too quickly. As I leaned back, I was still coughing from the water I swallowed. My throat was raw and my heart was pounding. My mind continued to race, it settled on confusion, which is hardly settling at all. I kept myself submerged until I finally warmed back up. I did not shake the chill that came from being spooked. Failing to make any sense of what happened, I decided to have a quick shower and get back to my room. As I made my way to the family bathroom, I took a wide berth around the pool, as though it had a mind of its own and could suck me in at any moment.

As soon as I was back in my room, I got under the covers and attempted breathing deeply. Whatever that was, was weird and really freaked me out. My solution to such trouble was simple, I would sleep it off. I thought maybe I would get lucky and just forget about the strangeness of it all. That is all it was anyway, an incident. Besides, what was the point in lingering over something so silly? There was already so much craziness going around, I would add it to the hidden list of things to forget.

[CHAPTER FORTY SEVEN]

Falling or being forced into the pool, the strange dream walk up to the cliff, and there was something else too. Something that was playing on the edge of my mind. I would have to remember it if I wanted any chance to make sense of what was going on. I was feeling far too overwhelmed to have such little understanding. By some miracle, I was able to fall asleep the night before. That was where the good things stopped. I woke up in a sweat that morning. I felt awful, my head pounded and my body was sore. I immediately messaged Henri and told him I was going to need to take the day off. He had no choice but to understand. I considered what to do. What could I even do? All I wanted was to feel better.

It was that morning that I first thought about getting off the island. I was merely a few weeks away from the end, why not finish the story early by booking an earlier flight? Plus, there was that message from Chris, I could always go visit him in Victoria. Perhaps I should. Perhaps it was time to leave this whole shit hole behind. I could pack my bag immediately and be on the ferry within a few hours. He would be happy to pick me up from the terminal. Oh, how I wish I had gone that day. I wonder if I even would have been able to.

I threw on Sgt. Pepper's Lonely Heart Club Band in an attempt to shake the awful mood in which I awoke. The music did little to distract my mind, but it did put me in a mood to move. I began thinking about where I would go. One connection led to another and I realized that there was only one place to go. I could get two birds stoned at once, as Ricky would say. For likely the last time, I would make the trek up to the cliff. I would also get the movement that my body so needed, and I would bring some peace to my mind. That peace would come in the form of discovering that my name was not carved into two trees up there, but only one. At the time, I did not consider my reaction if I were to find it on two. There was no way that I possibly could, so there was no reason to entertain such an insane idea.

The day was as sunny as the evening would be rainy. There was not a cloud in the sky. I dressed in a rush and soon found myself at the edge of the road. I was facing the path I must take. The only thing of note was that I saw the all-familiar Rolls Royce Phantom parked by the tennis courts; a large Cadillac was parked beside it. I figured the owner was visiting with family. As I began to fall into my old steps, I was struck by the silence of the woods. When it rains, all you hear is the sound of drops splattering off leaves on their way to the earth. On days when it is clear, you hear, at the very least, wind rushing over the cliff and through those same leaves. Most often, you could hear a plethora of birds chirping away, singing their songs. There was no wind and no birds, just utter silence. I could hear nothing but the sound of my familiar footfalls winding down the path. Normally they would have flown under the radar, unlike the birds. The wet leaves and soft pine needles often hid the sound of my steps. Not today, today each step was deafening.

In retrospect, I would have thought that finding a second engraving would have sent me off the edge. I imagine it would have been all too much, and that I would have returned to my room silently. I believed that once there, I would have packed my bag and left. Reality is infinitely different from expectation.

I approached the clearing cautiously. I felt a slightly stirring thought, 'I wish I brought my hammock'. It was the perfect day to set it up. It was oddly warm without the wind and with the sun shining so bright. Another oddity was how good I felt. My caution was quickly thrown to the non-existent wind and with gusto I approached the tree in question. The sun was behind the tree so I got close to properly examine it. As had happened so many times recently, my heart dropped. My name was engraved boldly. The arbutus's skin where my name was so crudely carved out was a deep red. I began shaking my head in disbelief, this did not last long.

I stopped the shaking of my head and found myself shrugging deeply. Something snapped within me, this was the final straw. There was some weird shit on this island, but enough was enough. I would leave. Not today, but the day after. I would first explain and apologize to Henri, although I was certain he would understand. I also wanted to say goodbye to the people who had shown me such kindness. The list was not very long, but those on it were of the upmost importance. I looked once more at my name carved in the tree, the one that I had or had not carved. I spat towards it with all the anger I could muster. It was a pathetic and animalistic reaction, but I told you I wanted to come as close as I could to the truth with these words.

I saw nothing but red as I walked back to my room. There was no appreciation for the trees and the earth that treated me well enough. There was simply no space in my mind for those things. In the first moments of my return, I was entirely focused on packing up my room. I wanted to get everything ready so that I could leave at a moment's notice. I decided to leave out only the clothes that I would wear the following day for travel. The packing itself went as smoothly as one can imagine, no surprise considering my limited possessions. I had not accumulated anything new while on the island, at least physically speaking. When it came to new ideas, thoughts, and understandings, that was a very different story, one that I have imparted much of in these words. I took down from the window the dream catcher Jen had so kindly loaned me. By this time, it was after work hours and I decided to go knock on her door. My intention was to return it.

I knocked, and called from the door, "Hey Jen, you home?"

There was only a breath's pause before the door opened. Jen's head poked out around the corner. She disappeared behind it.

The door opened slightly wider as she said, "Come on in, I'm just getting changed."

I walked in without a thought and saw that she was indeed getting changed. She was half naked with her back to me. I have no shame in admitting I did not tear my eyes away from her until she began to turn to face me. I am but a man, and besides, I had permission. She faced me with a smile as I held out the dream catcher. She shook her head immediately, as if there was no way she would accept it back.

She said, "Oh please, it's yours to keep. I really do think you need it more than me."

She paused for just a second before continuing, "Wait, why are you trying to give it back? You're not leaving, are you?"

I looked into her sad face, it wore the look of someone who already knew and understood.

I nodded slowly and said, "That's the plan. Do you have time for a walk? I'd like to say goodbye, and I have something to discuss."

She regained composure and responded, "Of course I have time for you. You're not leaving today, are you?"

I shook my head with confidence, "No, I figured I'd head out tomorrow. I don't want to be in too much of a rush."

A strange and unrecognizable look filled her eyes but stopped short of reaching her face. It may have been relief, but I am still unsure. Either way, I did not notice it at the time.

Jen donned a sweater and light jacket, it was still a relatively warm day. On our way out of the building, we stopped by my room. I put the dreamcatcher back where it hung while Jen stared in disbelief at the near-empty room. We said little as we weaved our way through the cottages that blocked our way to the forest. As soon as we got out into the fresh air, we were forced to listen to some loud and obnoxious music. As we walked along, it got louder and louder. The blaring music happened to be coming from the backyard of the cottage that we cut through to get to the Staff Beach trail. I knew from past experience that this must be where the owner of the Retreat and his family were staying. In my time on the island no one else stayed in this particular chateau. There was no need, never were all of the cottages filled.

Drunken screams of excitement intertwined with the blaring music as we crossed the cottage's lawn. We had a relatively clean line of sight toward the obnoxious happenings once we passed the building, we both looked as we walked past. Rather than seeing a group of people partying and having a good time, we saw a man. He stood close, with a dead look in his eyes. He leaned on the corner that we were looking past. His dick was sticking out of his fly, although not by much. It looked as though he had gone to take a leak and then lost track of what it was he was doing. I squinted my eyes and gave him my patented, and practiced, 'You look like a fucking weirdo' face.

For this strange man, coming into contact with Jen and I seemed to bring him an inch closer to reality. He began to move, slowly standing up from the wall. I was impressed he had the ability to stand without falling. By a miracle, he registered the look I was giving him and did not appreciate it. Fair enough. He raised both of his hands and gave us a double one-finger salute. Turning with less than no grace, he walked back to the party, his dick still flopping about.

Jen and I scarcely slowed our step, and it seemed we had both forgotten the interaction by the time we were in the forest. There were bigger fish to fry. I knew we were about to have quite the conversation. I hoped to get past the bad shit as quickly as possible, so that is what I started with. Telling Jen everything was a no-brainer. She had always been there for me when I needed her, and I knew that she would not mind my leaning on her one more time. I was oh-so curious as to how she would advise me, if at all.

I got right into it. I told Jen of my strange dream. Where in the middle of the night I walked up to the cliff and carved my name into the tree. I explained how it felt so similar to the visions, except that it was in my body. I shared my understanding of what happened at the pool the night before, it sounded even crazier to say aloud. I told her how that was what pushed me to go up to the cliff this morning to confirm or deny that I was indeed back up to the cliff to carve my name a second time. I questioned her on how there could be two different instances where I completely lost control of my body. What more was that I was forced to do things against my will, things I would have not have done were I in control.

It was in that moment that my brain made a much needed connection. I remembered something that I read, something that felt long ago, yet that I knew was quite recent. It was about a strange and dark form of mind and or body control. A small thing that I stumbled upon while I was researching an explanation for my dreams. It was not worth remembering at the time, and I happily swept it below the rug. It stayed there undisturbed for some time.

    At the original time of reading, I wrote the people who had these experiences off as being insane. Perhaps they were more sane than I imagined, or perhaps I was less than I hoped. I expected it was likely a bit of both. At its core was the question of whether or not you believed these actions were committed by someone else who was in control of the body. Did I believe that I was not in control? It was a tough one. I thought you had to be crazy to believe that sort of thing. But then if they were indeed controlling their despicable actions, were they not just as insane? This seemed to be a lose-lose situation for those fond of their sanity.

    One of those stories that really stuck out was actually the one that made me hit the little red 'x' on the tab. It was about a woman who murdered her husband. By all accounts, the woman was sweet as they came and would never hurt a fly. Sadly the same could not be said for her husband. He was your classic run-of-the-mill alcoholic, abusive as they come. One night when her husband came home indirectly from work, he had made a pit stop at the liquor store on the way home, his wife was waiting for him. Or that is at least what investigators assumed. What was left of the man's body was placed sitting up in his lazy boy. A collection of empty bottles lay smashed all around their apartment. The majority of them were dripping with blood and collected small pieces of flesh. The sweet wife had cracked. She smashed upon his head what seemed to be that month's entire collection of empty 40s and beer bottles. The sharper of the results were then used to mutilate her late husband's body extensively. It seemed that there was no part of the body left off the table, or on the bone.

It was unclear what eventual fate this woman reaped. The part of her story highlighted on the website was her defence. It was simple, she claimed she was not in control of her body when the ungodly act was committed. When pushed as to who or what it was that was in control, she claimed it was her husband's ex-wife pulling the strings. The ex-wife, who was allegedly in control, had allegedly been murdered by the husband in one of his worst drunken fits. I could not help but think that if her defence was that she had committed a gruesome murder because someone else was in control of her body, then her chances of success were slim. Someone whose body can be controlled by such a deity can hardly be trusted in normal society. At best, they would be locked up in prison or a psych ward. At worst, they would be scientifically studied.

At the time that I originally stumbled upon that article, I was aware it was quite similar to my visions. At least in terms of the feelings that some of the more simple cases experienced. I stopped drawing the comparison there because I only felt those sensations when I was in the strange dream world. Mine were visions outlining Georgia Island's history of colonial founding.

Oh sweet fuck, I must sound crazy, but I swear this is the truth. I guess you will either believe me or you will not.

It seemed that the comparison had grown in size, this sensation of being controlled seemingly spread to my reality. This direction of thought was doing nothing but worry me further. I decided to put a stop to it before I went all the way off the rails on the crazy train. Snapping back to reality, I looked at Jen and saw she was staring at me, concern in her eyes.

When my eyes met hers, she asked me, "Where did you just go?"

Half-joking, I said, "You don't want to know."

I was incredibly curious as to what Jen thought about my thoughts, "So, what do you think? I sound pretty fucking crazy eh?"

Jen gave a nervous smile and said, "Well, I actually just told you what I thought about it, but apparently I was speaking to myself."

I began to apologize and she waved me off as she continued, "I said, that's pretty freaky, I can understand your concern and why you're so stressed out. I think it makes a lot of sense for you to get off the island, it hasn't been good for your mental state. That's not to say that I think you're crazy, I don't think you're crazy. But this isn't the first time you've come to me with something rather inexplicable. Once again, I don't have any explanations for you. All I can tell you is that I'll be here for you until, and after, you leave Georgia tomorrow."

I had not thought that any words would be able to help explain my situation, and I was right. My situation was just as strange as it had been, but now it was different. Now someone I could trust knew what was going on in my head. Jen succeeded in reminding me that I was not alone, and it felt good knowing she supported my plan for getting off the rock. I considered whether to mention that dark and strange article I had just remembered. I decided against it, why bother? I would enjoy the rest of this walk with a friend and then probably get stoned in the evening with Jared.

I was right on with my prediction as to how the rest of my day would go. Over what would thankfully be my last staff dinner, I gave Jared and Henri a breakdown of when I was leaving. Neither of them were over the moon about it and Jared surprised me by being more upset than I expected. It seemed that I found a better friend in him than I took the time to appreciate. Henri could not have been more understanding. While I never got too deep into what was going on, Henri saw my shifts in mood and must have known I was struggling. I have never been much of an actor. Henri encouraged Jared and I to come hang out at his place that evening for one last fire. We both happily accepted.

    After dinner I stopped by my room briefly, there was not much reason to sit in the empty room alone. Besides, we were expected to get some heavy rain later that evening and overnight, better to get the fire going early. It was a good call, the rain came earlier than expected. Before it did, Jared, Henri and I were found laughing around the fire outside Henri's trailer. Louder than us, was the sound of the Retreat owner's party. Henri's trailer was close enough that I could once again hear their music blaring along with their screams of pain and joy. They were already partying all day. I could not imagine they had too much juice left. On the other hand, I could easily imagine they were hitting the slopes, they seemed the skiing type.

    In a simple throwaway sentence, I said, "Man, those guys are being loud as anything."

    That seemed to trigger a memory in my friends. Henri and Jared quickly caught my full attention as they launched excitedly into something that happened earlier that day at work. One of the housekeeping staff was in a rough state. They were up late the night before, most certainly using. Henri and him were tidying up the owner's cottage, a monumental task, when the owner came back to grab something. The big boss said something rude to our colleague and it was not well received. No one knows exactly what happened, but a glass was smashed at the owner's feet and apparently he was screaming at him, really letting the owner have it. It was unclear if the guy would be fired, but the end of the incident was witnessed by Henri, and so he was obligated to make a formal record of it. I did not know if it would be better or worse if he ended up fired. Either way, I was impressed by the spine that he showed by standing up for himself.

    At some point, Jared pulled out and lit a joint on the fire. I was more than happy to escape for as long as this altered state of mind would allow me. I would double my effort at getting off the stuff once I left this god-forsaken place. Henri pulled a rather shocking move by announcing he would be taking a puff. He never hopped into the rotation.

When asked as to why he was partaking, he shrugged and said in his beautiful accent, "Fuck it."

I was going to miss these guys. They were both damn good people. I find it hardest to say goodbye when you know it is unlikely you will see someone ever again. That has always been one of the toughest things to wrap my head around. You can make such a strong and genuine connection with someone so quickly, and if you do not happen to live close to each other or travel in similar circles the chances of reconnecting are slim to none. The more you travel and the more of these connections you make, the more numbing it becomes. In many ways, this is the beauty and the hardship of human connection in this modern age. If nothing else, it reaffirms that you must appreciate people when you can.

There was little substance spoken for the rest of the evening. When the rain came, it came fast and hard. We had just enough time to get beneath the canopy that stuck out from Henri's trailer. We watched in saddened awe as the rain slowly drowned and killed the fire. That was it. The last flame extinguished, it was time to head back to my room for the last time. Jared and I said a brief goodbye before each of us ran back to our respective accommodations through the downpour. Naturally, there was not a soul out. I was surprised to find staff accommodations absolutely silent. It reminded me of my last hike up to the cliff. Normally this early on a rainy day, everyone would be inside getting their drink and drug on. I thought no more of it. When I returned to my room, I immediately peeled off the wet clothing and hung them up to dry. I crawled under the covers and thanked everything and more that this was my last night on Georgia Island. It felt like forever ago that I arrived. At the same time, now that I was leaving, it felt like it was just yesterday. I slipped to sleep with warm thoughts of hugging my dog, my boy was waiting for me.

[CHAPTER FORTY EIGHT]

I awoke later that night to the same sound that coaxed me to sleep. It was a torrential downpour that pounded the roof ceaselessly. With a sad resignation, I quickly accepted my last night on Georgia would not be as peaceful as I hoped. In retrospect, it would have been more surprising if I was able to make it through the night uninterrupted. That was something that was simply never in the cards.

    I hopped out of bed effortlessly. Effortlessly in the literal sense, I put no effort in. Technically, there was effort, it was directed to fight the movement that raised me from rest. Yes, once again my body was being controlled by something other than my own mind. There were no ifs, ands, or buts this time. I was certain, beyond a shadow of a doubt, this was real. In that moment, I was certain that the other incidents were just as real. The question that accompanied this realization was 'why?' Why was I forced into the pool against my will? Why was I forced to wield a knife to carve my name a second time into a poor arbutus? Most importantly, why was I being raised at this hour? I wondered if I was going to be forced to slog through this vicious downpour? I could have asked a million questions, and questioned a million thoughts, I certainly had time to.

    As I thought, I was picking up my socks from the day before. They were not fully dried and I did not enjoy their cold wetness on my warm feet. Naturally, I assumed I would be pulling on the rest of my wet clothes too. I was not looking forward to their cold clinginess either. I wanted nothing but to get back into my warm cocoon, infinite comfort may be found in the most unwelcoming bed. I did not consider any alternative to putting on the rest of my clothing, and I certainly could not have imagined anything worse. When I went straight for my door and made my way out into the TV room, I was still only in my socks. This reminded me that things can almost always get worse. The absolutely absurd action of walking out of my room buck-naked, save for a pair of wet socks, made me reconsider the possibility that this was a dream. It also further extended the question of 'why?'.

      I moved with unfamiliar precision, as though whatever was in control of my body was on a mission. I was outside and soaking wet within a minute's quarter. My hair was drenched, along with my socks. The socks were almost immediately muddy thanks to pooling in the dirt lot. There was some pretty vicious wind accompanying the rain, and I saw that some trees were robbed of their weak, and or elderly, branches. I made my way down the normal walking path, the one that would eventually take me down to the bay. I felt ripe with anxiety, it felt so damn weird walking through the middle of the Retreat without any clothes on. I hoped with all my heart that no one would see me. With so few people staying at the Retreat, combined with the weather, and time of day, I was unlikely to be seen. The logic of this did not penetrate my anxiety.

      I came to the point in my late night creep where I could head down the stone stairs to my right and go past the upper pool towards the lobby's main entrance. Or I could head left and go deep into cottage territory, eventually to the trail for Staff Beach. For the moment, I did neither. There was a good-sized branch lying in the middle of the crossroads. I bent down and grabbed ahold of it. With one socked foot pinning the branch, I pulled hard, a baseball bat-sized limb cracked off. I got a feeling for the weight of it and then headed left. Staff Beach, here I come?

      Were I able to, I may have laughed. There I was, walking along the path that I normally drove a golf cart around while working. Now there was only a sock on each foot and a large bat-like stick in one hand. What a sight to see. Thankfully, a sight that no one did see. I was still moving in some set direction. Of which direction that was, I was unaware. Innocently enough, I figured I must be going to Staff Beach. That was certainly the rough direction I was headed. I guess the Matriarch's cabin was also been an option, albeit a strange one. There I was walking naked in public, who was I to contemplate strange.

It was not until I arrived outside the cottage where the owner and his family were staying that I considered it my destination. I was walking through the yard towards the Staff Beach trail when I changed direction. I made a right and turned the corner where Jen and I were flipped off by limp dick the day before. There was no music playing now, the cottage was dead silent. It seemed the place was all partied out. I thought it was likely for the best. Especially because it meant no one would see me. I could only imagine how freaky it would be to see someone in my current state creeping outside your cottage. I was momentarily out of the rain as I passed underneath the back patio covering. It was only then that I realized how damn cold the rain was. I was freezing, although not quite as cold as when I fell into the pool. With a stain of humour, I thought it would be nice if I was controlled to go to the hot tub after this. I was submerged back into rain as I approached the cottage's back door.

I stared through the glass double doors that opened into the cottage's living space. I was suddenly aware of emotions. It felt very similar to the emotions that I felt when the visions started. It was an anger that I felt. An anger that was somehow simultaneously dark as night and red-hot. Through this rage, I could see a single lamp illuminating the room. The light spilled upon two comfy chairs that bordered a long couch. The place was a mess, I felt bad for whoever it was that would have to clean up. I also felt thankful that it sure as hell would not be me. Amid the storm was a body. The body was slouched back on the couch, clearly dead to the world.

I tried the door with my free hand, the other still held the branch, now more like a club. The mechanism clicked and opened. It made no sound other than a vibration, thanks to the noise of the rain. I stepped in and onto the tile floor, my wet socks squelching with each step. There was no pause in my actions, not a single thought's worth. With brutal calculation, I walked across the room and raised the stick like I was wielding a sword. The first time it came down was directly on the person's temple. The body barely moved. It twitched slightly, and I never did see the whites of their eyes. I think that was the only grace I was granted. I saw and felt everything else. At this point, it was rather clear that I was dealing with a man. It was not a large man, and so when I dragged him off the sofa by his armpits, it was relatively easy. Adrenalin was pumping through my veins, that helped equally as much.

Were it not to have happened so quickly, I think I would have experienced more horror. Thanks to years of video games, I was relatively numb to violence. It was in this rush of action that I changed my mind decisively. I told myself that this was indeed a dream after all. It had to be, if it was not, then how could I possibly be living with myself as I write this. I left open the door through which I entered. With continued ease, I dragged the body out and onto the back patio. I took it out of the rain and beneath the overhang that covered the barbecue and patio set.

I left the body splayed on its back. I picked up one of the chairs from the patio set. It was the heavy metal set, high-quality, plus the weight would likely discourage anyone trying to steal them. I took the chair and placed one of the legs on the man's head. It came to rest on his right eye. I held onto the backrest for leverage. While balancing on my left foot, I raised my right foot high. I brought it down as hard as I could on the chair's seat. It sank down slightly. Once again the body twitched. I am certain that, had I looked, I would have seen some whites. Although they would have been out of place. I stomped again. The chair sunk down a bit more, enough that I was able to climb onto and stand upon the seat without losing balance. I jumped, slamming the full weight of my body upon it. The rain failed to fully drown out the cracks and squishes, I wish so badly that it had.

I wish I could say that at some point I blacked out, but I did not. Let us pretend I did. Even that which I have shared so far may have been too much, if so, please forgive me. I 'came to' back on the path along which the cottages were littered. I was still naked, but now my socks were gone. So was the branch. Rather than going directly to staff accommodations, I took a left turn, which a life time ago, had just been a right. I headed down the stone stairs that took me to the pool. Oh god, I thought, was I really about to go into the hot tub? That had been a joke, one that now did not seem funny. Rather, I entered the men's bathroom and made my way to the shower.

The hot water was lovely and short-lived. Before I could process what was going on, I moved back out into the main room. A towel was balled up in the corner, I picked it up. I made my way back out into the pouring rain and headed to staff accommodations. I did not wrap the towel around my naked body but rather continued marching along. I walked up the stairs to the building. Before entering, I dried each foot with the still semi-dry towel's middle. I took two steps inside and then launched the towel down the hall into the kitchen.

There was not a sound to be heard in the building. Anything that may have been, was drowned out by that all-consuming rain. I dried myself with my own towel and then got back in between the covers. It was as if I had never left. I guess I did not leave, I dreamt the whole thing. I was hit with a wave of exhaustion. It forced me swiftly to sleep. With my last free thoughts, I asked myself a hard question. If it was not a dream, at what point did I regain control? I was beyond a doubt that at some point, I was returned ownership of my actions.

[CHAPTER FORTY NINE]

I hate that first moment when you wake up after a traumatic event. For the first few breathes, you feel so safe and comfortable in bed. That moment always betrays you, and it betrays you quickly. Your heart sinks as you remember what it is that plagues your mind and heart. Whether it be something like missing out on a job that you desperately wanted, or the passing of a closely beloved. It is that first moment that does the most damage, that transition from bliss to brokenness that hurts the most. After the shock of realization, it can only get better. The dull pain of whatever horrific thing has occurred slowly becomes familiar until, eventually, you can live with it. I find that a rather opposite experience occurs when you wake up following a traumatic dream. You wake up in terror, genuinely believing that whatever transpired in your dreamscape will now have a direct impact on your life. You believe it literally is part of your life. As the realization that it was nothing but a dream comes to you, relief does too. I much prefer moving from a bad dream to any reality than any dream to a bad reality.

I awoke the morning after not knowing which way I was moving. Had I just dreamt one of the most horrific dreams imaginable? Would this fear in which I was gripped fade swiftly as I accepted it as nothing but a nightmare? I hoped badly that was the case. If the true situation be that I left my room naked the night before, then I could not imagine how long my life may take to get back to normal. More than that, there could be some serious implications, serious enough that I dare not consider them. I felt paralyzed in my bed, a sensation that was somehow worse than being forced to move. I noticed the rain had finally subsided. It poured so much overnight that I would be shocked if another drop fell today. Okay, enough about the weather. I had to get moving, and figure out what the hell those movements were going to be.

I knew what I needed to do, it was just a matter of execution. I had to get the fuck off the island. I already told people I was leaving, so that is just what I would do. I considered my options, the best two seemed to be organizing the Arbutus Falls van to take me to the ferry port or asking Henri to drive me there. Rather than either, I settled on neither. It would take too long to organize the Retreat's van, and I did not want Henri to be associated with my leaving in any way, just in case. First things first, I had to get up. I had to get up and check in on the thing that

I was putting off checking on. I had to check to see if my wet socks were finally dry. All it took was sitting up in bed to see that there were no socks. This all but confirmed my fears, not that there was much hope. Of course, there was always the chance that I misplaced them, or that I did not even have socks to dry in the first place. That was likely what I would end up telling myself in the future, especially when doubts crept in. I hopped off my bed and quickly stuffed the rest of my dry clothes into the bag that was awaiting them. I threw on my travel clothes at record speed and mentally prepared myself to leave my room, and then the Retreat.

I moved my backpack and my wheelie bag into the TV room before taking a final look around my room. It was as empty as it was the day I moved in. It was almost too empty. As I shut the door for the last time, I realized why. Something was missing, something that should have blocked a bit of the view out the window. The dreamcatcher that was so kindly loaned to me by Jen was gone. I shuddered at the very thought of her and prayed to never see her again. After last night, I did not want to think about her ever again, but I sure would.

I made it out of the building without running into anyone. It was early, just past seven in the morning. I essentially made it up and out of the Retreat without running into anyone as well. As I passed the sign that greeted me so long ago, when I first arrived to the retreat, I did see a golf cart ripping past the tennis courts. I wondered if they saw me, and who it was. Suddenly, a sound ripped through the air and startled the hell out of me. It was high-pitched and changing in patterned frequency. Were we in the city then it would have taken me no time at all to identify the siren. But out here in the silence of the woods, I was not used to any sort of loud wailing interrupting my peace, other than my now ex-roommates.

There was a small fire station just around the bend from the Retreat. I always assumed that this was the only one to service the entire south of the island, it was likely true. In my time there, I never heard them going out to answer any call in a hurry. It seemed that now they were. I was shocked there even was an emergency to answer. I had an idea of where it was they were going, but I could not understand the rush. There was no one to save, so why the hurry? I wanted to be out of their way when they arrived at the Retreat, so I began to my left. I walked in the direction of the ferry. The siren got louder and louder until it was passing right behind me. It was indeed going to the Retreat, no shock there. I walked on, literally leaving it all behind me, or hoping to.

     My plan was to hitchhike to the ferry. Although there would be few cars on the road headed in that direction, the chances were very high that one of the few cars would pick me up. The island actually had bus-stop-like stations where people could wait for a drive, organized-hitchhiking. Over the years they fell into disrepair and it became more common to simply pick someone up from wherever they were. This worked for me because I wanted to keep moving, I felt better that way. I was correct in the assessment of my odds of being picked up. It took ten minutes before I saw my first car, and they did not hesitate to halt. It was a man driving the car, and he seemed highly excited. He told me to throw my bags in the trunk. I did just that and then climbed into the shotgun seat.

     As the man pulled off, he said, "I'm going to go ahead and assume you're headed to the ferry. I'll take you right there, if that's right."

     I responded happily, "You've got it, thanks a million."

     He responded in a kind but alert voice, "You're coming from Arbutus Falls, eh? I just finished my shift up at the station, and the boys who just got on were called out to go over there. Any idea what's going on?"

     I could not help but think about how lucky this man was, his shift change could not have happened at a better time. He was likely avoiding seeing one of the most traumatizing things in his life. I'm sure he had seen some gory car crashes before, but there is something that is so much worse about the damage being caused by calculated intent, which in this case, it most certainly would appear to have been. I guess it literally was caused with intent, I was simply unsure of whose intentions they were. I felt horrible for his colleagues who would be unable to avoid the sight. They were not the only ones who would likely be traumatized on this day. It would be a dark day for the whole island, a day that would not be forgotten for a long time.

I responded with as much calm and innocence as I could muster, "I saw the truck going in. But no, I have no clue what it could be. I can't imagine there could be much of a fire with how much it poured last night, but I guess you never know."

He said with an air of deflation, "No, you're right. It was no fire. Apparently someone died, and we're the closest ones that are able to respond to it."

I mirrored his deflation, "Damn, what a shame."

We sat in silence for the rest of the drive, the cloak of death settled heavily upon us.

The kind firefighter dropped me off at the ferry terminal and I thanked him graciously. As he drove away, I could not help but wonder how he would react when he found out the nature of the death at the Retreat. I wondered if he would think back to the young man he drove over to the ferry terminal, I highly doubted it.

I would have to wait just over an hour for the ferry to Victoria. I used the time to try and give Chris a call. No luck, he must still be sleeping. Oh well, worst case scenario I would have to wait at Victoria's ferry terminal. Waiting there would be infinitely better than waiting here on Georgia. I was as antsy as I have ever been. I felt chained to the place, like a prisoner. I craved the feeling of looking off of the ferry and watching the island shrink as we pulled away from it. There was no way I would ever return. In my mind, the place was cursed, and for damn good reason.

The waiting room of the Georgia Island ferry terminal was tiny. It had four seats lining one wall and two sets of two on the other. There were large windows that let in lots of light and a single bathroom. There was an older lady and a pair of younger ones in there with me. The two young women looked as though they had all of their worldly possessions in tow. I was grateful for their presence, it made me feel as though I fit in. It made me feel like it was normal to be leaving the island on foot with everything I owned. I needed this sense of normality because the conditions in which I was leaving were anything but. The time crawled by. I kept checking my phone to see the time, and in hopes that Chris had hit me back. After what seemed to be forever, the ferry finally came into view. It grew bigger and bigger, the optical opposite of how the island would soon look. As it came closer, my anxiety grew. I guess it was visible, because the old lady looked at me with concern.

    She said, "Hey son, what's gotcha going?"

    I responded smoothly, "Oh nothing, I just get nervous around boats."

    She smiled wide and said, "Well, you're not in the best place then are ya, lots of boats on an island."

    As with how it was when I arrived on the island, the foot passengers boarded first. I wanted to seem as casual as possible, especially after the woman questioned me, so I did not rush to be the first person on. I ended up boarding behind the old lady and ahead of the younger women. The attendant checked our tickets nonchalantly and welcomed us aboard. I headed up top to the passenger area and found a spot to sit by the window. I watched with growing anticipation as the cars filed on one at a time. It seemed they could not have boarded any slower. It felt like time was at a near standstill. I watched on as the attendant signalled to pull up the boarding ramp. As it slowly rose, my hopes did too. Not by much, just enough to take a deep breath. I almost smiled as the ferry engine kicked on and propelled us out to sea. I checked my phone and saw that Chris finally responded. He said he would be waiting at the ferry terminal and that he could not wait to see me. What a strange concept that was. The idea that I was leaving this place to go hang out with my buddy from back home was impossible. How could I go from whatever happened over the last few months, and particularly last night, to hanging out with an old friend? It would be so incredibly normal, how strange.

[CHAPTER FIFTY]

I was right to think the normalcy of being with Chris would be boundlessly strange.
He greeted me so casually, "My man, how're you doing?
I greeted him likewise, "Chris! What's up buddy, I'm better now that I'm seeing you."
What else was there for me to do? I had no intention to tell him any of the strangeness that occurred over the last few months. I would tell him a version of the truth, the same one I would tell myself over and over, that I still am. I would share with him how the work itself was pretty shitty, that I had just one day off in my first month of being on the island, and that my expectations were nowhere close to reality. I would share that while the island was absolutely beautiful, the rest of the experience scarred me. I would tell him that some of my coworkers literally smoked crack inside our accommodations. Along with that, I would share that their nightly screams forced me to go to sleep early. I would speak of how I medicated myself heavily in a cloud of marijuana. This picture I would paint was dark in itself. I could only imagine how someone would feel to hear the story in its entirety. The true story. Perhaps you now know. So, reader, how does it feel to know the entire truth of my first move to the West Coast of Canada? Do you agree that I probably should have stayed home? I sure wish I did.

Chris was staying with a friend of his, and he assured me it would be no problem for me to crash there as well. The only caveat was that they were having a big party at the house the following night. I had no problem with the idea of a party. I would relish the opportunity to get drunk and forget. We went straight back to his friend's house to drop my stuff off and pick his friend up. From there, we drove thirty minutes, to Vancouver Island's west coast. Chris apologized along the way. They were going surfing, and he felt bad I did not have a board of my own. I explained as best as I could that I did not mind one bit. I was simply happy to be in the company of people I could trust. Especially him. It was good to be with someone who knew me before my time on Georgia, it allowed me to revert back to that version of myself. I could almost pretend I never went in the first place. I soon found myself amazed at how easy it is to pretend.

I helped Chris unload the surfboards from the roof of the little car. As my old and new friends paddled out to the waves, I found a nice tree to lean back against. I had never been surfing myself and was curious to see how good Chris was. I tried to get some cool pictures, and I sure did. I lost myself in the rolling of the waves, completely immersing my mind in the challenge of spotting them out there. After some time, the two of them came back to land. We loaded back up the car and headed into the city. Chris's friend had to work, so we dropped her off and then headed downtown. Neither of us had been to Victoria before. We decided to wander around the downtown streets with no particular goal in mind. We both noted it was not so different from Halifax, our home city. Just another sea coast town, even if it was four thousand kilometres from ours. We ended up at a brewery and each got a sample tray of local beers. We found a cheap place close by to get a bite to eat before heading back to his friend's house. It was a jam-packed day, as we ended up going to the student bar where our host was working. We met them for a drink once her shift ended. We stayed there later than expected and got back to the house just past eleven. Big preparations needed to be made to get ready for the party the next day, so we went to sleep.

The house's basement was mostly Chris's friend's room, it was a big L-shaped room. I slept around the corner from them on an inflatable mattress. It felt so good to be sleeping in a place that felt so safe. As I lay on my bed in a drunken haze I felt so far disconnected from Georgia Island. It did not even cross my mind that there was a chance my body could again be taken from my control. I fell asleep soundly, enveloped in an air of gratitude. I escaped the island, and considering what went down, I felt relatively unscathed. This would be the first night of many where the experience would fade. My current reality would take its place, and I was so excited to see where I would go. It sure as hell could not be any worse.

The party preparation could not have gone any better. I was slightly surprised that the majority of the party would actually be happening in our basement room. My mattress was deflated and stored, as the whole place was reorganized. Chris's friend was part of a successful punk rock band. The house in which we were staying was essentially the band's house. The place where my bed was got converted into a small performance area. A few local punk rock bands they were friends with were slated to perform that evening. What a fucking cool idea. I could not believe my luck. To be going from Georgia Island to attending what would likely be the coolest party I had ever been to.

The party did not disappoint. The bands absolutely killed it, and once they were done performing, they joined in on the partying. I had a great time with Chris, who sadly did not last too long into the night. With my friend down for the count, I made some new ones. I chatted with one of the bands for a while, and ended up elsewhere for a small after-party. I did not make it back to the basement that night, where my air mattress stayed deflated. One of my friends from the night before was kind enough to drive me back to the house to say goodbye to Chris and to pick up my bags. Chris was in no state to drive, so my new friend extended their kindness and drove me down to the ferry. I felt like a new man as I made my way into the Victoria ferry terminal. It was time to keep on traveling. The next step was to get the ferry all the way to the Tsawwassen terminal south of Vancouver and then take a bus to the airport. There I would hop on a plane to Calgary to meet my sister and her best friend.

It was after I boarded the ferry that I was brought out of my renewed reality and back to the reality of Georgia Island. It was a phone call from Jared. I felt obligated to answer it. Not only would it be strange for me to not, but I was also curious to get an update as to what was happening at the Retreat. It was now two full days since tragedy struck. He sounded pretty excited on the phone, not stressed at all. It was a small Retreat, and so naturally he knew some solid details about what occurred.

He started, "Dude, did you hear what happened? The owner of the Retreat was killed the other night, like brutally murdered. It was fucked."

I feigned surprise, "You're fucking with me. As I left the Retreat I saw a fire truck headed onto the property, but I didn't give it a thought since then. You're serious, eh?"

His excitement continued, "Oh yeah man I'm as serious as can be. They've already made an arrest and everything. It's all anyone's talking about.

They had made an arrest? What the hell, I thought. Who could they have possibly arrested? By no means was I upset about the news, but still, it was a surprise.

Continuing with my act, "Really? Who did they arrest?"

He went on to explain that they immediately suspected our co-worker who had the altercation with the owner earlier that day. When the investigators questioned the Retreat's management, they mentioned the incident and then further implied that the man in question was a drug user. The cops wasted no time at all in picking him up, they thought it was a no-brainer. There was certainly part of me that felt bad the guy was being blamed for it. I could not help but think that once the murder was further investigated there was no way they would successfully prosecute him. I understand that with sad regularity people are falsely convicted, but I had a good feeling they would not find the physical evidence required to lock him up. I could not imagine they would even charge him.

I drifted deep into my thoughts, and came to as Jared started to repeat my name.

I responded, "Oh, sorry man. I just got lost in thought. That's some really upsetting news."

He said, with a bit of nervousness rather than excitement, "You haven't heard from Jen have you?"

I told him that I had not, he continued, "Damn, okay. Well, I don't know how to say this, but, she's gone. No one has seen or heard from her. Henri and I were looking for her when she didn't show up to work. We went to her room and the door was wide open, it was completely empty, like no one had ever been there."

He went on a rant about how strange it was she would disappear right after the murder. He explained how it made sense that I left since I told people ahead of time. I simply agreed with him. I could not help myself, so I mentioned that it sure was strange, but that there was no way that she could have anything to do with the murder. It never hurts to plant a seed, especially with so much on the line. After what I saw a couple nights before, I knew the likelihood Jen would ever be seen again by anyone from Georgia Island was slim to none.

I ended the call with Jared by telling him to keep me updated on what was going on. He sounded so excited about the whole situation that I knew he would. It is a strange concept that even the darkest of things can excite a person. Anything out of the ordinary really gets our mind ticking, for better or worse. At the entrance to the Amsterdam harbour, the locals used to lynch and leave the bodies of people who broke their rules. The bodies were placed strategically so that incoming pirates or sailors would think twice before committing any crimes. People would actually travel specifically to see the bodies that were on display, it was a vacation of sorts. This is all to say that people being interested in tragic happenings is nothing new. The phone call had certainly brought me back to thinking about what happened. I fought the good fight with desperation, and was happy to find that I won. I returned my focus to where I was and where I was going.

I got to the Vancouver airport without trouble. As I went through security, I could not help but feel like I was fleeing the scene of a terrible crime. I had to applaud myself, I was doing a damn fine job of believing that all that happened on the island was the same that I told Chris. My thoughts focused on the excitement of getting to see my sister. She was flying all the way to Calgary to spend some time with her best friend. The two met at university and never looked back. I was incredibly grateful to be invited. My sister's friend had both a place in the city of Calgary and a place in Canmore. Canmore was a beautiful town tucked away in the Rocky Mountains. Funnily enough, years later, in what truly was a different world, Chris and I would meet up in Canmore for a couple evenings of reminiscing. Naturally, there would be nothing to say of Georgia Island, that was a long-gone history, and one better not revisited. Anyway, I could not wait to explore Calgary and then go to relax in a mountain paradise.

It was as we flew at cruising altitude that the feelings hit me. I could not help but begin to weep. I was in the window seat, and did my best to face the clouds as I cried. I had no intentions of bringing any extra attention to myself. Had anyone seen me, they likely would have thought that I was mourning the death of a loved one. In some sort of way, I was. I could have been mourning the version of me that was undoubtedly slaughtered upon the island. There was an innocence lost, and it was certainly gone forever. I thought back to that night. The one where the owner of the Retreat was murdered. I thought of the dream I had. The one where I was the one who so angrily took his life. I thought back to the shock that filled me when I looked up from the mangled body, that just ten minutes earlier was that of a man. I looked up and saw my good friend standing there in the grass, a big smile plastered across her face. It was a wicked smile, a smile of dark and evil knowing. She stood there, staring into my soul. Her eyes had gone black, nothing but pits. She held out her hands in a gesture showing she was ready to receive. At this point, I do believe I was still unable to control my body. I walked over to her. Balancing on one foot at a time, I stripped off my now blood and mud-stained socks. She accepted them, and then immediately turned to head down the trail that led to both Staff Beach and the Matriarch's cabin. I hoped it would be the last time I would ever see her hips sway as she walked away.

There was no doubt in my mind that I would never know what her role was in whatever it was that happened. In the moments when memories of Georgia would roll back into my mind's sight, I would ask many questions. What was the light that floated down the trail and penetrated me so long ago? What roles did Freshwater, the Matriarch, and Jen play in all that happened? How much, if any, was reality? To what extent was it nothing more than a dream? The one thing I knew was that I would never have these questions answered, and perhaps that was for the best. The one thing I hoped was that it was all behind me in its entirety. To this day, I sleep in relative peace.

[EPILOGUE]

It was three weeks later that I received another call from Jared. I was happily back home for the holidays. After a lovely time in Calgary, I decided to make up for time lost on the island by making pit stops to visit friends in Toronto and Quebec City. It was a lovely trip, but it sure did feel good to be back home with my dog. Anxiety flashed as my phone rang and I saw the caller ID. I pushed the butterflies down gently before answering and putting him on speaker. I immediately identified that he sounded stressed.

He said, "Hey man, we've gotta talk quick."

I responded, "Yeah buddy what's going on?"

My friend launched into a long-winded story about what was going on at the Retreat. He had flown home to Aurora two weeks after I left. He said the Retreat was temporarily shut down and that it seemed unlikely to be re-opened any time soon. I could not help but think to myself that it was some sort of a win, however empty it felt. The origin of his stress was that he received a phone call from one of the investigators looking into the Retreat owners murder. Ahead of the call, he heard they were no longer investigating our coworker with the drug habit. As I predicted, he was released without charge. On the phone call with the investigator, he learned that another one of our colleagues was under investigation.

He was asked a series of questions about Jen and I. He said he answered as honestly as he could. In the end, his phone call was essentially a warning. A warning that I should expect a phone call myself. We spent a bit more time on the phone, catching up about how he was feeling. He was similarly happy to be home, even though Georgia Island was a slightly better experience for him. We ended the call by agreeing we would keep in touch, of course we never did. I put my phone down and attempted not to freak out. I thought to myself, 'Okay, so you are likely being investigated for a murder that you may or may not have committed, fuck.'

It was for the best that I did not have to wait long to receive the phone call. I swallowed my nerves as best I could as I picked it up. The investigator introduced herself politely and gained permission to ask a few questions. I told her I would be more than happy to help in any way I could. The call could not have gone any better. There were two things she was focusing on. The first was investigating Jen as a potential perpetrator of the murder, not that she said this outright. To be fair, it was damn suspicious she vanished without a word at the same time the owner died. Apparently, they tried to track her down, but they lost her trail quickly. They believed Jen got on a plane to Colombia. After landing in Cartagena, she disappeared. They asked me what she was like and about how much time she was spending with the lady that I knew as the Matriarch. The investigator shared that the Matriarch was nowhere to be found and that they were assuming the worst. I answered her questions as honestly as I could, only slightly distancing myself from my friend. I felt there was nothing to gain by altering my story. Although naturally, I left out the last time that I saw her. There was no need to place both of us at the scene of the crime, especially if it was only a dream. I did not want to change too much. They were likely already privy to Jen and I's relationship, and to skew from that would do nothing but raise suspicion. The second thing the investigator focused on was why I left.

Once again, I was completely honest. I told her the exact same story that I told to anyone who wanted to know. It was so damn well rehearsed that I believed it myself. I guess in some ways it was now the truth. She was grateful for the details I articulated. The reason she asked about my leaving was not at all due to suspicion in my direction. Rather, she had heard from a certain Frenchman who worked at the Retreat that I did not have many good things to say about the place. She wanted my opinion as a favour to a colleague of hers who was investigating the Retreat. Apparently there was a possibility that the Retreat could be shut down permanently. I told her she was welcome to give me a call anytime if more questions were to arise. It was with a smile on my face that I put down the phone. An innocent man was walking free from a crime he did commit, what a strange concept.

As I write this, there are three years and many adventures between me and my time on Georgia Island. One of which was the volunteer program that I began roughly a month and a half after fleeing the island. Funnily enough, I ended up living less than fifty kilometres away from the Retreat, I did not pay my old home a visit. I was lucky enough to volunteer at the Nanaimo food bank, a non-for-profit farm, and an Indigenous Friendship Centre. The program was twelve hours a day, seven days a week. It was more intensive than my work at the Retreat but it was also much more rewarding. It was not until I completed the program that I was able to return my attention to the exposé concerning Arbutus Falls Retreat and Spa. My attention lived only briefly as I discovered no existing plans for the Retreat to reopen. From what I could gather at the time, the Canadian Government was using some sketchily paid taxes and the threat of more fines to leverage a below market sale. These few years on, the land is still in limbo, there has been no sale and no reopening.

The arguably more important of the two exposés met a more satisfactory fate. With the help of my mother, I polished and then published the real history of colonization that occurred on Georgia Island. Whether Jen or the Matriarch ever learned that their work was made public remains a mystery. The article has only received minor attention locally, and by this I am unbothered. If anyone is ever curious about the Island's true history, it is now available to them, and that is enough for me.

Understanding the importance of a written record has not left me. I went back and forth for a long time in regards to whether or not writing this document was well-advised. Eventually, I decided it prudent to record the facts. It was difficult to decide what to include and what to cut out when writing this story. At some point the line between fiction and reality became so blurred that I am rather unsure as to where these words stand.

I do hope that you understand the importance of my anonymity.

Thank you,

,

I am so grateful that you made it to the end of the book. I hope that you do not mind doing me one final favour. Please scan this QR code and share an honest review about what you thought about the book. Thank you!

Acknowledgements:

Thank you to my mother for being my first ever reader, and for her endless grammatical assistance. Thank you to my good friend Sam for identifying my experience at the Retreat as a worthy setting. Thank you Marleen for the ideas, and the invaluable brainstorming sessions while we strolled through the sacred valley. Thank you to my sister for completing my final edit, and for being my biggest fan. Thank you to my Bubbe for reading it twice to help satisfy her countless questions.

Manufactured by Amazon.ca
Bolton, ON